INYENZI

A STORY OF LOVE AND GENOCIDE

BY

ANDREW BROWN

MALLARD PUBLISHERS

First Published 2000

First Publication

Published by Mallard Publishers
P.O.Box 36012
Glosderry 7702
Claremont
Cape, South Africa

ISBN 1-875076-11-5

Edited by C.A.L. Harpur
Typesetting by Elfi Tomlinson
Cover design by Kate Wigley
Cover artwork by Anita Brown
Printed by Wescape Printing and Binding CC

Acknowledgments

My special thanks to Patti for her unwavering support and commitment to the completion of this work, to Ros for her editing and to Anita for her artwork.

Ubutabera (Intermedia): Independent Newsletter on the International Criminal Tribunal for Rwanda

Agence Hirondelle – Arusha, Tanzania

Philip Gourtevitch We wish to inform you that tomorrow we will be killed with our families Picador 1998

Human Rights Watch Leave None to Tell the Story: Genocide in Rwanda 1999

V Percival Environmental Scarcity and Violent Conflict: The Case of Rwanda Toronto 1995

MAP OF RWANDA

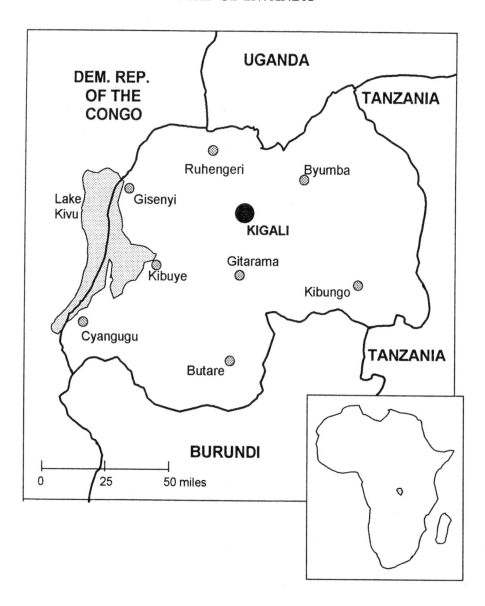

Then the LORD rained down burning sulphur on

Sodom and Gomorrah - from the LORD out of

the heavens. Thus he overthrew those cities and

the entire plain, including all those living in the

cities – and also the vegetation in the land.

Genesis 19:24, 25 NIV

The genocide was not an explosion of rage by the population

after the attack [on the presidential plane] but rather the

consequence of a deliberate policy of a political and military

elite.

James Stewart: prosecutor
Closing argument in the trial of Georges Rutuganda,
16 June 1999, International Criminal Tribunal for Rwanda,
Arusha, Tanzania

WORDS AND ABBREVIATIONS

Amarondo	- Interhamwe patrols organised during the genocide
Amasusu	- "bullets": also the name of a radical group of soldiers and police fomenting anti-Tutsi propaganda
Bourgemestre	- political representative of national government at commune level
CDR	- Coalition for Defence of the Republic: Hutu extremist party
FAR	- Forces Armeés Rwandaises: Rwandan government armed forces
Icyitso	- "accomplice" (plural = ibyitso): refers to supporters of RPF
Inguba	- "thunder": youth wing of the MDR party (Mouvement Démocratique Républicain)
Inkotanyi	- Rwandan Patriotic Front (RPF) soldiers; predominantly Tutsi
Interhamwe	- "people who work together/united people": militia involved in the genocide in Rwanda
Inyangarwanda	- "those who hate Rwanda"

Inyenzi	- "cockroach": pejorative term used by extremist Hutus referring to Tutsis during the genocide in 1994
Itsembatsemba	- "to leave nothing"
Gukora	- "work, mobilise": probably used as a code word to initiate the genocide in Rwanda in April 1994
Kinyarwanda	- Rwandan language
Kubohoza	- "to set free, to liberate": refers to the practice of forcing people to change political affiliation through threats and physical attacks
Masu	- club studded with nails
MDR	- Mouvement Démocratique Républicain: chief opposition to MRND
MRND	- National Republican Movement for Development and Democracy: Hutu political party in power under President Habyarimana
Minwa	- from the word "umunwa" meaning 'mouth': often refers to one who is spoken about but who does not materialise; used to refer to the UNAMIR during the genocide

Mwami	- traditional chief
Ntampogano	- type of club favoured by the Interhamwe
Nyambakumi	- head of an elected cell of people, usually about 1000 strong
RPF	- Rwandan Patriotic Front: Tutsi led rebel movement involved in ground war against government troops since 1990
Rubanda nyamwinshi	- "the great majority": a patriotic reference to the Hutu nation
Turatsembatsemba abatutsi	- "we will exterminate the Tutsi": used both in song and as a greeting amongst members of the Interhamwe
Ubutabera	- "justice"
Umuganda	- public communal work for the common good
Umwaanzi	- "adversary": with whom one can negotiate
Umubisha	- "the enemy": a mortal enemy to be killed in self-defence
UNAMIR	- United Nations peacekeeping force

The grey bedspread was worn thin, the weave loose and pulled up in places, as if someone had stood at the door and fired a gun randomly at the mattress. The tufts of dirty threads were pushed back and forth by the cross-draught of the small electric fan, like fragile sea anemones caught in the ebb and flow of a current. The heat pressed in from the walls, claustrophobic and stifling. The plaster seemed damp with sweat. The low wooden-framed window was open, but the air did not change in the room: the fan pushed the same weighted odours slowly about. The open window allowed only the sounds of the city to intrude: the irritable hoot of taxis, the shout of people on street corners, vendors, the call of pimps for the evening's business. A woman was carrying on a loud conversation from her second floor balcony, talking to a friend on the gravel pavement below, laughing and sighing, her forehead beaded and her exposed breasts heaving. Nairobi prepared itself for dark.

The man sat on the edge of the bed. His weight depressed the springs of the tired mattress to the lowest board. He picked at a hole in the material with one stubby finger, catching the thread under his nail and pulling it loose. He was distracted, scratching a widening dirty hole through which the stained blue sheet appeared. The small portable colour television set sat propped up on a wooden chair, the aerial splayed wildly in an attempt to pick up the broadcast from the central Kenyan Broadcasting Authority. The speaker hissed and squeaked like a caged animal. The volume was set high and the chair legs reverberated on the loose wooden floor whenever the newsreader spoke. An uncovered bedside light cast long shadows across the coloured walls, picking out the cracked paint and peeled corners and reflecting with a rounded glare on the screen.

The man was undressed. A trickle of warm sweat marked a line on his dry skin, running from the dark hollow of his arm-pit down the side of his chest, spilling across the folded ruts of his belly and disappearing into the shadow of his groin. His testicles hung heavily off the edge of the bed and with his free hand he slowly massaged the sac, rolling the balls under the skin between his fingers, abstractedly, comforting his tired body. The heat pressed in on the frame of his body. Someone coughed weakly outside the door as they passed along the passage. Cicadas grated and whined in the bushes, droning through the open window.

The grainy news report showed the Secretary-General making his way up the central aisle of the parliamentary chamber towards the podium. He seemed deferential, dressed conservatively in brown jacket and pants, unsmiling and dignified. He was watched by the members without applause. Men and women sat together in silence, resting their hands on the benchtops before them. They did not comment or pass remarks to one another: each one was sombre, watching the unassuming man as he stepped up to the podium. The camera showed his face up close, thin but kindly, a tight beard hugging his chin. The scene expanded to show the chamber, silent: there were people, parliamentarians, the man thought he recognised. He leaned a little closer and clenched his eyes in an effort to make out the faces. The television's reception was too poor and the definition of the peoples' features was imprecise. The Secretary-General opened a folded leather file and placed it, with deliberate movements, on the slanted wooden surface before him. He waited for a moment, as if in an effort to appreciate the burden that rested upon him, willing those who witnessed him to consider his burden. A pause, and a slow turn of the head, taking in the gathering moment.

> *I have come to Rwanda today on a mission of healing – to help heal the wounds and divisions that still torment your nation and to pledge the support of the United Nations so that once again we can become a partner and an ally in Rwanda's search for peace and progress.*

The noise from the television disturbed the woman lying stretched across the bed, languid and sleepy. Her movements were soft like chocolate that had been held in a warm hand, both smooth and greasy, both pure and corrupted. She rolled onto her back, her full breasts sliding loosely to either side of her torso. She uncrossed her bulky legs and a matted tangle of wiry black hair was exposed to the air. The woman opened her eyes and looked at the man's back, as if to say something. Seeing his taut and solid frame focused on the small screen a few feet away from him, she allowed her eyes to close again.

> *Four years ago, Rwanda was swept by a paroxysm of horror from which there is only the longest and the most difficult of escapes. It was a horror that came from within, that consumed and devastated entire communities and families. It was a horror that left you as survivors of a trauma which to the world beyond your borders was unimaginable, even though we all now know it happened.*

The Secretary-General paused in the delivery of his speech, once again sensing perhaps that the burden, the very gravity of his task, was beyond him. The naked man watched him without blinking. He watched him keenly. He felt a growing unease, not because of what was being said - it had been said many times before - but for other unpalpable reasons: the half-recognition of members of the chamber, the familiarity of the chamber, the fact that the administration of his country continued without him.

He did not feel fear, but a foreboding knowledge. Although he was not there in the chamber, he was also a player, a representative like the man on the news before him. He too would be called upon to represent his collective failings, his communal guilt. He felt as if the speaker was talking specifically about him, as if the speech was directed at him personally, addressed only to him. He almost expected his name to be spoken.

> *We must and we do acknowledge that the world failed Rwanda at the time of evil. The international community and the United Nations could not muster the political will to confront it. The world must deeply repent this failure. Rwanda's tragedy was the world's tragedy.*

The legs of the chair drilled the floor, jolting the floorboards as the speaker raised his voice. The vibrations hummed in the springs of the mattress. An intruder appeared from beneath the bed, disturbed by the noise or the movement. One long antenna almost brushed against the bare foot of the man as he sat unmoving on the bed. Light and dark brown patterns jigsawed across its smooth, hard outer shell. It moved forward with a short, rapid burst of legs, scuttling across to a point between the man and the television set. There it stopped and tested the air. It waved its thin feelers and its papery wings rustled beneath its carapace.

All of us who cared about Rwanda, all of us who witnessed its suffering, fervently wish that we could have prevented the genocide. Looking back now, we see signs which then were not recognised. Now we know that what we did was not nearly enough – not enough to save Rwanda from itself, not enough to honour the ideals for which the United Nations exists. We will not deny that, in her greatest hour of need, the world failed the people of Rwanda.

A shot rang out like the crack of a leather whip. The sound split the air, stinging the whore's ears. She bolted out of bed. She stood against the wall, bewildered and angry. Her mouth was open and her finger pointed in accusation at the man. He was oblivious to her shock. He sat back, tossing the hard-heeled shoe onto the bed, the bottom marked with a creamy, smeared liquid, a cracked brown wing sticking out from the one side.

"What are you doing? You are stupid ... can't you even behave?" The woman was too shocked to say anything more.

"*Inyenzi*," he said coldly, without looking at her.

Chapter One

There were warnings before the storm. Rumours filtered into the village, each seemingly unconnected to the other. The stories settled over time like the fine dust that collected in the aftermath of a train of oxen: imperceptible until it had gathered thinly in the cracks of elbows and the lines of weathered faces. A young man, on his way back from fishing near the lake, had come across a cleared opening in the forested hills that was burnt and without life. The trunks had been twisted by heat and the branches had lost their leaves. The ground carpeted with a dark oily dirt, like the ground of a slaughterhouse. He said it was a place for the dying spirits to meet. He told them that a sharp, biting smell still lingered about the undergrowth. The *nyumbakumi* dispatched a group of men but they returned without having found the place.

A mother of four children reported that she had heard terrible things while at the market in Rweru. She had been sitting with her friends on the grass next to the displayed cloths, laughing with idle talk. The wife of a MRND local official had joined them. She had spoken in whispers of terrible tragedies in the planning. Another young man returned to his parents' home from working on the green tea plantations in the south. He told them of rigorous self-defence training, using machetes and clubs. Workers on the tea plantation were taught how to use a rifle and how to march like an army company. On another occasion, a helicopter had terrified a woman and some small children in a maize field to the east of the village. It had swooped down low like a bird of prey, sending the woman sprawling amongst the brittle yellow leaves of the maize plants. Others had heard the chopping sound the machine made as it roared and screamed over the land.

Melchior considered these reports with disquiet. He murmured his prayers, kneeling before the small porcelain statue of the Virgin. A blue shawl was draped over her bowed, cream-coloured face and her eyes were downcast in humility. Her hands rested gently together, fingers intertwined in absolute passivity. Such peace, he thought, a contentment of being such as that which I cannot hope to attain. It was, he thought, an absolute assurance to be so resolved. He tried to let go of the anxiety that stirred inside him. He cast his eyes to the glossed face, to her small indented black eyes and thin pale lips. Her lips both irked and captivated him: they seemed lacking in life, or in love. The reddened mouths of the women at the beer bars in Rweru, by contrast, were passionate and filled with life. But she needed to be both compassionate and loving, and pure and reserved. He gazed at her visage intently, crossing himself in a flowing arc at the same time. Then the priest lowered his eyes and raised himself onto one knee, placed his hands on his leg and levered himself up. He dusted the cloth of his simple robe with his fingers.

The sacristy was a small, cramped room which led off the hall of the church, separated by a dark wooden door made of stained floorboards slatted together.The door swung on two heavy hinges which screeched as the metal hasps scraped together. The room was lit by a single unshaded globe, hung from unravelled wiring looped through a hook in the ceiling. There were no windows in the sacristy, which had been built as something of an afterthought, thrown together using the left-over bricks and boards. Water stains ran down the sides of the walls in thick brown stripes and the tin roof became dislodged in high winds. There were no ceiling boards and when it hailed the noise in the small room was deafening. But Melchior always retreated to the sacristy to pray and to escape the attentions of his community. A loose brick step and wooden box, draped with frayed red cloth, provided the room with the necessary spiritual form.

The porcelain statue of the Virgin stood on the red cloth alongside small terracotta statues. These figures were used to exalt one to higher levels of prayer and were widely regarded in the diocese as assisting in transporting one's prayers to the ears of the Almighty.

The walls were bare, save for two large wooden nails hammered into the cracked brickwork and set apart, for the priest to hang his robe. A wooden cross hung near the door. The cross was hewn from eucalyptus branches and carved so that the two pieces fitted together without the need for glue or nails, the one piece slotting into the other and becoming a single piece of wood. The priest had carved it himself, as a young boy, for his younger brother, Xavier, who was dying of malaria at the time, his body wasting away in waves of uncontained fever. As was his habit, the priest touched the cross now, gently and with sadness.

They had been raised as part of a large family in the green dense hills between Rweru and the border. The small settlement of Ritsire nestled into the crook of the hills in the north-western Kibuye province, a place where misted mountains rose from the grass plains and subsided again into the waters of Lake Kivu. The village burrowed into the side of the valley like a tick in the crease of a cow's thigh, feeding on the riches of life that surrounded it, sucking in the moisture that drained towards it from the misty sloping rises. Dark purple clouds often billowed high above the village and the air was thick and heavy before the storms. The winds seemed to hold their breath in anticipation. Then the pounding rains and the hail would clatter on the thatched rooftops, each drop and grain a separate drumbeat - hailstones the size of young potatoes, each raindrop a shower.

The village was close to the Ugandan border where the mountainous rainforest was still thick and wild, the peaks covered in mists. It was a place where life consisted of a tenuous balance of nature's gifts and her poisons. The villages in these hillsides were separated from the plains and each other by dense forested bush. They were joined only by winding tracks, formed by years of bare-footed walking. The tracks led around the bases of towering trees, over arched root stems and through curtains of creepers, peeling off one after the other to various destinations.

The village fell within the dominant catchment area for the country and the priest remembered the pounding force of unrelenting rain that had dominated his childhood. He had been summoned as a young boy to a meeting of his father's elders for suggesting to an impressionable friend that the spirits must have been drinking a great deal in order to produce so great and constant a flow upon the head of the village. He had entered the yard of the *nyumbakumi* with trepidation, nodding to the seated men. He had taken his seat on a rough plank spanning two low bricks: the elders questioned him with great solemnity and dignity, frowning and muttering with strained faces amongst themselves, pulling at their wrinkled cheeks and spitting seriously into the dust. They had filled their lungs with long draws on clay pipes stuffed with pungent tobacco and considered the matter before them. The young boy had become increasingly nervous and confused, until the village leader could contain himself no longer and the group of men had collapsed in guffaws, slapping their knees and wringing their eyes with delight, apparently unaware of the young boy's distress. In the weeks following the meeting, he had noticed the elder villagers smiling and whispering as they watched him running for home in the afternoon rains, nudging each other and laughing.

The priest had been named Lushodayana then: a scrawny child with clear and unusually wide brown eyes, scuffed knees and strong bare feet. He was part, initially, of a family of four boys and three girls, the second eldest son and fourth in the family. His father was a proud, stern man who earned a meagre wage, often in kind, as a school teacher in Rweru. He would return to the village at weekends and on holidays, austere and irritable with his children and their mother: he regarded himself as an intellectual and above the base lives of peasants. He grew angry and withdrawn upon returning to the village and being confronted with the reality of his family's rural existence. It was a weekly, self-inflicted cruelty which gnawed away at his being. It provided fertile ground for malignancy of the body and the soul to take hold.

Lushodayana's mother had struggled to provide the family with sufficient food from the small cultivated fields. The wet earth was worked communally by the villagers, hoed and turned into raw clumps of clay and soil, sprouting beetles, termites, snakes and larvae. The crops grew easily and quickly at their start: bananas, maize, rice in the swamp lands, cassava root, sweet potato tubers, taro and manioc. But once the delicate stalk and first green sprouts showed above the smoothed and patted earth, the roots and tubers were attacked from below and the edible green shoots devoured from above. The red and black locusts swarmed over the fields, the crickets and beetles sucked the life from the roots and the scale and corn bug spread over the stalks. When some of the precious plantings grew strong and dared to bear fruit, the glossy starlings, weaver birds, waxbills, crows and all the forest birds would descend to put an end to the villagers' toil.

Lushodayana spent his childhood working in these cursed fields, fighting an unending and unwinnable battle. The wealthier village members had a few head of cattle each: milk cows which produced small quantities of yellowed thin liquid, oxen for ploughing, clearing and carrying firewood, and a few select beasts for slaughtering on special occasions. Goats and wild pigs were left to fend for themselves in roughly-hewn enclosures set in the near reaches of the jungle, often falling victim to predators, snake bites or tick fever. It was a battle, fought day upon day to resist the returning tide of nature. The forest pushed and tested the borders of the village, springing on any opportunity to tangle a roof-latch with creepers, to break up the dried, smoothed mud-floor of a new hut or to drop thick, broken limbs on the straggled lines of maize.

He had seen cholera, malaria and other unyielding diseases pick at the lives of his siblings and friends. When he was still young, his older sister, then aged six, had been bitten by a tree snake while climbing in a wild fig tree on the side of a cleared field. Her hand had been painful for a short while, a thin red line running up from the bite on her fore-finger, like a thin scratch from a thorn tree, coursing between the knuckles and towards her arm, growing fainter and fading into the veins of her fore-arm. She had felt no pain after that, not until a few hours had passed, and then she had died, wracked by spasms and vomiting. He barely remembered her now. He had kept nothing tangible of hers and he did not even know where her small body had been buried.

It was the death of his younger brother, Xavier, when Lushodayana was himself twelve years old, that he remembered most acutely. His father had become increasingly withdrawn and his returns to the village, although prompt and regular, had increasingly been filled with bitter anger. A feeling of cold dread had risen up in him on seeing the thin figure approaching the house on a Friday afternoon, stalking like an insect along the side of the road. Lushodayana's mother would still be in the fields and he would have to welcome him home. His father would enter their home scowling, dismissing his son with a wave of the hand and demanding drink to quench his thirst from the journey from Rweru.

"Have you nothing better than water from the ditch?" he would growl, having drunk his fill. His father would cast the mug to one side, cool water leaking out onto the ground. Then he would inspect the dwelling, swiping his hand across the simple furniture, prodding the clay walls, scuffing the ground with the toe of his polished black shoes. His figure would grow taut and his manner menacing while he awaited his wife's return. She would try and appease him, dropping her head and running to meet his every need, but her deferential manner only showed him her weakness and would enrage him

20

further. Lushodayana's mother would soon be reduced to tears and his father to ranting and irrational accusations. He had not ever struck her in front of the children, although the air was always filled with the fear of physical power.

Xavier had been a quiet and nervous boy. Lushodayana had tried to protect his younger brother from the vagaries of the real world, trying to cup his hands around his fears and contain his anxiety. The continual effort of keeping his brother beyond the circling borders of his father's rampages was exhausting. He kept him out of his sight as far as possible and physically placed himself between his father and the timid boy.

His father taunted the weak boy, referring to him as his older brother's 'shadow': "Your shadow skulking behind you will have to learn to walk on his own two feet like a man one day," he would say derisively. Sometimes his father would lunge for the boy with a strong clawing hand, sending him yelping like a frightened animal out of the house, his father's abusive laughter beating about his head.

Xavier was seven years old when he contracted malaria. He was already thin. His frail arms poked out from his shirt like broken sticks and his eyes were wide and big, filled with uncertainty and reliance upon his older brother. Lushodayana kept him from his father's harm and from the blows of other bullying children, but malaria was a slow and insidious threat against which he had stood powerless and frustrated. The family had no money to get the child to a hospital in Kigali and, like many of his peers, he was left to fight the illness alone, lying in a darkened room with a wet cloth across his face. Xavier slowly wasted away as the fevers wracked his small frame and Lushodayana felt the full weight of his sibling's burden on his shoulders.

He had sat beside him, day after day, touching his drawn face and willing him to survive. He made the wooden cross, carving the wood as he sat on the floor alongside the small mattress, talking quietly about the day's events. When the cross was complete, he placed it standing against the wall next to his brother, so that he could take hold of it and would take strength from its presence. But he knew, in his desperation, that there was not enough strength in his brother to sustain a recovery. One early morning, before anyone in the family had roused, Lushodyana slipped under Xavier's blanket and held him in his arms. His brother's body felt as if it were heated by a fire from within, a constant source of burning heat surging up through his chest. His skin was dry, his life's water burnt off by days of sweating and shivering. He held his head against his chest and rocked him, softly murmuring his name, until the sun started to rise over the forest. Xavier opened his eyes to see another day approaching: he felt his brother holding him. Then he let go and moved into the other world. Traditional beliefs dictated that Lushodayana should then have left his brother to the spirits, but he was unable to give up the despair at his loss. His failure to protect his frail brother bore down on him. When Xavier had closed his eyes with nothing more than a small sigh of breath and in that moment of parting, Lushodayana had felt the hand of the spirit on his brother – not the kindly paternal hand of comfort, but the hard-gripping and arbitrary hand of the omnipotent.

The door screeched as Melchior stepped out of the sacristy into the cool hall. His father's surliness and bursts of aggression had taught his son to fear the vagaries of human conduct. His brother's early death left him with a suspicion as to the actions of the deities. The reports he was hearing were not new - young men training with guns and machetes, threats of rebellions and crackdowns. The stories which trickled into the village concerned him not because of the content of the rumours themselves, but rather because they suggested the arbitrary influences of the forces of the dark - the spirit that had made his sister choose the tree with the snake in it, rather than the tree alongside it, the will that had chosen his brother to be infected, rather than the child next door, the influences that acted without cause, or without there seeming to be cause. The reports he heard were not of the acts of people, but the work of forces that possessed the shuttered, evil parts of the souls of the deceased - those forces that accepted no offerings, and nor were any given, for the goodwill of a dark spirit was of no use and could not be trusted.

He had been taught at seminary school that the random and unreasoned happenings that befall humankind are predetermined by a singly entity which was all-pervasive and all-knowing. God was in control of the human spirit, which was itself a single and undivided soul, incapable of being constituted in different parts, united and utterly integrated. When death struck the innocent, it was to allow the untainted spirit to rise into His opened hands. When it struck the guilty, it was to precipitate their judgment. He had asked his teachers whether the concept of original sin did not weight the scales unfairly against true morality, but his question was never answered clearly - he was doused instead with biblical jurisprudence which, in the result, excited the intellect but left his emotions unmoved.

He had difficulty in marrying the two sides of his belief: on the one hand, his wary childhood respect for dark and light spirits, the divided, portioned souls of those deceased, and on the other hand, his adult learnings of God, the Son, the man, the united spirit, the integrated trinity. His life in the forests had made him comfortable in allowing opposing forces to weigh against each other, without one taking precedence over the other, the one pushing up against the other, neither relenting, neither overpowering.

It was a deeply personal and delicate balance, one which could not be shared with his teachers, steeped as they were in concepts of cause and effect, singleness and unity. His own construct would be viewed as having sprouted from dialectical influences, as being leftist and secular, or even worse, as representing an unfaithful malingering, a retention of base and savage beliefs. A leftist, although undesirable in the Church, might be engaged intellectually, but a malingerer, an exponent of base beliefs, would be regarded as a ritualist and paganist. Such a person could not be accommodated within the Church. In moments of honest reflection, he supposed that he was in truth both a ritualist and a paganist: the ritualism came from his adult teachings and from the daily routines of the Catholic church. The paganism emanated from his childhood beliefs, which were as much a part of his being as the limbs on his body.

The reports of arbitrary evil touched the most vulnerable areas of his intellect. The will of God was challenged more fundamentally by such incidents than by any other tragedy: unnecessary and indiscriminate evil which struck ordinary people, still striving for wholeness, in the midst of their struggle. No will nor reason was manifest by the holy trinity in such acts. In those moments it seemed that the dark spirits pushed that much harder, that moral teachings were forced to relent and give way to baser fears, and that control was to be relinquished.

Melchior stepped out into the bright sunlight. The compound was clean and uncluttered. He felt alone and isolated from the community of the church and somehow removed from the village congregation which he served. He feared that his father had left him tainted by aloofness. At times he felt that his identity was determined by his position and by his learning. He feared that he would never feel at ease in any form, whether as a priest or an ordinary villager.

In truth, his learning had been a patchwork of irregularly attended primary and secondary school classes and an opportunistic foray into spiritual advancement. He had first attended an informal school in Muyara. The school had been started by a Dutch missionary who had arrived under the auspices of the Red Cross Society after the floods and the resultant famine in the 1950's. Lushodayana was not taught by the missionary himself, but tales of his eccentric behaviour abounded amongst the pupils. It was only when Lushodayana had finished his schooling that it dawned on him that the Dutchman had, in all probability, been in the throes of dementia in his latter years (probably from advanced syphilis). His sudden and dramatic exit from the school had probably been less the result of a calling of God as the call of some fantasised nightmare from his addled mind.

Muyara was a small town to the east of his village, Ritsire, and to the north of the prefecture town of Rweru. The school had had one classroom, a disused storeroom at the back of the stone church. The church and its storeroom were the only stone structures in the town. The police house and the drinking saloon were the only other solid buildings, made of fired brick. The remaining houses and shops were made of hardened mud, wood or a hardy combination of lengths of sticks, bound together with twine and cemented over with a mixture of straw, mud, dung and thinly-spread cement dust. The schoolroom had bare concrete floor and walls, save for the wall at the front, which was painted white with shiny paint and served as a chalk board.

The children, of all ages between four and twelve, sat on the floor on small woven mats, frayed at the ends from the attentions of small hands, picking and twining. The subjects taught in the school could not be differentiated, the one from the other: the lessons began with a prayer, ended with a prayer, and melted in between. Stories about wars in other countries drifted into didactic explanations of addition and subtraction (which never lasted long), French vocabulary, geography, reading, writing. Subject content was presented in small, sampled pieces, each a taste of the possible realms of knowledge, the edges of possible learning.

Lushodayana was taught by the Dutchman's successor, a local man who insisted on being called 'father', although he did not have any children and was not an ordained priest. His real name, they discovered from the woman at the beer saloon, was Kuturanda Muyigenzi: he had left for six months training in Bujumbura and returned with a suddenly acquired and heavy French accent and an affection for foul-smelling cigarettes. He was a small, compact Hutu man with hasty eyes and a high forehead. His body moved, even when he was standing still, with abrupt, impatient jerks, as if he were possessed by an irritable physical spirit which wanted to be released. The pupils sometimes cruelly referred to their teacher under their breath as *Twa*, from the race of pygmies that came from the bush to trade wild coffee and meat for sharpened machetes and cloth.

The 'father' took over all the functions of the Dutchman, including the small services held on Friday evenings and Sunday mornings. He stood at the front of the simple church, shouting incantations in French, flaying his arms in the direction of his attentive flock. He berated them for their apparently numerous sins and called on God's forgiveness for their fallibility. Collections were deposited in large open basket which accommodated the offerings of cobs, unshelled nuts, fresh coffee berries and other crops. The basket was passed along the rows and returned to the sweating preacher bursting with freshly picked fruit and tubers, earth still clinging to their roots.

The preacher's brother had a son, Victor, who was a year older than Lushodayana. Their homes opened out onto a communal yard and the boys had grown up alongside each other. Victor had been slow at first to show any affection towards the younger boy. They gradually formed a lopsided relationship in which Victor led and Lushodayana followed, carrying out the older boy's orders and following his rules. They often played together in groups, kicking a weathered soccer ball or throwing mud-balls into the river. Victor tended to play with the older boys if they were available and liked to be part of the games, chasing in a pack. But he would immediately complain and feign injury if ever chosen to be the target of a playful attack. Melchior remembered Victor lying on the ground laughing, tears running down his cheeks after he had split a ripe mango open on a playmate's head, only to scamper screaming and protesting when the bruised fruit was mashed onto his face and neck in retaliation.

Victor assisted his uncle in the services, passing the basket, dusting the wooden benches before and after each service, polishing the wooden crucifix at the front of the church and sweeping the bird and bat droppings from the entrance-way. He was also responsible for lighting the sandalwood and camphor-tree fire that smoked quietly in the back corner of the hall, filling the air with a thin haze and a rich, warm smell. The smell lingered in the church throughout the week, giving the church hall an atmosphere that Lushodayana found comforting - secure like the smell of an elder's pipe or the coals brought inside to the sleeping hut from the fire tended outside in the cold night air.

Lushodayana started to attend school more regularly after a while, starting the hour-long walk along the rough forest track early in the morning to reach the church school before the lessons started, and before the preacher had roused himself from his bed and struck his first foul cigarette. Lushodayana would slip into the church and walk quietly towards the crucifix. He would sit on a front bench and draw in deep breaths, as if trying to absorb the essence of the smell, the very heart of the feeling that overcame him, a reverence and a sense of comfort. He would remain in this state until he heard the laughter of children, arriving for school, pushing and joking with one another. Then he would slip out of church, unseen and quick like a scavenger. The preacher Muyigenzi saw him leaving the church hall early one morning. After that the door to the church was customarily left ajar and the floors of the church unswept until school had started and the boy had completed his morning ritual.

One rainy Sunday morning, Victor - whether on impulse or out of mischief – tossed a handful of fresh marijuana stems and leaves onto the corner burner in the middle of one of his uncle's fervent sermons. The scalding vegetation hissed, its bubbling liquids emitting a heavy, pungent cloud of sweet smelling opiate which quickly enveloped the assembly in beguiling scents. The preacher, himself not a stranger to the opportunities that nature at times presented, soon recognised the intruding odour. He was outraged. He strode down the aisle and grabbed his cowering nephew by the collar of his unwashed jacket. He lifted his helpless kicking feet off the ground and flung him from the doors of the church, sending him sprawling in the dirt outside.

Melchior did not see Victor in church again after that: Victor was to have little to do with the Church until the terrible events that unfolded many years later.

The preacher spoke to Lushodayana at the end of the next day's lesson. "I have seen you, sitting in the church in the morning, thinking of the ways of the Lord and thinking of the small part which you might play in His plans. My brother's son thought that his task was a favour to the church, a meaningless ritual for his uncle, the work required of a child only. He failed to understand that the task was an opportunity, given to him not as a favour but as an honour, and he failed the honour given to him."

The preacher's thick eyebrows moved swiftly about his face as he spoke, and he grasped the boy's shoulder and forearm as he spoke, his eyes moving intently as if searching for the boy's affirmation. The heavy smell of old smoke rose from his skin and clothes.

"It is an important and honourable task, father," he said, as if to satisfy the intense gaze of the older man.

"Yes, you are right, the work of the Lord is always important and it may not be abused, not by anyone." The preacher held the boy's arm tightly, he could feel his fingers starting to tingle as the blood slowed to a trickle in his hand. "I would like you to have the opportunity, I would like you to be afforded the favour of working for the Lord, bless His name and His Son, Jesus Christ, the Son and the Holy Ghost, amen. Those who follow in His shadow shall not fear the valley of death as they are in His form and are not evil but shall take over the earth."

Lushodayana took the preacher's words and his new position as supervisor of the corner-burner seriously. It required, he felt, a measure of dignity and obedience, and he performed his simple tasks with a strictness that found favour with the preacher. He spent time searching the nearby hills and valleys for succulent twines, crushed barks and leaves. He broke them and rubbed them against his palms, cupping his hands over his face and breathing deeply to discover what undisclosed scent might be released under the persuasions of red hot ember. If the result seemed attractive, he stored the plant in his sack, for testing on his home fire. Some plants he burnt on the open flames, skewered on a sapling branch. Others he packed into the coals or draped on the hot rocks around the edge. Some of the leaves were too harsh when burned directly and required to be distilled for a day or two in warm water. He splashed the water delicately over the smouldering coals, enjoying the drama of the heat spitting the cold drops into the air. Some smelled of earth, some of sky, some of dense green sap and others smelled of old dung. But, once the natural fibre had given off its secrets, he would return to the hills to collect fresh quantities. So he managed to imbue each service with a subtle and unique combination of aromas.

The tenor of the preacher's voice, and the sermon itself, seemed to be governed by the scent emitted by the burner. There were days when the preacher would implore his congregants to follow Jesus for His sweet love, the light release of blossoms wafting about his temples, uplifted and filled with hope for his mortal servants. But the smoke from the thicker stems of angel's creeper and liam brought sermons of foreboding and threats of harshness in the face of disobedience. On one occasion, Lushodayana allowed the leaves of a beetroot plant to smoulder against the hot metal rim of the burner. The fiery veined leaves emitted a pungent, corrosive odour which resulted in a sermon of hell and damnation which terrified the small faithful gathering.

On another occasion, Lushodayana was excited to find a frangipani tree in the *bourgemestre*'s garden in Rweru on a visit to the market. He detected the sweet smell of the fallen blossoms from some distance and he filled his pockets with the pure white flowers with yellow centres. When he snapped off two of the smaller branches, a white ooze filled the wound and dripped onto the dusty ground. When he tested the flowers and branch on a fire, the result was disappointing: the blossoms burnt quickly and emitted a thin unpleasant smell. The charred pulp of the broken branch gave off a biting smell which attacked the membrane of his nose and throat like a poison. His siblings demanded that he carry the offensive stick outside and dispose of it away from the huts.

Melchior had returned to his childhood church after completing his studies at the seminary in Butare, to find that the institution of the burner had fallen into disuse. He discovered the rusting remains of the low tin barrel behind the cemetery but it had been eaten away by the elements. Now in his own church in Bukumara, he burned scented candles instead: sandalwood, rose and vanilla aromas lifting from the small cups of wax placed at the doors and on the simple wooden altar.

The preacher had been influential on his choices as a growing boy, particularly as the relationship of trust grew between them. Melchior had found security and friendship in the man, to the exclusion of Victor, who had retreated ever-further from him. He was now aware of how the incident with Victor and the marijuana leaves had unintentionally shaped his own life. It had provided him with an unexpected opportunity and had directed him towards the open doors of the church. Yet their contact had become increasingly sporadic and their involvement with each other's lives now seemed remote. Victor's father was a violent man, prone to lengthy bouts of drinking during which he became abusive and vindictive. When he was fifteen, Victor had moved to live with his aunt in a neighbouring village to avoid his father's tirades. But Melchior had always felt that the decline in their friendship had more to do with personal differences than the short distance which lay between them. Melchior still saw Victor occasionally: when Victor visited Bukumara he would usually call on the St. Jean church for a mug of tea.

Melchior's own father had died an unforgiving death soon after he had started his duties at the church. Victor's uncle, Muyigenzi, became increasingly central to the young boy's world. He became part of the family and increasingly joined them for meals, staying to talk to his mother after the children had gone to bed. His mother never tired of the preacher's wordy speeches and enjoyed satisfying his simple needs. Unlike Melchior's father, Muyigenzi was filled with exaggerated praise and wonder for her uncomplaining work. Melchior was in his second year of study at seminary school when he received the news of his mother's death. He returned to Ritsire to find Muyigenzi cleaning the house and packing his mother's clothes neatly into packets. The preacher's own clothes hung familiarly on the walls.

Melchior accepted this state of affairs without comment, comforted by the knowledge that his mother had been appreciated right up until the last moments of her harsh life. Muyigenzi took over the house as if he had been married to his mother and had always lived there. Melchior was happy to let that position remain as it seemed an appropriate return for the preacher's unwavering support.

Muyigenzi had been instrumental in securing a place for Melchior at the seminary in Butare: he had called it "a place blessed by the Virgin Mary herself".

"The seminary was established in memory of the Ugandan martyrs. It is greatly respected for its holistic teachings," he told his young ward solemnly.

The preacher had written to the seminary on his behalf. The response had been guarded. Melchior had not received schooling at any recognised school or college and the seminary was wary of making a commitment to a rural applicant. Muyigenzi had then travelled to Butare to speak to the seminary committee directly. His energies had ensured that the young scholar was admitted into the preliminary year of study. This year at the seminary would take the place of his last year of formal schooling.

"I have secured a place for you, Lushodayana," Muyigenzi had told him excitedly. "I would like you to attend the seminary and finish what I could not," he had said, his hands on the young man's shoulders.

Melchior recalled the uncertainty he had felt then. It was a feeling that had never truly left him. But the preacher's own excitement and overbearing insistence had made all questioning impossible. By the end of the year, the arrangements for his move from the small village of Ritsire to the intellectual centre of Butare had been completed. His mother was filled with gratitude and pride. She wrung her hands in pleasure whenever her son's anticipated move to the city was discussed. Melchior's own feelings were less sure and he had left his home with some trepidation. His physical separation from his village marked the beginning of his adulthood. It was to be a road that stretched far beyond the naïve pleasures of Butare: it was a road that reached all the way across Rwanda and back, to Bukumara and the horrors that awaited there.

Office of Trial Prosecutors
INTERNATIONAL CRIMINAL
TRIBUNAL FOR RWANDA
Presidential Avenue
Arusha
TANZANIA

PRESS RELEASE - 5 August 1997

TO: Accredited press corps
     ICTR Building

The OTP formally issues the following press release, as at 5 August 1997, for the information of all members of the accredited press corps:

Operation Naki has resulted in the arrest of a further suspect in Nairobi.

Mr Victor Muyigenzi, the former head of the communal police for Rweru, Rwanda, was arrested in a hotel in Nairobi on 27 July 1997. Mr Muyigenzi has been sought by the OTP and is being brought to the United Nations Detention Facility on suspicion of crimes of genocide, conspiracy to commit genocide, crimes against humanity and serious violations of Article 3 common to the Geneva Conventions of 12 August 1949 for the Protection of Victims in Times of War and of Additional Protocol II thereto of 8 June 1977. It is the intention of the OTP to bring an indictment against Mr Muyigenzi in the International Criminal Tribunal for Rwanda under the provisions of United Nations Security Council Resolution 955 of 8 November 1994

The OTP hereby formally confirms the identity of the arrested suspect.

The OTP further hereby formally responds to the following selected queries raised by members of the accredited press corps at the press briefing of 4 March 1998:

1. *In response to a query regarding details of the arrest of Mr Muyigenzi on 27 July 1997 in Nairobi:*

The OTP is not at liberty to disclose the details of the investigation into or arrest of Mr Muyigenzi at this stage, save to state that Mr Muyigenzi was located in a down-town hotel room which he had taken in the name of a prostitute whose services he had engaged.

The OTP is able to confirm that the group AJIR, the Association pour une Justice Internationale au Rwanda, was of assistance in locating Mr Muyigenzi. The OTP cannot provide further details as to the involvement of AJIR at this time. Mr Muyigenzi was arrested by Kenyan police officers acting in conjunction with special investigators and members of the OTP.

2. *In response to a query as to OTP's intentions in regard to the charging of Mr Muyigenzi:*

It is the intention of the prosecutors' office to bring a formal indictment against Mr

Muyigenzi for acts of genocide arising from the period of his office as head of the communal police for Rweru during the period April to June 1994. It is the intention of the OTP to utilise the new rules applicable to trials under the ICTR to bring this matter to a speedy trial and to secure a conviction against Mr Muyigenzi.

3. *In response to a query from Associated Press as to the request for transfer to Rwandan criminal courts:*

The OTP confirms that it has received a written request from the office of the Prosecutor General of the Rwandan national criminal courts that Mr Muyigenzi be transferred to the Rwandan penal jurisdiction. The OTP has declined the request and intends to bring an indictment against Mr Muyigenzi in the ICTR.

4. In response to a query concerning the evidential basis of the charges to be laid against Mr Muyigenzi:

The OTP refers to the charges named in the formal press release above.

The OTP is not prepared to disclose the evidential basis of the charges or any further details in regard to the specific offences: this information is withheld by the OTP at this time for the protection of both the prosecution witnesses and the suspect.

The OTP is prepared to indicate that it will be pursuing a special charge of crimes against humanity (rape) on the basis that the rape of Tutsi civilians constituted a part of a widespread and systematic attack against the civilian population (or a portion thereof) on political or ethnic grounds, as recently accepted in the judgment of Chamber Two in the case of <u>Sisobenda</u>.

5. *In response to a query from the Nairobi Daily News framed as follows: "The OTP previously stated that the operation in Nairobi was based primarily upon the investigation into the role of Colonel Batho and the prefect in the massacres. It did not appear from the releases from your office that Mr Muyigenzi was a target in the operation or that he had formed part of the investigation.*

To what extent is your office prepared to proceed with this trial on the basis of the information you have at hand?":

The Criminal Tribunal is not involved in a public relations exercise and it takes its mandate and its function extremely seriously. It is not the intention of the ICTR or the OTP to bring charges against a suspect, charges which necessarily accuse a suspect of the 'crime of crimes', unless the OTP is in possession of substantial and convincing evidence upon which it believes it can obtain a conviction of the defendant.

Furthermore, the OTP is not to be restricted to the trying of high profile suspects who, by virtue of their positions in the former political structures in Rwanda, are regarded as being more worthy of prosecution than other suspects. Any suspect against whom sufficient evidence of genocide exists will be prosecuted by the OTP to the full extent of its ability.

6. In ·response to a query from the *Nairobi Daily News* framed as follows: "Does the OTP regard the indictment of Mr Muyigenzi as being the 'second prize' to the arrest and indictment of the bourgemestre or prefect?":

The response of the OTP is as above.

7. In response to a query from the *Burundi National News* as to how Mr Muyigenzi managed to flee and reach Nairobi and as to whether the suspect received any aid from governments in the region:

The flight of Mr Muyigenzi from Rwanda is a sensitive diplomatic matter which does not concern the OTP directly. The OTP is able to state that it appears, to the best of its knowledge, that Mr Muyigenzi fled north-west Rwanda during Operation Turquoise into the refugee camps of Goma. It is believed that the suspect succeeded in making his way through Congo to Kenya. The OTP is not in a position to provide any further details as to how Mr Muyigenzi may have reached or gained access into Kenya.

8. *In response to a query from Nairobi Daily News as to current status of investigation into Colonel Batho:*

The OTP declines to respond.

END OF PRESS RELEASE
9/1877h/AP

Chapter Two

Lushodayana, anxious and solitary, witnessed both the manifestation of strange and unpredictable evil and the exhilarating depths and forms of human emotions during his stay in the university town. There he was exposed to the restricted taste of adult freedom. As a child at play in his village he . had been free within the grounds of his responsibilities, which he accepted not only because they were given to him and expected of him, but also because they were necessary and beneficial. But the freedom of the adult world was unbounded, it seemed, by the borders of beneficial responsibility. It seemed both untrammeled and unchallengeable, and without recourse. It seemed to him that the streets teemed endlessly with people, all keenly seeking their own interests, moving and shifting, watching one another and restrained by nothing more than weak and unexpressed social expectations, controlled by nothing more than the premonition of sanction. There was no structure, no one who could define their position in relation to any other. The absence of control and an identifiable system of communal practice made him feel light-headed and fearful, like a man on a strung rope-bridge with nothing to hold onto, free but intensely vulnerable.

He wandered through the alleys and was accosted by vendors who touched his bare arms, calling out to him and drawing him into their domain. He was more wary of them now. On his arrival in the town he had stepped off the bus into the hands of a young man with glass beads strung around his neck. The man was friendly and helpful, taking his bags and ushering him through the crowd with promises of taking him to the seminary. Lushodayana followed his talkative guide, warmed by the man's apparent care – but the man had taken him to a jewellery store in the back-streets. He had refused to let him leave until he had bought some expensive bracelets, using up nearly half of the few crumpled notes he had in his pocket. He had arrived at the seminary feeling sullied and miserable. The expedient activity of the town frightened him - it made him anxious to see so many different people, never meeting the same person twice, always dealing with someone new, someone unknown. In the village, families shared their history, survived through the same experiences and told the same stories; in the village, there was a sense that the individual's interests coincided with the concerns of its inhabitants as a whole. Here on the tarred roads of the town, there seemed to be little commonality and success was a deeply personal and coveted affair.

Local politicians refer to Butare as 'the city of the intellectuals', although it is a quiet town by any standards. The town boasts the National University and the National Museum of Rwanda, the esteemed Groupe Scolaire secondary school, as well as several theological colleges, seminaries and a veterinary college. It is traversed by deep ravines and valleys which divide the town into different neighbourhoods, the shallower sides scarred with criss-cross paths kept bare by the passing of hundreds of feet. The main road, running through the town towards the border with Burundi, is tarred and well-maintained, dusty red gravel lapping at its sides like water at the edges of a lake. The rough alleys and secondary roads snake away from the tarred road, disappearing down into valleys and sliding behind the facades of houses.

The war changed the face of Butare considerably: the town was desecrated by the *genocidaires* in their upsurgence and scorched in their retreat towards Burundi. But when Lushodayana arrived at the seminary as a young student, the houses in the middle-class suburb of Buye stood proudly side by side and the museum building that marked the northern entrance to the town was clean and unscarred. Buye was home to foreign diplomats, aid workers, professionals and politicians. Its tree-lined avenues were quiet and shady. The tarred main road passed alongside Buye and the dominating museum building, and stretched through the business district of the town, flanked by rows of shops and the established Faucon Hotel. A wide side street led off to the large open-air market and, further on, to a training school for junior military officers. The main road made its way from there past the Prefectural Offices, the university campus, the nearby Ihuliro Hotel and bar where the students gathered to drink in the early evening, the National Police Post near Ubutamenwa and onwards to the border and Bujumbura.

The main road and the commercial district were the busy parts of the town, filled with the shouts of students and hawkers and the rumble of traffic moving south to Burundi or passing northwards towards the interior of Rwanda. Trucks carrying timber, crates of tea and raw coffee beans, belched smoke from their undercarriages, hooting and revving their engines as they lumbered through the town. Music spilled out from the fabric shops, drum beats merging with the lilting voices of women, mixing in turn with the pipe tobacco and diesel fumes to form a sensual blanket embracing the length of the district. But once off the main road, the noise receded quickly, the smells drifted away and the more restful nature of Butare exerted itself. The views enjoyed by even the most humble dwelling across the hills and valleys had a comforting effect on the dense neighbourhoods. During the day, the still heat was disturbed often only by the rustle of bicycle tyres on gravel, the bark of a dog or the sound of children playing. But at night the darkness was treacherous and absolute.

The Catholic seminary was situated on Avenue des États, a pretty tree-lined road leading from the commercial centre past the Cathedral. The grounds were green and manicured. Banana trees lowered their heavy load of fruit over the split-reed fence onto the avenue and the nuns tended the crisp grass lawn, sweeping across its closely-cut surface like skaters, taking small quick steps so as to avoid showing their feet from under their habits. They diligently swept the courtyard and raked the lawn clear each morning, moving between the rows of pruned red and yellow rose bushes, stroking the leaves of the day-lilies clean of white fly and picking the dried heads of the dwarf daisy bushes. The air was filled in the early mornings with the low hum of bees and other insects drawn by the bounty of the garden, and with the scent of yellow jasmine from the shaggy creeper which clung to the walls of the bell-tower. The south-western corner was dominated by a mpingo tree: cared for by generations of seminary scholars and teachers, it had grown to over 40 feet in height and nearly three feet in diameter. Its trunk was pale grey with a long fluted bole that suddenly branched into a myriad of spiny leaves and spidery limbs and arms. During the second dry season the leaves were replaced by white blossoms, sweet-smelling and delicate, softening the hardy tree. The nuns collected the blossoms in woven baskets and place them in twined bunches about the altar, permeating the chapel with a pleasant scent.

The compound was isolated from the bustle of the markets and shops, the hooting and revving of impatient drivers and all the noisy self-driven purpose of men and women caught by the lure of town living. When Lushodayana walked about the courtyard, or sat on the bench next to the fishpond, he could still hear the noise from the avenue, but the sound did not intrude upon the regularity and structured quiet of the school. The seminary confines provided Lushodayana with a protective shell in which he could concentrate on matters which were to him both small and yet overwhelming, both mundane and yet profound. The school provided him with some shelter from the uncertainties of the reality outside and from the arbitrary events which had disturbed him as a child.

But the tensions which defined the country remained manifest. He was woken each morning before dawn by the insidious shouting chorus of the FAR militias, running in formation through the streets, loaded weapons held above their heads, green khaki uniforms and arrogant faces in unbroken lines, the banshee cry of men with power. The young student was wary of these groups of soldiers. He would turn in his cramped metal cot and pull the pillow on top of his head waiting for the cries to subside. He did not venture outside the seminary compound until the sun had risen and the muddy boot-prints had dried on the road outside.

The formal army and the militias, with their set hierarchy and chain of command, provided a security that was in some ways attractive to him. It allowed one to be part of something that already existed and did not need to be created, and which was not dependent upon your role within it. Once you were incorporated into its structure, it required your unwavering services - you were not expected to act independently (such conduct would be scorned) and you would not act alone. The army was an effective body because it had rules and sanctions which bound all of its members equally, and it operated out of self-interest. But the security it offered lacked compassion, it was inflexible and dry, toughened for its singular purpose like the end of a bull-skin whip. The militiamen's power did not come from any faith, but from their belief in their own group identity, their loyalty to nothing but themselves and their own identifying control. They wreaked their loathing like pirates on the peoples of Butare.

He had hoped that the Church would provide him with a similar form of purpose and security, while allowing him his own doubts as to the veracity of its motives. It would allow him to think and ponder the wisdom of humankind and its constructs, and to consider the lot of those around him, from a position of safety and unthreatened authority. A crisis, caused by the arbitrary shifts of nature or the expedient whims of men, would require the intervention of army personnel to take charge and direct the resolution. But a man of the church would be expected to comfort, to console, to counsel as a more passive witness and player, free from the obligation to maintain control, but ever a willing participant in its benefits. The combination of authority, respect and limited intervention, appealed to him and drew him towards his studies.

The seminary programme only catered for a small number of local and hostel students, both male and female, and was divided into a year-long pre-theology level, a two-year seminary level and a year of pastoral ministry as a requisite for ordination. Lushodayana was immediately captured by the debates that were purposefully raised in the first year of the course. His father's stern and unforgiving intellect had made him shy away from debate at home and he was reserved and uneasy when faced with the stated opinion of a teacher or friend. But the polite, measured manner in which debates were raised in the seminary school drew him from his shell and the rarefied nature of the issues discussed filled him with a sense of comfort and ease that overshadowed his solitude. He began to question and debate, no longer content to accept whatever was placed before him. He attended courses on liturgical practice and pastoral supervision at the seminary itself; other lectures, on philosophy, history of the church, theological reflection and comparative religion, were held at the university. He learnt about sacramental practice, spiritual life, conscience and Catholic morality, and contemporary social issues.

The Liturgy of the Hours and the Eucharist were celebrated each day in the small chapel by the entire seminary. Similarly, meals were taken together in the dining hall adjacent to the nuns' hostel. He developed passing friendships with some of the hostel students, although the spiritual development expected of seminary students was deeply personal and social contact between students tended to be minimal. Their conversations were limited to classroom debates and theory-based discussions over mealtime. The students enjoyed little free time, as the day started early with personal prayer and was filled with course work, communal chores, pastoral work and prayer. Occasionally they would relax in the courtyard or a small group would visit the university library, stopping for tea at the market.

Lushodayana was given a small room in the male students' hostel, with a cot, cold-water basin and an unstable wooden table and chair. This sparse space was his home for three years, where he felt gently rocked and numbed by an unchanging routine and an omnipotent authority. The small window looked out onto the central courtyard and faced the nuns' hostel and dining hall. The seminary buildings were divided, significantly, into two sections, one wing containing the chapel and male hostel, the other the dining hall, a smaller female hostel and the classrooms. The two wings were separated by a courtyard and joined on the northern end by a paved path leading past the bell tower. The administrative offices and stores fell behind the male hostel, between the hostel building and the boundary of the seminary grounds.

Soon after he had commenced his pre-theology level, he was assigned to an Advisor. It was the duty of the Advisors to guide and nurture the new students through the orientation programme and to provide them with an example, a sage from whom advice could be sought. The Advisor was also responsible for the individual seminars on sexual development and clerical celibacy. The Rector, a thin, emaciated man with a deeply pock-marked skin and lesions on his nose and cheeks, apparently had some doubts as to whether the young man from the rural north would survive the four-year course. Lushodayana discovered that the Rector had resisted his acceptance at the seminary school and that Muyigenzi had traveled to Butare to persuade him to reconsider. Although the Rector was never rude towards him, he dismissed Lushodayana with little attention. The Rector assigned him to an Advisor named Gratian, a plump middle-aged monk whose flexible style and loose mouth had caused him to fall out of favour with the higher echelons of power in the Church for some time. It was to be a fortuitous matching, as his senior's easy manner and daring humour appealed to his ward and provided him with relief from the otherwise pressing expectations of the seminary.

Gratian had sublimated his natural manly passions into an interest in culinary matters which bordered on the irreverent. His round head perched solidly on a rotund soft body and his podgy fingers habitually fiddled about his mouth and chin. The presence of food in his mouth was no deterrent to speech and he spoke freely regardless. One could often not even be sure that his mouth was full, as his cheeks were naturally puffy and flaccid and his speech was replete with sucking, tongue-filled sounds. The monk sweated when he ate, small trickles running from his short cropped hair past his bulbous ears in tell-tale streaks - even thinking or talking about food resulted in little beads of perspiration appearing on the bridge of his nose. He inhabited a densely packed chamber down the passage from Lushodayana's own room on the first floor of the hostel. His chamber contained an array of pilfered leftovers, open packets of nuts, half-eaten fruit and boiled sweets. The monk always had sweets about his person and liberally dished out the sour yellow and black ones to anyone who showed interest – the sweeter red, green and orange sweets were reserved for the owner.

"Have a sweet," he would coo effeminately, watching the offered person's hand closely as it delved into the half-opened packet. His fingers squeezed the unwanted sweets forward and held the more desirable ones tightly in the rear. Lushodayana soon learned of his master's harmless idiosyncrasies and Gratian would wink at him slyly as he observed the person offered withdraw a shiny black or off-yellow sweet and nervously push it between their lips.

"Physical relations are vastly over-rated", Gratian proclaimed grandly during the privacy of their 'clerical celibacy' seminars. "The act is base and demeaning and there are many other far more worthy practices to be mastered."

Lushodayana knew that he was about to be tested. "Such as communal prayer." Gratian sat back, with the slightest hint of a smile on his fatty lips, and waited for his pupil's response.

"We are taught that communal prayer is an important part of expressing one's inner spirituality, Father," Lushodayana replied, smiling to himself as Gratian melodramatically cast his head back in mock agony. It was this kind of conduct, rather than outspoken insurrection, that resulted in Gratian being isolated by the Church leadership. He could not be challenged directly, as his disdain was oblique and always masked, but the Rector did his best to restrict his influence, giving him those students who were most unlikely to complete their studies. This, together with the widely rumoured incident involving the Mass wine and the fact that he none-too-secretly referred to the Rector as "His Majesty", served to perpetuate Gratian's isolated position on the outer fringes of the Church.

Gratian found it hard to hide his dislike of the Rector or his assistant, Bertin, a short, stocky man who espoused the virtues of physical training and was wont to flex his muscles under a thin cotton shirt at any and every opportunity, particularly when the female students were passing. Bertin stalked about the seminary grounds at night in the hope of catching a student out of bed and took delight in reporting any incident, no matter how trivial, to the Rector. He habitually carried the gnarled femur of a male gorilla with him, which he would hold across his neck and shoulders, twisting his body from side to side in a macabre form of exercise. The shaft of the bone at either end was blackened from constant contact with his palms, and tiny grey pieces of bone flaked off and speckled his shoulders like dandruff. Bertin insisted that he had had a hand in the demise of the fearsome creature itself, but Gratian assured his ward that it had been bought in a run-down junk store in Kigali. The bone was to prove Bertin's downfall in the end.

Gratian took a keen and protective interest in his student. It was as if the older man saw the solitude and doubt in his pupil's soul and found some resonance there. At first Lushodayana was overwhelmed by the intrusive nature of his advisor - he would sense the large man's presence, unannounced, in his room, not by smell or by noise, but just by the sudden closeness filling its spaces. He would turn over in his bed and Gratian would smile, without saying a word, and then leave as quietly as he had come. But there was a consistency, a dependability, to his affection for the young man which provided Lushodayana with a balance during the course of his residence at the seminary. He felt secure and comforted by Gratian's interest in him and he was the one person that the young man felt able to speak to: it was Gratian to whom he spoke, from the wrenching depths of his heart, about the loss of his brother, the terrible burden that he felt, and the unrelenting pain the ghostly memory caused. Gratian's loyalty shaped his life at the seminary and his influence extended even so far as to the choice of the name 'Melchior' - one of the wise men - for his student at the end of his pre-theology year.

"In anticipation of your ordination," Gratian said. "I believe that you were wise before you came to this place, and I hope that we will do nothing to change that upon your leaving here. It is a name well-fitting to a man of your being entering the world. Wear it with confidence and grace."

Gratian shielded him from the authoritarian vagaries of the Rector and Bertin and, in his own way, filled the space left by the absence of family. Hostel students were allowed two weeks away from the seminary in order to celebrate Christmas at home - apart from this break Melchior did not see his village or his old friends and family. The few stolen weekend hours for 'self-reflection' broke the regularity of seminary life but did not provide an opportunity to have meaningful contact with anyone outside of the confines of the school itself. He would accompany Gratian into the town on occasion, drinking tea or sweet mulled wine in the open gardens of the university, or visiting his mentor's friends, listening to their ribald jokes and serious discussions.

Gratian, and their outings together, provided some relief from the strictly regulated life of the seminary course, but even when they sat drinking wine and laughing at some irreverent remark, they knew that the breach was temporary, and short-lived at that. They would soon return to the compound with its strict controls and the watchful eyes. Melchior drew comfort from the protected existence within the seminary, but it conflicted at times with his youthful curiosity and desires. On some days, when he awoke to bright sunshine and the smell of warm earth in the air, he was seized by a desire to step outside the cloistered walls and walk uninhibited and alone through the sorghum fields.

Melchior awoke on one such morning and stood at the window, staring out onto the swept courtyard. He could faintly discern the whirring sound of bees and brown locusts moving amongst the tendrils of the jasmine creeper. The courtyard was empty, save for a silver-backed mongoose digging amongst the roots of the banana trees, scuffing the dirt behind him in small puffs of dust. Melchior was about to turn back to the cool interior of his room when he noticed a figure at the gates, turning the stiff brass handle one way then the other. The gates were locked at night and had not yet been opened. He saw a movement of yellow and red, and then a voice called out from the other side of the courtyard. A nun approached, the keys clinking gently in her hands. The two said something to each other, a friendly greeting, and he heard the figure outside laugh, an easy fluid sound floating up towards him. The gate swung open and she walked into the compound.

There are moments when one senses a shift in one's world, perhaps a small, subtle change in a life, the introduction of a fact, a person, an event, seemingly insignificant, but in the moment, one knows that nothing can ever be quite the same as it was before. As he watched her, standing to one side while the nun closed the gate, he felt that shift, an instance of absolute quiet in which he was moved, imperceptibly, in a new direction.

Her presence was powerful and clear: things around her seemed blurred and obscure. He absorbed every aspect of her, her long yellow dress, decorated with red flowers, falling simply from her shoulders to her ankles, offset against her deep olive-brown skin, her hair braided into a mass of thin dark plaits which seemed to glisten with a life of their own. He was mesmerised by her poise, strong and sure, and by the confident manner in which she entered his unknown world. She asked the nun a question, who pointed towards the chapel in reply. The visitor walked with unwavering strides across the swept gravel path, followed by his burning gaze, and disappeared from view in the direction of the chapel. He stayed at the window for a while, relishing the warm excitement he felt moving about his body.

He did not see her again that day. He waited until the very last moment to leave the school to attend lectures at the university, bustling into the classroom after the lecturer had arrived, but she did not reappear. The visitor occupied his thoughts throughout the day and he was distracted during the classes, his eyes staring inattentively at the empty blackboard. She walked in front of him, her tall body and thin neck, elegant and smiling, looking at him as she strode past him. His mind played out the scene, repeating it over and over again without pause, addictively feeding off the images, shutting out the surrounding world.

He managed to shake off the obsessive image after classes and consider the intriguing figure more rationally. It occurred to him that she might be wealthy, that her secure outlook might in fact have been nothing but disdain, contempt for the basic nature of the lives of the nuns and students in the school. But he dismissed the idea, as her demeanour was engaging, rather than cold, and the manner in which she had lightly curtsied before the nun suggested a respect rather than a rejection. He found her presence at the compound both strange and uplifting, as if an unexpected and rare rose had suddenly flowered in the nuns' garden, a welcome and unexpected intrusion. He did not dare ask the nuns what business she had had at the compound, and kept his thoughts secret, like a precious stone held under his garments, touched and smoothed for comfort.

A week passed before Melchior saw the visitor in the seminary again. She was wearing the same yellow dress, her lanky body neatly enclosed in its simple cotton, her dark hair pushed back and held by a bright band of fabric. This time she was met at the gate by a nun who embraced her lightly before taking her hand and leading her towards the women's quarters. Melchior stood before the fish pond, pretending to meditate on its cold inmates, straining his eyes to the side to watch the nun and her companion as they ambled up the path between the rose beds and the lawn, into the shadow cast by the bell-tower. The young woman stopped and picked a sprig of jasmine flowers from the cascading creeper and pretended to place the flowers on the nun's drab habit. There was a forbidden squeal from the nun as the two women stifled their giggles and turned to see if anyone had witnessed their small indiscretion. Melchior stood alone in the courtyard and took the opportunity to look up at the visitor directly. As she turned and hurriedly walked into the building with her companion, Melchior felt a sharp pang, a physical sensation of pain, sink into his chest. He must have looked so stern, so disapproving, he thought. Why could he not have entered their game, been light and mischievous as well ? Gratian would have laughed out loud, approached them and made some enthusiastic comment. He felt desperate, but the moment had so enraptured him, that he had been unable to use the opportunity at all. His breath felt short and his thoughts were confused.

He left the courtyard and sat for a while in the cool chapel. He wondered why it was important to him that the young woman did not think him staid or disapproving of her joke: she did not know him and he did not know her - what did it matter that she saw a young priest standing, watching her without rebuke? But these rational thoughts did not quell the despair he felt at his ineptitude and he was filled with contrary emotions, anxiety mixed with excitement, despair mixed with hope.

The week dragged slowly and he was dispirited. Gratian tried to tease his secret from him, first flippantly and then more seriously, concerned by his ward's distractedness. Melchior answered him grumpily and spent time on his own in his room. It scared him that the contented structure of his life at the seminary could have been disrupted so fundamentally and so easily, and it raised again his doubts and fears about the path he had chosen.

The following week the young woman appeared again and was again met at the gate by the nun. She wore a thin cotton dress this time, light and cut just below the knees; her hair hung loosely, more wildly.   Melchior moved without conscious thought, placing himself on the path that she would walk to the nuns' quarters, oblivious to anything other than her approach. Young male students were not expected to engage in any conversation with the nuns, other than as was strictly necessary for the performance of their duties. He had not dwelt on the boundaries that were instilled in the seminary to contain the exigencies of human sexuality, but the forbidden nature of casual contact between the male students and the nuns was an unspoken and accepted tenet at the school.   The nun and her companion walked towards him, deep in conversation and apparently unaware of the young student who stood in their path, fidgeting with his hands. His chest pounded and his hands were sweaty and hot. He wrung them together and wiped his palms down the sides of his robe. As they drew close to him, the young woman looked up at him. He felt her gaze strike through his being, her large brown eyes seemed to glisten and her mouth pulled ever so slightly - in the hint of a smile, he fancied.

"*Hello*," he said in Kinyarwandan. He deliberately addressed her informally, using Kinyarwandan rather than the more formal French, trying to project an air of ease, of youthfulness and confidence, which would appeal to the young woman. It seemed to him it would be more engaging than formal address and might dissipate any reticence the young woman may have felt at being addressed by a student of the church.

"*Bonjour, monsieur*," the young woman replied, lowering her eyes from his face in a sign of respect and visibly tightening her hold on her companion's arm. The nun looked up, apparently startled, before they walked swiftly past him. He caught the scent of body powder, silky and clean. The nuns would not use any such cosmetic and the scent was enrapturing. He stood quite still, not even looking after them, and let the perfumed air settle about him. His reverie was broken by the sound of the two women giggling, holding onto each other and tripping into the building. Just as they moved out of sight, Melchior thought he saw the young woman turn her head in his direction, a strong face looking back.

He smarted from her use of the formal French in the face of his use of local parlance. Did she think he was unrefined for addressing her in Kinyarwandan? He was suddenly agonised by the thought that she might think him simple or uneducated. Perhaps she thought him a rural peasant, seeking refuge in the church. Did she even know that he was a student at the seminary? In all his tortured thoughts, he did not consider why he was so ensnared by the young woman who had appeared at the seminary. Within the space of just one or two visits, and without them ever meeting, without him even knowing her name, she had become a central part of his thoughts. His daily routines seemed motivated by her next visit, by the prospect of saying a few words to her, by the hope even of discovering her name.

The afternoon after he had spoken to her, Melchior was working in the library, reading through a text in French that had been prescribed for the next day's religious literature class. He had chosen a cool corner of the library, where the sun was unable to penetrate and the surrounding wooden shelves and leather bound volumes provided shelter from outside noises.

He looked up at the rustling sound of folded fabric and saw the nun, the young visitor's companion, moving towards him, apparently intent on finding some work hidden amongst the volumes on the top shelf. Melchior forced himself to return to his work and placed his hand on the side of his face, in order to avoid any chance contact with her. He had already shocked her, he was sure, by addressing her companion in her presence so directly and he did not want to worsen matters further. He heard the nun move along the shelf behind him and he thought he detected a slight mildewy smell from her clothes. He stared at the page in front of him without reading the small black print, laid like thread across the book.

"My cousin comes to visit me every Tuesday morning at ten o'clock," she said simply, still searching for a book, almost as if she was talking to herself. "She is a student at the teacher-training college in Avenue de Liberté. It would be better if you did not interfere when she visits me again."

The young man sat quietly while the nun continued her search around the corner of the small desk, until her back was turned to him. Her features were undefined beneath her roughly cut habit. Perhaps she too was lithe and strong beneath those clothes, he thought.

"What is her name?" he asked in a whisper. The nun turned to face him. Her face was not playful as he had seen in the courtyard and her expression was sour. "I was going to complain to our Mother but my cousin asked me not to get you into any trouble. But if you continue to interfere with her visits I will say something, so please leave us alone." Then she turned and walked swiftly away, leaving him far more elated than chastened at the thought that the young woman had wished to protect him from the disciplining hand of the Mother.

Sensitivity arises from an appreciation of the inherent vulnerabilities of those around you. It brings with it as well the necessary understanding of one's own limitations and has as its partner all the doubts of the insecure. Melchior was unable to hold onto his initial elation and his thoughts were soon filled with questions: Did she regard him as being too unsophisticated ? Perhaps her protectiveness was born of sympathy rather than interest ? He felt both uplifted and miserable at the possibilities. The nun's words seemed almost like a message for him to approach the woman outside of the seminary. Why else did the nun tell him that she was at the teacher training college ? But then perhaps she was drawing a distinction between his restricted lifestyle and the exciting choices facing her cousin as a student of the college.

Melchior attended his weekly session with Gratian in a state of despair. "We are not going to talk about anything else besides what it is that is going on and making you so stupidly miserable," he announced before his pupil had sat down. He looked at Melchior menacingly. "And if that means that we have to sit here not saying a word for the next hour, me staring at your sad little face and you trying to look away, well then that is what we will do." With that Gratian folded his arms with a huff from his protruding lips and stared mercilessly at him.

Melchior sat for a while, enduring his mentor's chilly look. "All right," he said, "but only if you stop looking at me like that." He took a deep breath and started to tell the priest about the visitor to the seminary. He spoke of his obsession with her and the conflict which her presence had drawn up inside of him. At first Gratian misunderstood the thrust of the dilemma, thinking the conflict was between his pupil's adherence to the discipline of the church and his youthful desires. However, it soon dawned on him that the young man was not considering the restrictions placed on him by the church.

"Dearest God in Heaven !" he exclaimed, clapping his two podgy hands together. He heaved his weight off the chair and scrounged in a cupboard, breathing heavily and muttering to himself distractedly, before producing a bottle of sweet mulled wine and two plastic cups. He poured them both a generous quantity of the dark plum-coloured wine, even though it was still morning.

"My poor boy, you are quite right." He gulped a huge mouthful noisily. "The life of any young man is complicated enough without adding the ridiculous rules of the church to his burden. Good God, here I am worrying about what His Majesty would say or what the bone-man would think, and you have a real crisis on your hands. There is one thing that transcends all the rules, that blows the top off the highest church roof, one thing that is inconsolable, one thing that can tear open the heart of a man and scatter his thoughts to the wind, one thing that you can never take away and one thing that you can never plan. That thing can destroy you in an instant, it can lead you into the sky and then drop you like an oyster shell, it can heal you and it can break you." Gratian was animated, waving his arms in wide gestures, slopping wine onto his hand.

"Gratian," Melchior interrupted, "I am not in love with this woman. I haven't even met her, I don't even know her name. I'm not upset because I love her, I don't love her. But that's the very reason I feel so miserable - not that I want to meet her so that I can fall in love with her, I won't fall in love with her. It is not knowing her, not meeting her, not knowing her name, it's that absence that is making me miserable."

"Do you think love is when you marry the woman you have been living with since you were a child ? Do you think love is the woman you sit next to in class for months ? Do you think love ·is like bringing a family together, that always belonged? Of course this is love, this is exactly what love is, it is an obsession with a fleeting event that you cannot hold onto, it is like a mist that clears as you reach out and take it in your hand. Love is a hot breath as you pass, a half-seen stare from afar, a fruit that is ripe for the eating only for one day of the year, a hot meal of lamb knuckles and gravy before it cools." Gratian stifled his giggle when he caught sight of the young man's cold stare.

"You are not helping. I know you think this is all very exciting and lots of fun, but I am unhappy and you are not making anything any better. Love is not like food and anyway I'm not hungry."

Gratian laughed out loud and poured himself some more wine. Melchior put his hand over the top of the cup. His head hurt from the early morning drink and his unsettled thoughts. His tutor's enthusiasm had not made him feel any better.

He observed the visitor over the next few weeks, feeding if not satisfying his burning hunger for contact with her with glimpses and stolen glances when she visited the seminary. He ensured that he was in the courtyard for her visits, but he was careful to be seated beneath the mpingo tree, away from the gate, or resting on the chapel steps, so as to watch her movements from a distance. It was impossible to get anywhere close to the visitor whilst she was in the company of her cousin. Melchior started to take late afternoon walks after studies in the hope of coming across her on her own. He walked up the paved main road, past the shops and hotels, and towards the old colonial suburb of Buye, tree-lined and graced by old pre-independence residences. Then he would turn along Avenue de Liberté towards the low squat dormitories and buildings of the training college. He would walk slowly towards the college, observing the movements of the people drifting along the road, searching unabashedly for the merest glimpse of a familiar walk, a movement of the hand, a turn of the head. He felt the young woman's physical presence was etched into his mind, that her smallest movement would alert him to her presence. But he would walk past the college without catching sight of her and the walk home was quick and abrupt, embarrassment shrouding his hunched shoulders. He felt foolish after these unsatisfying attempts. He conceded to himself that it was just as well that he did not meet her on his walks after all, as he would probably only say something inappropriate, if anything at all, and the sophisticated student would think all the worse of him.

The morning after just one such unsuccessful foray to the college, Melchior rose early and walked to the open air market in search of cloth for curtains for his room. His frustrated attempts to see the young woman, and the confused emotions which she caused to well up within him, had darkened his mood. He felt that he was no longer in control and small things, which would not normally have played on his nerves, suddenly irritated him. He reacted sharply to questions from his fellow students, whether asked in concern or not. His small room seemed suddenly unbearably sparse, his daily routine drab and without meaning. Gratian's enthusiastic interest in his troubles only irked him and he had lost his singular sense of security. His dreams were once again troubled by visions of his brother and he woke, tired, his face grimy with sweat. He approached the market determined to regain his protective sense of order.

The market was already filled with people laying out their goods. The strong smells of fish and fresh blood emanated thickly under the tin-roofed shelter, pink stained water trickling along the cement gutters, women scraping the scales from fish caught the day before, hessian bags of dried silver fish open, glinting in the new sunlight, twitching under the attentions of blue and green flies as if alive. The sellers were laughing and talking in loud voices, excitedly chattering with friends and passers-by, wielding their sharpened flat knives, wiping their broad faces with the back of their arms, flicking fish entrails into the stained buckets next to the piles of silver-grey fish, their eyes glassed-over and their bodies limp, slit down the middle and flapped open to reveal their pink flesh. Further down women were hanging goat carcasses from thick metal wire strung over the rafters of the shed, large purple and red animals swinging like bats from the roof, no fluid dripping from the meat, slaughtered and drained, heads and hooves removed to be sold separately. The heads were lined up along the cement shelf, skinned, smooth pink faces grinning splayed teeth and eyeless sockets, the butcher-woman attacking the leg joints of a carcass with long hard cuts, crunching and twisting the bone out of the body and pushing it to one side.

Chickens screeched and thrashed in the small crates, layered one on top of the other, white and brown feathers rising on draughts above the crates and filtering down over the floor and concrete tops like a fine snow. The fowls pecked and thrashed against the plastic sides of the crates as they were caught and turned upside down, their feet and beaks tied with twine and then finally hauled, quiet and shocked, swinging from the wooden beams awaiting purchase and slaughter.

Melchior greeted some of the women who were joking amongst themselves, swaying their hips and opening their mouths wide in carefree guffaws, their hands busy with their work, their faces alight. He moved past the shed into the central open square of the market, bounded on all four sides by kiosks and tables selling cloth, small collections of clothes, mechanical parts. Music blared from one small store selling tapes, the tape recorder centred in the middle of a wooden table and pointed out into the open market. Next to the shed the flat tables of dry food stalls bent under the load of sacks, opened and spilling out rice, beans, dried peas, tea, corn flour, chilli seeds, pumpkin pips for roasting, salt, unground pepper, piled hills of dried and fresh corn cobs, spices, tobacco leaves and ground tobacco. Other tables had small piles of fresh tomatoes, potatoes, cassava, taro, sweet potato, bananas, mangoes and green beans. The aroma of spices and brewing milky tea with cloves filled the air, the comforting smells of food combining with the shouts of buyers and sellers, talking and negotiating, offering prices in the middle of jokes, interrupting jokes with counter-offers.

He pushed past a group of women filling packets with sweet potatoes and tomatoes to get into the middle of the market, where other women sat cross-legged on small woven mats, relaxed before their spread of colourful cloths, yellow and brown mats, scarves and *bubus*. He walked slowly up and down the paths between the cloth, stopping to look and to feel some bright yellow cloth, bordered with emerald green. The women carried on talking and laughing, ignoring the young man as he paced carefully between the laid out stores. He stopped before one set of cloth and lifted the edge to reveal a printed fabric that was half hidden underneath - a simple cotton cloth, thin and light, printed yellow and red. He pulled the fabric from underneath the pile and, half-crouched, ran his hand over the silky layer, his fingers pausing over the floral print, almost surprised that the print did not feel any different to the rest of the fabric.

"That would make an interesting cassock," a woman said in French, lightly, behind him. He rose too quickly to his feet, flushed and still holding the fabric. He almost lost his balance as the blood drained from his head. The speaker must have noticed that he was unsteady on his feet, as she took his arm and looked into his face, not teasing now.

"Are you all right?" she asked in Kinyarwandan. "I didn't mean to startle you."

Melchior turned and looked into the face of the seminary visitor. Her beauty, her closeness to him, took his breath away. He looked away, down at the cloth still in his hand. It was the fabric of the dress she had been wearing when he first noticed her at the seminary, yellow with red flowers. He felt the blood rise suddenly in his cheeks. She was laughing, an open, free laughter that made her deep brown eyes fill with tears and her smooth cheeks bunch together.

"My name is Selena," she said, still smiling. Her braided hair framed her face and her skin seemed to shine with a light of its own. He felt his mind clear and his chest open, like a traveller whose pack has been lifted from him, allowing him to straighten his back and see his surroundings clearly for the first time. He looked at her open face without any shame or disguise. Then he bent down and carefully placed the cotton fabric he had removed back in place amongst the folded cloth on the ground, carefully arranging the corners in line with the rest.

When he stood up again, she was still close to him, standing and smiling. Her expression was open, without any hint of judgment: she was smiling not in sympathy nor yet laughing at him, but somehow joining him, stepping into the intimacy surrounding the cloth and her dress. Melchior felt strangely safe within the gaze of this lovely woman, at ease, as if he would always be free from her judgment.

"My name is Melchior," he said not taking his eyes off her face. They looked at each other in silence, each held in the other's unwavering gaze until the woman selling the cloth clucked loudly in disapproval.

"Are you buying my cloth? This is not a hotel. Buy the cloth or move out of the way !"

Selena laughed and said something to the woman. Her hazel-brown skin was unblemished and her dark eyelashes defined her eyes with startling outline.

"I feel that I should apologise for making things difficult with your cousin," he said, still standing alongside the cloth seller.

"No one has to justify themselves to anyone else, least of all you, you who have chosen such a demanding and disciplined path. I on the other hand have chosen an easy and well-travelled route. You have not embarrassed yourself: I am honoured that you felt a wish to speak to me." She paused before smiling. "And I am very pleased that you like my choice of cloth," she said, laughing and pointing to the fabric folded on the ground. Melchior felt a blush turn in his cheeks, but her vivacity made him laugh in spite of himself.

"I will look out for you, Melchior, when I next visit my cousin," she said. The turned towards the bustle of the market without waiting for a reply. He watched her walk away, soon to be lost in the crowd of people moving across the colourful open square.

NAIROBI DAILY NEWS

13 February 1998

RWANDAN MUYIGENZI TRIAL
SET TO START AMID CONTROVERSY

Legal correspondent
David Nsilese

The grey edifice of the
Criminal Tribunal building here
in Arusha, with its yawning
entrance and concrete strips,
gives this building the
unfortunate look of a baleen
whale; an unfortunate 'but
perhaps not inappropriate
comparison to an animal which
ploughs through secluded seas
catching the flotsam and jetsam
of past events.

One piece of flotsam presently
in the bowels of the beast is
the former communal police
chief, Mr Victor Muyigenzi: his
trial is due to start on Monday
next week and has attracted the

interest of the local and international media.

This reporter has reliably learnt from sources within the office of the prosecution that Muyigenzi is to be indicted on charges ranging from genocide and crimes against humanity to the rape of Tutsi women on a grand scale. Perhaps it is this last aspect which has captured the media's attention, or the relationship between Muyigenzi and the infamous (and enigmatic) prefect, Colonel Batho, who has evaded capture and prosecution despite the purported best efforts of the international policing community. This reporter has repeatedly and pertinently demanded information of the status of the investigation into Colonel Batho, but has met only with the stony stares of bureaucratic walls.

It has been reliably discovered by this reporter that the true target of the operation which netted Muyigenzi was in fact his superior, Batho, and that the indictment of Muyigenzi is regarded within the hierarchy of the tribunal as being a poorer substitute.

The anticipated trial of Muyigenzi takes place against a backdrop of a raging debate as to the ethical objectives and ethnic underpinnings of the tribunal. The arguments, played out in the closeted hotel rooms inhabited by the foreign members of the press corps and reflected on the pages of the newspapers and television screens of the local networks, are old and rhetorical, but nevertheless strike at the very heart of the moral rationale of the tribunal.

It is a debate which arises amongst African and Asian members, but which seems strangely irrelevant to our paler brethren who, from time to time, emerge wan and anxious into the bright skies of northern Tanzania; for these paler palates the mere existence of a funded tribunal is a sufficient palliative for the guilts of an international community.

For Africans, the moral rationale of the tribunal is a critical issue upon which the potential healing of the wounds of the land of a thousand hills, and indeed central Africa itself, is dependent. The creation of a tribunal operating outside of both the geographic and jurisprudential boundaries of the country which has experienced the tragedy is deeply troubling for some critics: "You put the country on trial, by doing this you perpetuate the crime of colonialism, you say that the victim is not qualified to deal with his own tragedy and you, the international elite, must now move in and wrest control in order to judge the wrongs that have befallen this backward and barbaric region. You wrest all control from the very people that must heal themselves and you deny them the chance to do so; it is an injury upon all injuries." So says Jean Ngari, correspondent for the Africanist Movement of Kenya.

The response, that the tribunal has managed to focus world attention on the atrocities suffered by Rwanda and that the tribunal represents the United Nation's will to re-establish order in the region, does not impress Ngari: "Europe and America cannot find fault in the Rwandan criminal code nor can they accuse the Rwandan courts of partiality; they are reduced to pointing fingers at the punishments and complain that the execution of *genocidaires* in public is unacceptable. What is the Western world saying by this: that Africans can kill one another in a genocidal orgy without intervention, but come judgment day, only they are equipped to hand out the punishments? Entire communities were massacred and they saw fit to 'register their concern'; now we come to the healing process and the West imposes its own view of what should constitute healing. Perhaps we need retribution; the West has no idea what we need."

Ngari's criticisms of the
United Nations tribunal have
been thrown into sharp relief
by the decision of the tribunal
clerks not to accede to a
request from the Rwandan
national government that
Muyigenzi be transferred to the
jurisdiction of its criminal
system.

This decision has precluded the
Rwandan courts from prosecuting
Muyigenzi before the Rwandan
people, according to the rules
of the Rwandan people; most
importantly, the conviction of
Muyigenzi before the tribunal
will limit the punishment which
can be meted out to him. When
the United Nations considered
the proposed creation of the
ICTR in 1994, Rwanda voted
against the motion - the
significance of that simple
statement is perhaps only being
felt today.

Furthermore, the Registrar is
thought to be taking seriously
the challenge raised by the
body of defence lawyers to the
newly sanctioned presence of a
Rwandan national government

representative in Trial Chamber One. The fact that the Rwandan government has not been represented in Arusha until now is itself an indictment on the process - the fact that the Registrar is listening to the objections of the *genocidaires* to such a move is simply incomprehensible.

The last word from the Africanist Movement? "The tribunal in Arusha is nothing but a perpetuation of colonial control and interference, the kind of interference by Western powers which led to the genocide in the first place, which allowed it to continue and which has destabilised the entirety of central Africa."

Chapter Three

The light fabric curtains hung in the priest's small room now, yellow catching the sun and shining brightly, a small segment of colour in an otherwise darkened and drab space, and a reminder of an association that had blossomed in inhospitable ground. From that first day that she had entered the compound and he had caught sight of her from the window, he had felt a change affected about him, like the subtle touch of a breeze from an opened window. His thoughts and perceptions had been moved, perhaps only slightly, by his knowledge of her existence in the world, seemingly insignificant information, its imperceptible weight adjusting the scale and changing his course ultimately more profoundly than he could ever have anticipated.

Gratian had been unimpressed by his account of Selena. "You don't know the woman. Tell me, what do you know about her? Does she cook?" he asked, his face screwed up into mounds of thick skin and jowls. "She's of no use to us," he continued presumptuously, without waiting for a reply, "if she cannot cook." This half-serious jesting on Gratian's part gave way, however, to a deeper concern when he appreciated the impact of the young woman's presence on his ward. He observed his pupil watching for her, sitting by the window in classes at the seminary, straying by the gate whenever he could. Some weeks after their meeting in the market, Melchior was standing on the steps of the chapel, delaying his entry for prayer, when he saw her leaving, walking alone across the courtyard towards the gate. He took a step away from the chapel only to be grasped forcefully on his arm.

"His Majesty is watching," Gratian hissed at him as he pulled him back up the steps. Melchior sat miserably through the prayer session, his head half-bowed and his lips still. He could not account for the strange upwellings he felt within him, the physical need he felt to talk to her, the desperate unsatisfying emptiness of fleeting glances. The bench seemed hard and he moved restlessly, sighing and rubbing the back of his neck. At one point he looked up to see Gratian glaring at him, but he could not contain himself. Halfway through the prayers he walked, crouched, down the side aisle and out of the back doors into the cool evening air. She had left long before and he sat on the steps, trying to contain the sudden yearning he felt to cry like a child.

It is not possible to feel only one emotion intensely and to remain cut off from others, to let one river flow but keep the others dammed – the internal mechanism by which we block our spontaneous emotions has only one key and only one door. Selena's arrival left him feeling alive but exposed, vulnerable to all the hardships that he had experienced, exposed on an open plain and without shelter. Years of emotion, for the death of his brother, his sister, his mother's slow melting away and his father's scorn, seemed trapped inside him, pushing up. The protective walls were suddenly frail like rice paper that can be torn with a brush of the hand.

He heard movement from inside the chapel as prayers ended. He realised his hands were shaking and his cheeks were wet with warm tears. He ran from the chapel up the stairs to his room, before anyone could see him. But his mentor was close behind him and no sooner had he sat on the edge of his cot than the door opened and Gratian came and sat down next to him, the metal cot groaning in protest at the weight.

"It is very important that you tell me what is happening to you," he said softly. "His Majesty saw you watching that young girl and everyone observed you running out of prayers. You have been distracted and irritable lately. I must tell you that I have already been called in to speak to your philosophy lecturer at the university because of your poor concentration in his last seminars, and I am sure that His Majesty will want to speak to me about your latest dramatic exit."

The young man felt the tears well up once again, he opened his mouth to speak, strands of spittle threading from his teeth and lips, but was unable to put words to his wounds.

Gratian looked at his tortured face and placed his thick arms around his shoulders. Melchior buried his face in his master's folded cassock and flesh and let go of his feeble restraints: he wept with deep sobs, his gasped breaths wracking his body, a wet stain slowly spreading on the priest's garments. Gratian held him wordlessly, waiting patiently until the sobs became quieter, the jerking breaths more even, and still he kept him in his embrace, until finally he was at rest, as if he had fallen into a slumber, exhausted and drained.

Melchior pulled his smeared and moist face out from his mentor's chest and half laughed in embarrassment. Gratian ran his fingers affectionately through his ward's hair: "If this is just about this girl who has caught your interest and can't even cook, I will be very disappointed, I can tell you that," he said, trying to appear stern.

"I am feeling very strong ... feelings, I feel out of control," Melchior paused and took a deep breath. "She does have something to do with it, Father, but only because she has started something inside of me. It is about her and it has nothing to do with her. She has opened a door that I did not even know was there, and inside I have found feelings that ... I have found self-pity, shame, hurt, I haven't found feelings of love, I haven't the feelings that should be there. I don't think about pastoral care, I don't think about the lame and the sick, I don't think about the work of the Lord, I just think about ... me, my brother .."

Gratian interrupted him loudly. "You want to heal other people when you are yourself wounded ? How can you heal another if you are not able to heal yourself ? How can you take the time to listen to someone else's pain if you have never taken the time to listen to your own ? You have shielded yourself against that healing process, you have distanced yourself from the world and yourself on the pretext that you are unselfish, that you have the will only to help others and not to consider your own needs. Your solitariness is your guard against the truth, and now someone has come into your life who has challenged those barriers. You feel an uncommon need to make contact with another person and you find your own barriers in your way. If you push them aside in order to get to your goal, you open all the doors, not just the door to get to her. You cannot be selective, my little one."

He listened to what the priest had to say; it resonated somewhere within him, but it frightened him to think that his perspectives could be challenged, fundamentally, by the mere existence of another person, a stranger who had no interest in the emotional outcome of their unintended assault. It made her seem all the more powerful. "Perhaps she is an angel, after all," he said, half to himself. "Perhaps this is my test."

Gratian exploded in mirth. "So it is just love after all," he guffawed, breaking the serious tone of the moment and giving his pupil's leg a stinging slap. Gratian heaved himself off the bed and looked at the pale orange clouds thoughtfully. "I think that perhaps you should talk to this girl of yours," he said to the evening sky. "This is dangerous territory, I need not tell you that. Friendships between young men and women are fraught with calamitous potentials and His Majesty will not approve, I assure you. However, if she can cook," he said conspiratorially, "maybe it would be useful for you to see her again." Gratian coughed theatrically and turned to the young man, who looked up at him with wide grateful eyes. "Do not expect too much, you understand, but perhaps a meeting can be arranged. In the interests of personal growth."

Melchior had to wait nearly two frustrating weeks for his next chance meeting with Selena. He caught her as she entered the seminary grounds and walked with her from the gate to the nuns' quarters. He explained Gratian's agreement to her in fervent whispers. It occurred to him afterwards that she accepted his rather strange plan remarkably easily, given that she had not been privy to the unburdening of his feelings and that they had only really met once before. But at the time, his only concern was to receive her affirmation of the plan. She seemed to enjoy the forbidden intrigue, but, she told him, she did not cook herself as she was in residence in the hostel.

"But because you want to see me, and I cannot refuse a man of the Church," she laughed gaily, "I will see what I can do."

Two days later Selena's cousin from the nun's residence, whom he discovered had been given the rather unimaginative name Sister Mariana, came up to him after supper, as he was leaving the dining room. She was curt as she told him that she had delivered a plate of food to Gratian's room. She pursed her lips in disapproval and turned her back on him without waiting for a response. By the time he made it to Gratian's room, the enamel plate was empty, wiped but not cleaned, ready for collection.

"Well?" he asked expectantly.

The priest turned his nose up. "The meat was salty and the potatoes were not properly cooked," he declared authoritatively, wiping his mouth with the back of his ample hand. Next to the plate was a small brown envelope, the seal still damp.

The meeting took place during the next Saturday afternoon on a bench near the chapel in the shade of the mpingo tree. Gratian sat in the middle of the bench, sucking noisily on his sweets, while Selena and Melchior spoke quietly, separated by his soft frame.

"This is an impingo tree," she said to him across the girth of the priest's belly. "The tree of sound and music. It is a member of the rosewood family. It is solitary by nature, often enduring harsh conditions where other trees would falter. It takes root in infertile and rocky soils, its roots feed the soil with nitrogen, through the bacteria that live in the roots. It gives back more than it takes and so it is blessed, blessed with wood so fine, so pure that only the very best woodwind instruments are made from it. Blessed as they are, impingo are in danger of disappearing, they are so sought after."

Selena stroked the bark of the tree gently, speaking more to the tree itself than to her attentive admirer. He was enthralled by her knowledge, by her confidence and the way her fingers stroked across the rough fibres, feeling, brushing. He watched her with fascination.

"It reminds me of you," she said lightly, laughing and leaning across to touch his arm to show that her jibe was not meant to hurt.

Gratian growled and Melchior blushed deeply. He looked up into the tangled branches of the tree in an effort to hide his sudden reddening discomfort. He was affected not so much by the comment as by the touch of her hand, the sudden direct acknowledgement of their being together and the fact that she could talk of him as someone she knew, someone who could remind her of something else, a part of her consciousness in some way. No matter what would happen now, he realised, he would remain within her memories as someone she had met and grown to know, someone with whom she had spent time, someone in whom she had been sufficiently interested to take the time.

She pulled open a small leather bag and pulled out a large red and green mango and a short stubby knife. She cut a generous chunk of orange flesh and offered it to the priest. Then she cut a piece for Melchior, leaving a quarter of fruit on the oval stone. She raised the fruit to her full lips. The juice ran over her fingers and wet her lips as she sank her teeth into the flesh. Melchior felt a flush of heat across his cheeks and looked away, but not before he noticed Gratian raise his eyebrows, his chunk of mango caught halfway into his waiting mouth.

The meeting was short, at Gratian's insistence, and the small party reluctantly broke up. But Melchior made certain that he had his master's agreement in principle that a similar meeting could take place again. "She certainly is a lively one," was the priest's only comment after his first introduction to the young woman.

Selena had taken close note of Gratian during their short meeting and her next offering consisted of sweet foods: a wrapped packet of sugared biscuits and almond croissants and some butterscotch on the side. Melchior felt like a child bribing a parent for small favours, naughty and safely loved, delighted by the priest's enthusiastic exclamations as he unpacked his treasures and sampled the butterscotch. Gratian gesticulated in the air with half a croissant, wafer crumbs scattering across the floor, his mouth filled with crispy pastry and flaked almonds: "This is going to lead to trouble, mark my words," he said, spraying pastry.

The next weekend was devoted to pastoral service in a village some distance away from Butare and Melchior had to wait for another week before he could meet with Selena again. The Rector was away for the weekend at a conference and Gratian left them alone for a while, a packet of mangos clutched in his fist as he made his way towards the male hostel. She sat close to him, touching his shoulder when she spoke, imparting the warmth from her body.

A small glossy sunbird fluttered about the thin branches of the poinsettia, its delicately curved beak catching at small flies with bright clicks that ran together like the first fall of hail before a cold storm. Its wings made a whirring sound as it alighted and left the branches, falling into space and returning. When it sat still, for a moment, in the sunlight, the iridescence about its neck and chest shone purple, black and green. They sat quietly watching the bird.

"When you look at a sunbird like that, perfectly smooth, beautifully coloured, finely structured, and you believe that it is the construct of a higher being - then admiring the bird is nothing more than honouring the Maker," Selena said, breaking the silence. Melchior frowned and looked at her, but Selena held his gaze and continued. "You say 'Look how finely He made that wing, observe the delicate skill of the beak.' When you look at a fine woodcarving, you cannot hold the statue up itself, disassociated and paganistic, and exalt that this is a thing worthy in itself of respect. No, you hold it up and exalt the name of its maker."

Melchior agreed with her entirely, because to praise an object as the object itself was heretical, for everything was the work of a creation. But he sensed that Selena was not presenting his own views to him as confirmation, so he averted his eyes and waited for her to finish.

"But when I look at a bird like that," she continued softly, gesturing towards the flitting figure amongst the bright red flowers, "I see something that has made itself, something that has its beginnings a long time ago, thousands of its own generations before its arrival, slowly moulding itself, perhaps unknowingly, into the shape of today. You, I think, cannot look at the sunbird without seeing the God behind it, whilst I cannot look at the sunbird without marvelling at the absence of a god behind it. I see the thing itself, in its own beauty and fineness."

"Do you think that makes us very different?" he asked sincerely.

Selena thought for a short while. "No, I think we both see the beauty of the thing and can both sit here and appreciate its form. If one of us stood up and threw a stone at it, because it was irritating us with its noise, or because we were cross about something else, that would make us very different."

Melchior remained quiet. He was once again humbled by her appreciation of her surroundings. Despite his avowed love of God's Creation, despite his courses in one aspect of the Creation or another, he was not the one who had looked about him and had taken the time to study the movements of a glossy sunbird or any creature placed before him. Even before the seminary, his acceptance of his natural environment had been unconscious and his struggle to overcome its challenges had been overwhelming.

Selena came from an educated family from central Rwanda. Her father was a doctor at the central hospital in Kigali, whilst her mother taught secondary school students at a private school attended by the children of the political elite. She was the youngest of three children, her two brothers had both married, one lived in the middle-class suburbs of Kigali and the other had moved to Kinshasa doing contract work as an engineer. Although she was close to her family, her position as the youngest and only girl had made her fiercely independent and, she readily admitted, headstrong. She had learnt to fight stubbornly for her interests and even to stand up to her brothers physically if necessary. She had a keen sense of her own strength and resilience, which allowed her depths of experience unavailable to more timid personalities. She retained a humility and compassion about her, whilst dismissing the petty judgments and reservations of others. In many ways it was a flawed strength, as her exuberant happiness could give way to equal depths of suffering, emotions that rose acutely and cut deeply when enthusiasm was disappointed by the ever-present shortcomings and emotional disabilities of those around her. It was this sense of a flawed strength, a perseverance that carried with it its own destructive weakness, that attracted her to the young seminary student: he seemed to her both so sure and so deeply vulnerable. Differences mattered little, she thought, if you end up on the same square.

"Meeting you has opened up something inside me," he told her honestly. "It will not be easy because of the rules in the seminary school, but I would very much like to be a friend and see you."

"You don't have to tell me these things, they are unspoken and clear," she replied.

His initial revelation - that he had found someone who would hold a memory of him forever - was strengthened and nurtured with the prospect of a real friendship: the potential of more deeply personal contact, of straying from light and unsatisfying topics and into their thoughts, their perceptions, their dreams for themselves and their predictions each for the other. He had a sense that, whatever the outcome, he would have shared significant moments with someone from a worthier world, someone beyond his small confines and troubled person, and that it would stay with him forever. Even small comments that she made, concerning her work, her daily stresses as a student at the college, her plans for her career when her studies were complete, allowed him to feel somehow part of a life outside of his own, a conspirator in the success of another person.

He was able to talk honestly to Selena, about his past and about his uncertain hopes for the future. She in return was always direct and, whenever she disagreed with him, was quick to take up the issue until it had been resolved.

But their continued contact made Gratian nervous. "Don't get too close to her, that's all I'm saying," he blurted out in the middle of the individual seminar. "You have nearly finished your seminary course and after the pastoral service you can be ordained. Don't destroy that hard work."

"You mustn't worry, Father," he replied unconvincingly. In truth, he craved their contact and, whilst the pain he had felt and confessed to Gratian had abated, his emotional turmoil remained. "You told me that I need to heal myself, well, this is my way …"

"Healing involves a painful process of self-recognition," the priest interrupted. "Don't think giving into your young manly urges constitutes healing. I hope you can distinguish between self-realisation and lust." He squinted his eyes as he uttered the word.

"Yes, Father," he replied lightly. "The one is a light to lead you along the Path, the other is the stone that waits to trip you in the darkness."

"I sometimes wonder if you believe any of these things that fall from your lips so wisely," the priest snorted. He held his hand up to stop his pupil's indignant retort. "Because if you believe everything that is presented to you in this deconstructed place, without doubt or question, you're a fool. Now let's carry on."

Despite the priest's concerns, Melchior became more brazen in his meetings with Selena. They would sit openly on the bench beneath the mpingo during his hours of 'self-reflection', talking and laughing. On some weekends he would leave the seminary and they would meet in a teashop at a pre-arranged time or in the cafeteria of the university after one of his lectures - on one occasion he returned to the seminary late and slipped into the chapel after prayers had started. They never seemed to exhaust their conversation and their meetings were always cut short, discussions left hanging, histories untold.

It did not take long for Bertin to intervene. They were sitting together in the shade within the compound, when Melchior saw him come around the corner of the chapel, swinging the gorilla bone determinedly in front of him. He walked across the courtyard directly towards them.

"This will mean trouble," he said softly to Selena, who turned to look at the approaching figure.

Bertin came to a stop in front of them, his hands holding the leg-bone behind his neck. "I think you should leave, little girl," he said nastily, flexing the thick muscles along his arms.

"She is my guest here," Melchior protested, trying not to be intimidated by the squat man.

Selena touched his arm gently to stop him from saying more. Then she stood up and smiled at Bertin. "Don't worry, big boy, I was just leaving." She brushed past him and left him standing, dark with anger.

Melchior stood up to leave but Bertin swung the bone in front of him, pushing him roughly on his chest with the end of the femur.

"If I find you with that whore again, that will be the last day you spend here. Do you understand? This is not a brothel, this is a church. You watch out or you will be very, very sorry." He pushed him with the bone once more to make his point and then stalked off towards the administration office.

Melchior was incensed by Bertin's rudeness and his threats. "Don't say that I didn't warn you that this would happen," Gratian responded. "And don't think that you can hide from that man: he has his little spies everywhere. If you try and meet her in town or at the university, he'll find out. I promise you that."

Melchior was distraught. Bertin seemed to be following him wherever he went. He would turn and find the man a few paces behind him, or he would approach a corner and hear the slap of the bone in his hand coming the other way. He went for a walk in the market and was relieved when he returned to see Bertin talking to another student. But soon after he felt a tap on his shoulder.

"I am pleased that your walk to the market did not take you near the college; I hope you enjoy the four oranges you bought." Melchior looked down at the plain paper packet in his hands. It was impossible to say who had followed him, but Bertin knew all his movements.

A few days later Selena's cousin approached him after prayers and slipped a crumpled note from Selena into his hand. Her college master had been approached by Bertin, who had informed him that she had been making a nuisance of herself at the seminary. She was to refrain from visiting the seminary under any circumstances. Melchior seethed with frustration, pacing up and down in Gratian's room while the priest read the note and pondered his pupil's predicament.

"You will have to be patient, Melchior," he said, handing the paper back to him. "Don't be miserable, please. I will see what can be done, but you must behave perfectly for the next while. Put her out of your mind and concentrate on your studies." Melchior looked at him forlornly and nodded.

He tried for the next few days to tend to his studies and it seemed that Bertin was slowly losing interest in following his every move. One night he considered slipping out but Gratian sensed his intentions and urged him to wait.

"One of the pre-theology students has fallen pregnant," he whispered conspiratorially. "You must not tell anyone this, but I happen to know because the doctor in town is a friend of mine. No-one knows who the father is. She will probably be having an abortion, but the Rector is obviously very upset. The girl is staying in the hostel for the next few days, but the Rector has imposed a kind of quarantine. Then she will leave the hostel and not return." Melchior was puzzled. "I can't say anything more, but just give me a few more days."

Two days later Melchior observed Bertin hurrying towards the Rector's office, frowning, his hands free. One of the students reported over-hearing harsh words between the Rector and his loyal assistant. At mealtime that evening, the Rector made an announcement before the prayer.

"I regret to announce that Mr Bertin will be leaving us to take up a position in the business world," the Rector said shortly. "Mr Bertin has been a part of this institution for many years and he will be missed by us all." Bertin was not present and the Rector immediately started the evening prayer.

Melchior was elated and had to restrain himself from leaving his position to question Gratian about his persecutor's sudden exit from the seminary. Throughout supper he tried to catch the priest's eye, but the big man studiously avoided any contact, keeping his head down, engrossed in his meal.

"I had absolutely nothing to do with it," he said once they had reached the privacy of his room. "I have absolutely no idea what made Mr Bertin decide to leave." Melchior could not keep still, laughing and skipping in front of the priest.

"Come on, Gratian, you must know something. I mean, this is the most exciting thing that has happened at this dreary place since you were found asleep in the rose garden."

Gratian frowned, as if trying to remember some insignificant detail that had slipped his mind. "No, I can't recall any incident involving the rose garden. And I really don't know why he left." He paused for dramatic effect. "There are always wild rumours when these things happen, of course."

"What rumours?" The young man almost shouted, grabbing the priest by his wide shoulders. "Come on, Gratian, tell me! What rumours?"

"Well, the rumour is, and I am sure that there is absolutely no truth in it, but the rumour is that while the young pregnant girl was under quarantine, she was again illicitly visited by her lover. A man was seen leaving her room under cover of darkness. On further investigation, a rather old and worn leg-bone was found under her bed." Melchior's mouth dropped open and he started to giggle. "I think they said that it was the femur of some large animal. Only God Himself knows what it was doing there. Anyway, as I say, it's all just mad rumours, I'm sure." Gratian's face gave nothing away, but his eyes sparkled with mischievous delight.

With Bertin out of the way, contact with Selena quickly settled into a firm arrangement and Melchior's confidence in their friendship grew. He found he was able to apply himself to his studies with renewed energy and his drive to meet the expectations of the school was fuelled as much by an intention to complete his studies as by a desire to protect his friendship from further interference.

They did not speak of the circumstances surrounding Bertin's removal from the seminary, save for one occasion when the three of them were together at the tearoom at the university. A young girl had been raped and murdered in the town, her body casually thrown into a ravine.

"How can anybody do such a thing?" Melchior had blurted out naïvely.

"Well, look at Bertin," Selena said seriously. "He was a man of the church, his duty was to uphold the discipline of the church, and there he was on top of some girl who could have been his daughter."

"Something went wrong in the Garden of Eden," Gratian responded. Selena clapped her hands together in delight. Unlike Melchior, she relished these dangerous conversations with the priest, encouraging his irreverence and vocally developing the themes. Melchior looked about the tearoom nervously to see if anyone could hear them.

Gratian continued with his impromptu lecture regardless. "What did we get in the Garden?" He raised his eyebrows towards them. "We didn't get Knowledge from the tree, we got a piece of the apple that came from the Tree. The Tree was filled with fruit, but we got a bite of a single apple. That doesn't give us Knowledge, that gives us a glimpse of knowledge, a whiff of knowing. Yes, I like that, a Whiff of Knowing. That's what we got." Gratian paused to slurp his tea. "There is nothing, and I mean nothing at all, as frustrating or as dangerous as the flicker of knowledge, because that is knowing without understanding. I know that this is so, but I do not understand why it is so. That is what we got."

"But you see," Selena joined in, "when God said you can have this and this and this and this and this ... but you can't have THAT ! Then God knew that surely the one thing we are going to try and take was the one thing we can't have. He must know that, He made us after all. We didn't need a snake to persuade us. All the snake did was help us get the apple out of the Tree. We wanted it from the moment we were told we couldn't have it. And He knew that."

"Hah !" exclaimed Gratian, "crafty old bugger." Selena whooped at his irreverence, wiping her eyes with a serviette. "But you see, here is the problem. Before we get a taste of Knowledge, the little whiff of knowing, we are walking around the Garden with nothing on, enjoying our sexuality. And then what happens? We get this little piece of the fruit and what knowledge does it impart to us? Do we then know about God? Do we know about the Earth? Do we know the answer to our own happiness? Do we then know anything that is even slightly useful to us? No, from the little piece of knowledge that we get, we know only that we have no clothes on."

Selena was laughing out loud, banging the table with her fingers and howling with delight. Gratian loved her unrestrained reactions to his discussions and continued at the top of his voice.

"So now we know that we have no clothes on. What do we do, we grab a fig leaf, a tiny little fig leaf and we hold it up against our genitals in a desperate attempt to cover them up. There we stand in the Garden before God, before our own spirituality, our own essence of being, clutching little green leaves and our sex peeking out from around the edges. I mean, can you imagine me standing there trying to hide myself behind a fig leaf? Now you tell me, does that make for healthy sentient beings in the long run? I don't think so. And so we end up with people like Bertin, whose intellect and spirit and instincts reside in separate rooms with separate entrances."

Melchior never told Selena about how Bertin came to leave the seminary, although he sensed that she had an idea that Gratian had played a part. A strong bond developed between the three of them and their growing friendship was not to be disturbed again during Melchior's time as a student at the seminary.

However, as the final seminary year drew to a close, Gratian warned him that the location for his pastoral service lay in the hands of the Rector alone and that it would provide His

Majesty with an opportunity to separate him from his undesirable friend. Melchior recognised the inevitability of this when he was called to see the Rector. The Rector did not get up when he knocked and walked in. He stood waiting in the plush study with dimmed side-lights and dark wood table.

"Melchior, you will soon have completed your studies and, provided that you complete your last courses satisfactorily, you will start your pastoral service immediately after your two-week break. I have discussed the matter with the Church elders and we have decided that you should perform your service at Bukumara, in the north-west near the village of your birth. Bukumara is presently without any minister and it is probable that you will be assigned to that congregation on ordination in any event."

The Rector looked straight at the young man, as if daring him to protest or defy the decision. Melchior felt a strange strength in him - somehow he was above this man and his petty secular concerns. He would go to Bukumara and he would make a success of his pastoral service and his ministry, and he would retain his friendship with Selena.

He was surprised when he told Selena about his meeting with the Rector. She got angry and threatened to challenge the Church on its decision. She demanded to know what right they had to send him away and shouted at Melchior for being so calm. Finally she broke down in tears and hugged him for a long time. "I am sorry," she said, drying her eyes. "I am not making it easier for you. You mean a lot to me and it seems so unfair that some old man who hasn't got a friend in the world can post you off somewhere far away just because he can't cope with your friendships."

They agreed that they would use his two-week break before pastoral service to be together and visit her parents in Kigali. But the last few weeks of his studies were difficult and he had to force himself to concentrate on completing his course work, distracted by the anticipation of saying goodbye to Gratian and the excitement of planning a holiday together with Selena.

Gratian had tears in his eyes when the time came. "I told you that you would hopefully leave here as wise as when you came: well, fortuitously, I think we didn't do anything to mess you up, my little one. You do good work in Bukumara and keep a big warm bed for me." He gave Selena a sloppy kiss on the cheek: "Just because he has gone doesn't mean our little arrangement must end," he said earnestly, his fingers playing about his chin.

Selena and Melchior boarded the bus in Butare bound for Kigali. Although the journey was not long, they stopped along the way at different villages, walking through the rough streets to find the market places, sharing food and tea, and telling childhood stories. Melchior felt alive and vibrant in her company and the shared time was like a drug that fed and sustained them through their journey. They savoured every passing moment, knowing that at the end of the two weeks they would have to part.

When they reached Kigali they disembarked at the central bus station and walked through the shaded streets to Selena's home in the nearby suburb. The house was a large, stately colonial structure surrounded by high trees and the interior was cool and expansive, filled with soft chairs, an attractive and welcoming comfort. Selena's parents exuded her same ease and warmth. Her father was a large, open-faced man who welcomed the young guest into his home without any qualification. Her mother was a smaller woman, dwarfed by her husband and tall daughter - the pictures of Selena's brothers showed similarly tall, well-built men. Melchior pictured this small woman bustling between her strapping family, feeding, providing, supporting, all from a level over a foot below them.

Selena took her mother to one side and, after a brief whispered conversation, Melchior was shown to his own room, a carpeted space complete with a sprung bed and mattress, a bedside table and a light with a frilled light shade. The room had a stillness about it, a homeliness that made him think of his mother. A momentary pang of sadness passed.

They spent his last week in her parents' home, visiting relatives in and around the city, taking walks around Kigali, visiting the natural history museum, the botanical gardens and the market. Melchior felt a closeness to Selena and her family by the end of the week that made the thought of parting both more immediately painful and yet somehow more manageable, knowing that a stable unit existed that was and always would be 'family'. Selena seemed to sense this too, as for the first time she spoke about his move to Bukumara and her planned return to continue her studies in Butare.

"I will write to you, Melchior. I am a persistent writer," she said at the supper table, nodding to her mother for confirmation. It was his last supper at their hospitable table. "I write to my parents at least once every two weeks and I visit them when I can. It's not that far from Kigali to Bukumara." Melchior smiled wanly, desolate at the thought of such occasional contact.

"We have been and we will always be the closest of friends," he said, trying not to blush in front of her mother. "That can never be changed and no amount of physical distance can take that away from us." He noticed Selena's mother squeeze her daughter's hand as they left the table.

After supper they helped Selena's mother clean up. Selena was wearing a loose top and her smooth skin glowed hazel on her neck and chest, before the light shadow of her hair darkened the colour. There had been little physical contact between them, despite their emotional closeness - she occasionally took his hand, or touched his shoulder to attract his attention, but she was careful not to infringe upon any physical space. But now Selena turned and saw him watching her.

She smiled and took his hand in hers. "Don't worry," she said simply.

She said goodnight to her mother and they went to sit in his room. They sat together on the bed. The cicadas whirred in the branches of the trees. They sat and listened to the evening noises without speaking. Her leg was pressed against his and his hand was still resting in hers. She pressed his palm gently. Her braided hair rested against her neck and shoulders and he stretched out his hand and stroked the loose braids. The braids slipped through his fingers, smooth and tight. He did not look at her, but gently caressed her beautiful hair, his eyes filled, his hand trembling slightly.

"Melchior," she said softly. She pressed his palm once more.

He looked up and his eyes fell across her strong face, her smooth cheeks, dark eyelashes, her trusting gaze upon him; a shine of warm pleasure, holding his look until he felt himself dissolving into her coloured irises. He felt as if he were moving outside of his body, floating away from his straining muscles. She firmly placed her hand over his, enfolding his fingers in her palm and lifted his hand up to touch her cheek. Then she smiled and gently kissed his fingers, her lips dragging against his fingertips, the hint of moisture. His chest felt full, as if it were swollen in pain, bursting in fact. Perhaps he was falling ill, he thought distantly, removed from the reality of his thoughts. The first signs of malaria perhaps? A waft of new smells, of a woman's hair, not his mother's smell of caustic soap and dust, but a light clean smell of shampoo and fresh water. He breathed in and filled his body with this new smell. His body shook. An image of a snake moving through the cropped grass, cold and warm, filled his mind, shivering in the heat of close bodies. The sound of plates being stacked away in the kitchen.

She moved his hand gently over her breast, the firm feel of flesh under her cotton top, the nudging point of her nipple pressed into the palm of his hand. Then the gentle scraping of his skin against her uncovered chest, an imperceptible shudder of muscle as his fingertips touched the rounded curves of her breast, moving, exploring beneath, around, the smooth tight skin between, soft and filled. He was sensitive to the released close smells, jasmine scents, the exciting suggestion of more human scents, warmed and flowing from her supple body, moving beneath his touch, adjusting and reacting to the finest brushing contact. His body felt tight, his skin felt taut and hot, small flinching waves of nerves streaming up his back and legs, small spasms of muscles in his calves. Then the prickled feel of hair against his clenched stomach, scratchy. His head felt dizzy with other smells and tastes, heavier and more sultry, full of adult senses, his thoughts filled with confusing colours and images, of people and of animals, of the humid air of the rainforest, the moist paths outside his home, the dripping fern leaves alongside the river bed, the soft mud beds, star points of lights in a dark sky.

"Melchior," she said softly again. He realised that his eyes were closed and as he opened them, he looked up to see her clear bright face, her eyes wide, open and softly embracing him. "I want a small part of you with me for ever," her full lips, dark flesh ringing her soft mouth, whispering to him. His mind suddenly cleared and his muscles relaxed, fluid, an overwhelming release of emotions flowing from him, a gentle cry on his tongue.

Before

CHAMBER THREE

INTERNATIONAL CRIMINAL TRIBUNAL FOR
RWANDA

CASE NO. ICTR-98-3-1

In the matter of:

PROSECUTOR OF TRIBUNAL

versus

VICTOR BUSISWA MUYIGENZI

SUMMARY OF INDICTMENT

The accused stands indicted on the following charges, the details of which are further reflected in the Full Indictment hereto, which Full Indictment remains sealed, for the protection of the prosecution witnesses and in the interests of the accused in terms of Article 21 of the Statute of the Tribunal, save for release to this Honourable Court and the defence.

1. Genocide: in terms of article 2 of the Statute of the Tribunal, the accused is charged with the following acts, committed during the period April to June 1994 in the prefecture of Rweru, Rwanda, and which acts were committed with the intent to destroy, in whole or in part, the national, ethnic and/or racial group, being the civilian population designated as Tutsi ('the group') of Rwanda:

    1.1   killing of members of the group (article 2 (a));

    1.2   causing serious bodily or mental harm to members of the group (article 2 (b));

    1.3   deliberately inflicting on the group conditions of life calculated to bring about its physical destruction in whole or in part (article 2 (c)).

Alternative charge (1): conspiracy to commit genocide as aforesaid.

Alternative charge (2): direct and public incitement to commit genocide.

Alternative charge (3): attempt to commit genocide.

Alternative charge (4): complicity in genocide.

2. Crimes against Humanity (Murder): in terms of article 3 (a) of the Statute of the Tribunal, the accused is charged with the act of murder, committed during the period April to June 1994 in the prefecture of Rweru, Rwanda, and which act formed part of a widespread and/or systematic attack against the national, ethnic and/or racial group, being the civilian population designated as Tutsi ('the group') of Rwanda.

Alternative charge (1): conspiracy to commit murder as aforesaid.

Alternative charge (2): direct and public incitement to commit murder as aforesaid.

3. Crimes against Humanity (Torture): in terms of article 3 (f) of the Statute of the Tribunal, the accused is charged with the act of torture, committed during the period April to June 1994 in the prefecture of Rweru, Rwanda, and which act formed part of a widespread and/or systematic attack against the national, ethnic and/or

racial group, being the civilian population designated as Tutsi ('the group') of Rwanda.

Alternative charge (1): conspiracy to commit torture as aforesaid.

Alternative charge (2): direct and public incitement to commit torture as aforesaid.

4. Crimes against Humanity (Rape): in terms of article 3 (a) of the Statute of .the Tribunal, the accused is charged with the act of rape, committed during the period April to June 1994 in the prefecture of Rweru, Rwanda, and which act formed part of a widespread and/or systematic attack against the national, ethnic and/or racial group, being the civilian population designated as Tutsi ('the group') of Rwanda.

Alternative charge (1): conspiracy to commit rape as aforesaid.

Alternative charge (2): direct and public incitement to commit rape as aforesaid, in that the accused is charged with planning, ordering and encouraging subordinate militia and communal police members and other persons to commit rape upon Tutsi women.

5. Serious Violations of Article 13 common to the Geneva Conventions of 12 August 1949 for the Protection of Victims in times of War, and of Additional Protocol II thereto of 8 June 1977, alternatively, complicity in these crimes: in terms of article 4 of the Statute of the Tribunal, the accused is charged with committing serious violations of the article, during the period April to June 1994 in the prefecture of Rweru, Rwanda, including:

5.1 violence to life, health and physical and/or mental well-being of persons as well as cruel treatment such as torture and mutilation (article 4 (a));

5.2 outrages upon personal dignity, in particular humiliating and degrading treatment, rape and indecent assault (article 4 (e) qualified);

5.3 pillage (article 4 (f));

5.4 the passing of sentences and the carrying out of executions without previous judgment

pronounced by a regularly
constituted court, affording
all the judicial guarantees
which are recognised as
indispensable by civilised
peoples (article 4 (g));

5.5   threats to commit the acts
referred to above (article 4
(h)).

6. The personal liability of the accused
for the aforegoing acts is further
asserted by the prosecution in terms
of article 6 of the Statute of the
Tribunal on the basis that the accused
planned, instigated, ordered,
committed or otherwise aided and
abetted in the planning, preparation
or execution of the crimes referred to
herein.

OFFICE OF THE TRIAL PROSECUTION

Per: *N GWEDLE.*

N Gwedle
INTERNATIONAL CRIMINAL TRIBUNAL FOR
RWANDA
21 February 1998

Chapter Four

The east side of the church compound nestled into a banana grove: the broad-leaved trees started against the low walls surrounding the compound, to the north and south, as if trying to embrace the compound in a protective fold, and stretched down the slope of the hill towards the valley below. The acacia and sausage trees of the eastern savannahs gave way to denser, greener riverine trees, sycamore-fig and occasional fever trees, leadwood and wild pear, and deeper into the forest the taller, stately canopy trees rose above the scramble of the forest floor. The fields were carved out of the vegetation and bordered by clusters of banana trees. Colobus and vervet monkeys moved amongst the tree tops, hunting for berries and small insects, and when the fields were fallow, bustards and peafowl nested, using the flattened area to keep a wary eye for predators.

The church roof was the most immediately visible part of the village, pushing up between the tall eucalyptus trees which flanked the side of the cemetery and stood between the curve of the dirt road and the compound wall. The compound was centered on the hilltop and the roof of the church, although not tall, stood above the banana trees and provided the first indication that a settlement existed in the otherwise unbroken greenery of the hillside. The low stone wall enclosing the compound, four or five large stones high, had been hewn from the rocks of the surrounding mountains when the church was first built under colonial rule. The surrounding wall and the church itself blended together in shades of slate-grey, brown and moss green, a home to small speckled lizards and black whip snakes. Glossy starlings, shimmering with greens and blues in the sun, nested in the eaves and overhangs of the church roof, staining the short sills with white and brown streaks. The stifled cry of chicks could be heard every time an adult bird flew near.

On the west side of the compound, the red-brown road curved at a tight angle, winding up from the valley floor below and passing the compound in an unexpected turn to the west. The road was rutted and, during the rainy seasons, deeply scarred and eroded by water, forming deep ditches which followed the contours of the road, weaving and dipping and leaving hard smooth outcrops of rock and clay which afforded little traction. Once the rain stopped the road dried in the sun, baked hard in the contortions it had formed, folded and rutted like a mountain range, jarring and almost impassable, save on foot. The road served as a path for villagers to reach the compound, walking or pushing a thick-barred black bicycle with their wares piled on the seat or handlebars. It was seldom that a car passed this way and so the road was left in its disused state. On the other side of the road, in its elbow, the natural vegetation had been left untamed, thick and woven together. The trees, bushes and creepers formed an almost impenetrable mass which swept down the steep incline away from the hilltop.

Inside the compound itself, the red earth was swept clean. A tidy vegetable patch grew between the end of the church and the compound wall - straight rows of corn, potatoes and beets grew well in soil which had not been exhausted by years of intensive, desperate sowing and reaping. On the other side of the church building, behind the sacristy and next to the row of three latrines, their green stable doors peeling and cracking in the sun, a line of creeper beans curled around poles cut from young saplings and crisscrossed to form a green mat against the wall.

A large eucalyptus graced the compound at the open gateway, its smoothed streaked bark leading up to the dark green leaves high above the church. A low brick shelter had been built in the compound in more recent times. It stretched along the western side of the enclosure and was divided into three rooms of roughly equal size and one slightly smaller room at the end closest to the latrines. The three larger rooms were used as an unfurnished classroom, a store and an administrative office – the Kinyarwandan word for 'office' was painted in small white letters on the door and a piece of wire bent over a nail in the doorpost kept the door closed.

The office was a small unpainted room with bare walls, save for a picture of the Archbishop of Rwanda - a faded regal portrait which was distributed to all the Catholic parishes - next to which hung a square fabric of needlework depicting the Virgin Mary with a bright yellow halo and a blue swallow taking flight above her head. There was only one chair and a school-room table, with the name of the school etched in black pen on one leg. The table had been scarred by the hand of bored pupils and frustrated teachers over countless years with obscure names and small diagrams scratched across its surface. The three-tiered metal filing cabinet provided the only sign that the room was ever entered or put to the use its name suggested.

The smaller room at the end of the low building was the priest's private room: his bedroom, washroom, kitchen and sitting room in one undefined space. A spring bed, covered with a patchwork bedspread, designated the one corner as being the bedroom; a low wooden crate with a basin, cloth and soap against the far wall indicated the washroom. A soft couch, with a split at the back, which indiscreetly showed its stuffing, had a small table next to it, equipped with reading light (for when the single line electricity cable worked) and a candle (for the many times when it did not).

Melchior had arrived at the St. Jean church as an outsider. He was young and newly ordained. He knew no one in Bukumara and, although not far from his home village of Ritsire, the church fell within the Ngoro commune and diocese. The church structure in the diocese was unfamiliar to him and the village had been without a pastor for several years. The villagers had continued to use part of the church building – the hall and the sacristy – while the remaining rooms had been left to the attentions of birds and rodents. He had set about transforming the compound back into a community centre for the village: his first week had been spent cleaning the office and classroom of rat droppings, wiping the smeared walls and windows, raking the compound in the way the nuns had done at the seminary.

His first service had been poorly attended - a scattering of elderly men and women, bent from work in the fields, took up the middle few benches in the church hall. It seemed that the physical site of the church echoed its relationship with the village, set above and away from the daily lives of the people.

He found himself initially unable to break down the reserve which came with the villagers' measured respect and humility.

Gratian had impressed upon his pupil the need to approach pastoral work simply and with the understanding that it was a service provided to the community: "God did not place the flock before you so that you could fulfil your need to herd it. You were placed in the midst of the flock because it was already there and may receive some assistance from you," he had intoned. "Remember, your task is to serve. Be guided by the needs of the people that you serve, not by the patronising notions that are spewed out by those like His Majesty."

Melchior approached his work with his master's directions in mind: he made the church hall available for the village meetings and offered the use of the office to the *nyambakumi*; he tended the graves in the cemetery, clearing away the encroaching grasses and planting flowering bushes at the entrance; he visited those who were sick and attended on deaths in the village with sympathy. Mass was held regularly each morning. He introduced religious teachings in the classroom on Sundays and encouraged those who attended to discuss all matters relating to their lives. These meetings were increasingly well-attended and became a forum for the resolution of disputes and the discussion of issues affecting the village. Save for commencing with a prayer, he did not try to introduce any religious content to the meetings and instead used them as an opportunity to learn about his pastoral community. The central government had done little to develop the north-west of Rwanda as the area was predominantly Tutsi. The meetings often evinced the villagers' dissatisfaction at the inaction of the *nyambakumi*, a loud and unpleasant man who represented the ruling MRND at a local level and who enjoyed the power that his administrative position afforded him, without necessarily attending to any of the administration that was his responsibility. He had seemed surprised when the priest had offered him the use of the office in the compound - he had not understood what the priest intended him to do with an office and Melchior did not push the offer. "But he is *Umuhutu*, what does he care about us?" the villagers grumbled at the meetings. They had attempted to retain the powers of the Tutsi *mwami*, but his traditional responsibilities were ignored by central and local government structures.

The village was beset with health problems, particularly dysentry, malaria and infection from flatworm larvae, due to the moist conditions in and around the fields. Bukumara was too small for its own clinic and the sick had to be transported by car or cart along difficult roads to reach medical help. Melchior used the small church budget to purchase a quantity of medicines which he kept in his room and dispensed without charge to children and the elderly.

He wrote to Gratian and received encouragement and advice from his mentor. His contact with the world outside of Bukumara was limited to his former advisor, occasional visits from administrative and church officials, and Selena. The severity of his longing for Selena was tempered in the beginning by the excitement and challenge of his work in his new community. During the first few months in Bukumara he felt that he was pushing his feelings to one side, focusing on the church and the community and in so doing, running just a few steps in front of a breaking wave of unspent emotions. He wrote to her of this fear - that soon he would be swamped by his need to be with her. Selena wrote back and urged him to accept their position as being for the best. Neither one of them openly referred to their physical encounter, but between them lay the simple fact that, as a practising priest in charge of a community, there could be no further lapses. They had known when they had parted in Kigali that they would remain apart in space and that their love was to be that of friends and not that of lovers. As the months passed their letters became less emotive and, although always open and honest, each was sensitive to the vulnerabilities of the other: Selena did not make mention of her social activities, and he did not ask. She became for him a confidante, removed from his immediate world, someone to whom he could open himself without exposure, before whom he could cast his doubts without judgment. Their separation seemed to allow their friendship to deepen and develop in a new direction, rather than fade away.

He was surprised how content he was with the simple lifestyle he had adopted. The pace of life was slow and the problems that faced him were real, immediate and earthly. He had the time to think, and the time just to work without thinking – he felt himself maturing, and healing. His relationship with the village took on a reciprocal balance: he helped in the communal fields, tended to the sick, listened and counselled, and in return he had his hair cut, his clothes mended and took his supper at the eating house in the village. Simple meals of potatoes, maize bread and, on some occasions, braised goat's meat and beans; although always offered, he did not drink the banana beer, for the sake of appearances rather than from any principle.

"Perhaps a Primus would suit you better, if banana beer is not to your liking" was the standard joking reply from the owner, Michel Ndayede, a jovial heavy and broad-faced man. Michel's passion for beer in all its forms was well-known. He brewed the banana beer himself in large open drums, simmering over blackened hardwood coals before being stored in the warm shed for the fermentation to continue, producing a glutinous bubbling substance which was then strained for the liquid beer. Michel would stand before his guests and lock his hands together under his large belly, as if holding it in place, holding it back from slowly drooping like gum from a cut tree to touch the ground at his feet. He would gently rock the protruding mass from side to side, listening for the slap of hidden liquids. Then he would raise his meaty hands in resignation, "Ha ! Still it is not full !" and with dramatic gestures pour himself another serving of beer, to the never-tiring delight of his patrons.

The eating house was a point of assembly for the men, and many of the women of the village. On any one evening, the room and the surrounding open wooden balcony would be filled with people eating, talking and drinking. Conversations passed back and forth, over the heads of others, as people joined and left groups, the pitch and tone of the voices rising and falling, floating out into the clear skies outside. Michel would often have his radio tuned to a music station, the speaker crackling and spitting in an effort to project the bass notes and higher pitched voices of the singers.

Melchior enjoyed sitting with his evening meal, eating it slowly and listening to the villagers discuss the matters of the day, gesticulating with easy movements, laughing aloud and freely joking and poking fun at others, grinning at jokes made at their expense. What tensions may have formed during a hard day of work in the fields were released to float, without complication, into the night, forgotten the next day and not to be brought back again. Swallows had built a mud nest in one roof corner, carefully placing rolled balls of red-brown mud taken from the fields to form a bulb and tube, open at one end, that set hard and provided a secure home for several seasons. As dusk settled in the birds flew in fast weaving circles outside the eatery, swooping low along the road, rising suddenly and steeply into the darkening sky. As the light faded their acrobatic flights were taken over by small, soundless bats, competing with the speckled geckos and long-legged wall-spiders for their share of the fat-bodied moths attracted by the lights. Michel would point to a gecko, cleaning the powdery residue left by a moth's wing from its head, or to a wall spider, its fangs deep inside the soft body of some luckless creature, and proclaim in a loud voice: "You see, here is where all of Rwanda comes to eat !"

Melchior finished his chores at the church and pulled the door of his room closed. The afternoon's rain had passed and the earth smelled rich and full. Smoke from evening fires drifted up from the huts towards him and he could hear the voices of children playing in the sparking light. The compound was neat and contained and he drew comfort from its clear borders. He made his way down the rutted road from the compound towards the eating house, hungry and looking forward to chatting to Michel. A jackal barked in the fields, hunting for dropped vegetables and the stale bread left over from the villagers' lunch.

He approached the lights of the eating house and noticed the *nyambakumi* sitting with a group of men to one side on the wooden balcony. The group was drinking and talking amongst themselves, separated from the other patrons who kept their backs to the group. The eating house seemed quieter than usual. Melchior stepped up onto the balcony and nodded towards the group of men. It was hard to tell in the subdued lighting, but none of the men were familiar to him. Then one, seated in the middle of the group, leant forward and his face caught the light coming through the opened doors of the house.

"Hey, Melchior, how are you? Come and talk to us here."

Victor Muyigenzi sat with a half-eaten plate of goat's meat and boiled potatoes before him, a cup of banana beer in his hand. The men, perhaps six in all, stood and sat around him, also drinking beer, but only one other had a plate of food, also unfinished. The men seemed wary and unrelaxed, the food was good (goat's meat was a fine meal) and Michel's beer was always strong and satisfying, but they had left some of the best parts of the coal-charred meat and only Victor seemed to be drinking his beer. The others seemed to hold their mugs without any desire to drink the contents.

He nodded towards the *nyumbakumi* who was sitting opposite the group of men. Victor looked well, Melchior thought. He had not seen him for almost a year now, as his visits to the village became less frequent and his work in Rweru presumably more pressing. He would sometimes visit the village on official business but more often Victor would come to visit on a day off, and he would always make his way up to the compound and spend a while talking to the priest, discussing his life in Rweru. Victor was proud of his successes, proud of his courage in leaving his isolated childhood playing grounds and moving to the centre of the commune. He never tired of telling the priest of the first year he spent in Rweru, working as a fee-taker on the taxis during the day and attending clandestine meetings of *Inguba* at night. Life had been hard for him during that first year in the town, Victor told him, and there were nights when he would sleep on the back seat of the taxi with no food in his stomach and little prospect of anything to eat when he awoke the next morning, ready to start again with a day on the jarring roads of the commune.

Some days he would accompany the drivers on longer journeys into other communes, and on one occasion he accompanied the *bourgemestre* all the way to Kigali and returned to Rweru with a handsome fee. His employer was a hard man who always checked the mileage on the aging Ford sedan and carefully worked out the earnings due to him, before sliding a few coins to one side as payment for the young man. The work had been tiring and endless, days of work without break at the hands of a tough master. Victor had initially joined *Inguba* when he was told that the owner of the taxis was himself a leadership figure in the MDR and that his membership of the youth wing would assist him in obtaining a job. The advice had been correct, because when he laid his member's card on the table, the owner's attitude had immediately changed and he had started work the next day.

Towards the end of his first year in Rweru, Victor had been one of many victims of a *kubohoza* drive on the part of the ruling MRND. The *kubohoza* had targeted the members of *Inguba* and one night a group of twenty members of the *Interhamwe za MRND* arrived at his room in the backyard of a house near the central taxi rank, sporting distinctive blue and yellow bubus and chalked faces, beating the ground with thick sticks and calling for him to show himself. Victor had been terrified and thought that the group planned to kill him. Unfamiliar with the tactics of *kubohoza*, he had feared for his life and tried to escape through a window. The group laughed when they saw him jump out of the window and try to run across the yard, tripping over a low-strung wire fence. He collapsed into the dust and was set upon by the group, who beat him with sticks about his back, chest and legs. He was not struck on the face or head and none of the blows were so severe as to break a bone, but he was left with cuts and deep purple bruises which took weeks to disappear altogether. Then the leader of the group entered the room and searched through his belongings, returning outside with his *Inguba* membership card and the MDR cap which he wore when attending meetings. The card was set alight and left, burning, next to him on the ground. The cap was speared through the middle and the stick was pushed into the ground at the door of the room, the sharpened end of the stick showing through the fabric at the top of the cap. Then the group left.

The next day, whilst he was cleaning a taxi at the rank, the *Interhamwe* member who had entered his room approached him. Victor's body ached from the blows meted out the day before and his muscles were too bruised and crushed for him to try and run away. He looked anxiously about him for the rest of the group. The young *Interhamwe* smiled at him and told him not to worry, he was on his own. Then, still smiling, he said: "The youth meeting is tonight at the commune centre at seven o'clock." Without further explanation, the man turned and moved off across the paved taxi rank towards the market and disappeared into the crowd of people moving in and out of the stalls.

When Victor attended the meeting that night he saw several of his former *Inguba* peers, uncomfortable both from the beatings that they had all received and from the apparent ease with which they had changed allegiance. Although the new members felt contrite, like children who have been punished for their errant ways, the members of the *Interhamwe* did not treat them any differently and they were immediately welcomed as full youth members, as if they had decided to join of their own accord. Nothing was said of the *kubohoza* and they received MRND badges and pamphlets. From then on, Victor regarded himself as *Interhamwe* and an MRND member. In his discussions with the priest, Victor conceded that his original loyalty to the MDR had been an alliance of expedience made merely in order to obtain employment and that, once he was forced into the fold of the ruling party, his true political colours were allowed to manifest themselves. Melchior knew Victor to be a proud and defensive man and was careful not to point out the obvious expediency in both of his choices during their discussions.

Victor told him that a few weeks later the youth group had discussed a further *kubohoza*, this time at a more high profile level. The local leader of the MDR was to be targeted and forced either to join the MRND or at least to disavow his allegiance to his party. Victor pointed out to the meeting that the man was his employer and owner of the taxi rank at which he worked: he could hardly be part of the planned action. The youth wing leader discussed this difficulty and agreed that, if Victor formed a visible part of the action he was likely to lose his job. After the meeting, the youth leader took Victor to meet the MRND communal administration head, Colonel Batho. The colonel had been the commander of 16 Battalion in the Forces Armées Rwandaises during the war against the RPF and had been injured by a grenade during a skirmish along the Ugandan border, which had left one arm weakened and his face scarred, a thick keloid scar running from under his chin to his left temple. The injury had severed the muscles holding his left eye in place and the eye remained staring to the side. Victor could not tell if the colonel had any sight in this eye and he strained to keep his own eyes focused on the big man's right eye, not daring to stare at the deformed left side of his face.

The colonel had moved to the Offensive Bureau of the FAR General Staff and had commanded the Presidential Guard. It was rumoured that he had the political protection of the *akazu* - the 'little house' – the close entourage of relatives surrounding President Habyarimana that was controlled by the president's wife. The approval of the president's wife converted the recipient from a successful autocrat into an untouchable. The powerful and enigmatic colonel was suspected of acts of cruelty on the battlefield, nefarious business arrangements in the civilian world and a number of scandalous affairs with wives of members of the political elite, but his indemnity was absolute. When he left the FAR and joined the political structure of the MRND in the commune, his rise to *bourgemestre* was assured.

Victor stood before the imposing man, large and muscled save for his left arm which had withered from lack of use and hung lifelessly at his side. He greeted the young man and listened intently to the problem the youth leader described.

"There are going to be many changes in Rweru and the whole country in the next while," the colonel told the two men, "changes that you cannot begin to conceive or anticipate. Your country and *rubanda nyamwinshi* will need the courageous assistance of its young men." Victor had not heard this phrase, 'the great majority', used before and understood the colonel to mean the country as a whole. It was some time later that he understood what the colonel meant when he used the phrase.

"The time is coming soon when we will crush the RPF and its *ibyitso*." The colonel spoke in sweeping phrases, his deep, resonant voice holding the young man in thrall while he fixed him with a lone fierce eye. "Resources in our beautiful country are limited. The environment in which we live can only support so many people and no more. The countryside is ravaged by erosion and depleted by the over-grazing of cattle owned by the wealthy few. God intended the legitimate people of Rwanda to use these resources for their common good. He did not intend that foreigners should force their way in, raping the land as if it were their own, leaving nothing but the crumbs for those who have always lived here."

The colonel pointed at Victor: the time to hold onto the security of employment in jobs outside of the established political structures was over, he said. "You should take part in the planned *kubohoza* without fear of reprisal. Think of it as your tender of resignation", the colonel asserted without smiling, "and when it is over, come and talk to me again."

The *kubohoza* took place two nights later. Victor felt a surge of excitement as the group gathered together at the commune offices and passed the tin of white chalk from one to the other, smearing the substance like paint in thick smudges across their cheeks and forehead. Then they each took a stick from the pile that rested on end against the wall of the office, only Victor noticed that this time several of the sticks had nails protruding from one end. He chose a heavy stick without any nails and joined the party outside, who were encouraging one another with chants and bottles of beer. They joked and shouted, gathering strength and courage from one another, preparing themselves with nervous energy for the 'work' that awaited them. Then, on a signal from the leader, the group moved quickly out of the grounds of the commune offices. Victor drank beer as they marched down the road, trying to quell his fear. By the time they reached the house of the taxi owner, he felt dizzy and nauseous. He stood back behind the group as the men pushed into the small garden and spread out around the sides of the house. Some went around the house to the back to prevent any escape. The chanting started up again and the lights went on inside the house.

Victor felt nervous and tried to keep out of the light. The door of the house suddenly opened, casting light on the path and directly onto him. He stood bathed in light, holding his stick - the only one in the group who was not shouting and the first one the taxi owner saw before the nailed sticks rained down on his head. He noticed how the blows seemed to stick to the man's body, momentarily, before being pulled loose by his assailants. The man sank to his knees and stared, dazed, straight at the voiceless young man standing at his garden gate. Then he fell face first onto his path.

It seemed very quiet to Victor. He saw the youth members contorting their mouths into screamed chants, he saw an older woman appear at the doorway, wringing her hands, her mouth open and her chest heaving, but he could not hear anything. A child appeared behind her, holding onto the back of her skirt. He did not hear any sounds. It was very still where he stood. The taxi owner lay without moving on the path. His eyes were open but he did not blink. A stream of blood emerged from his hair and ran across his forehead, coursing over his nose and dripping onto the path. The small trickle of blood started to flow more quickly. One of the young men struck a blow on the fallen man's head and left the club impaled in the crushed skull. Victor dropped his stick and ran home in the dark.

The next day the youth leader woke him from a fitful sleep, knocking sharply on the wooden door-frame. Nothing was said of the events of the previous night. "Colonel Batho has taken over the *icyitso*'s taxi business," the man said. "You can carry on working as a fee-taker for now, if you want, but Colonel Batho has asked me to tell you that there is a position for a trainee in the communal police under his command. He strongly suggests that you apply for the position. It is in your interests." Victor had felt both honoured and frightened by the message from the colonel. A week later he had donned the uniform of a communal policeman.

Victor was wearing civilian clothes now, but three of the men in the group wore the uniforms of communal policemen. "Good evening, Victor," said the priest. He remained standing, uncertain as to the nature of the delegation from Rweru. "Is this official business or are you here to sample Michel's beer?" He smiled in an attempt to lighten the inquiry.

Victor sensed the priest's unease. "Please, sit down and join us, Father. Please," Victor insisted, indicating to one of the men to get a chair. The man carried a chair over for the priest who sat down across the table from the head of the Rweru communal police. "How are you keeping, my friend?" the policeman asked, apparently intent on avoiding the priest's initial question. "And what are you drinking?" he asked, before the man could answer.

"Spiced tea," the priest said and Victor sent one of the men off to see to the order. "I am fine, Victor, as you see me. I am fine, the same as always. We struggle on here against the forces of nature. As you see from the road, we have had strong rains and part of the communal land was flooded at the bottom of the valley." Melchior noticed the grey Pajero parked alongside the eating house, mud clinging to the wheel rims and running board. "I see you have your own transport these days." Victor did not reply.

The tea arrived in a tin pot, milky and smelling of cloves, together with a bowl of brown sugar and an empty tin cup with a teaspoon. The priest heaped a spoon of sugar into the cup and poured the tea out. The rich-smelling steam hung between the two men as Melchior sipped the hot tea. "How is the head of the communal police?" he asked. The unanswered query as to the purpose of the visit remained between them. That and the presence of the other men, was complicating their interaction.

"I am well, thank you. As you see me," he smiled. "We are kept busy with RPF infiltrations..." he paused, " ... and with domestic problems, of course. We have asked the prefect to send us more arms and money for additional trainees, but so far, there are only four of us, plus a few volunteers," Victor gestured to the men about him. "Colonel Batho keeps the administration of the commune well ordered, like a military operation," the policeman said – ruefully, Melchior thought. "Well, it is to be expected, he is an ex-FAR soldier," the priest said sympathetically. "Fighting an unseen enemy calls for good administration."

The squat, dark man in civilian dress sitting next to Victor turned aggressively on the priest. "What would you know of fighting the enemy?", he demanded, flecks of his spittle flying onto the priest's arm. Melchior moved his tea a little to his right. The man thumped his arms, thick and muscular like the roots of an old tree, on the table. "Have you ever received any honours for fighting *Inkotanyi*? You church priests ... you preach the good life but who can protect our country from foreigners? Who will hold back the pillaging hordes who are waiting on the borders, moving through the bush at night, stealing our food, stealing our women, slaughtering our young children ... ?"

The priest looked at the man with a frown. "What are you talking about?" he asked in amazement. "Foreigners massing on our borders? Children slaughtered in the night?" The thick-set man's eyes widened in anger and he half-rose from his chair as if to strike the priest. The light caught his head and Melchior noticed a large, smooth patch of skin, the size of his own palm, surrounded by dark closely-cropped hair on the right side of the man's head.

Victor intervened, putting his hand firmly on his companion's chest: "Venant, calm down. This man is a priest and my friend. He is not *icyitso*. He meant nothing by his comment. He is just isolated from the developments in Rweru and in Kigali. Is that not right, Melchior?"

"Certainly, I meant nothing against Colonel Batho. I don't even know the man," the priest responded. "It is true, we are not kept up-to-date with developments in the country. I sometimes receive orders from the Archbishop in Kigali months after they have been issued." His squat neighbour growled under his breath and gulped down a mouthful of beer.

"I advise you to be more careful about what you say, churchman," he said menacingly, wiping a thin line of foam from his thick top lip.

Melchior lifted up his tin cup and drained the last of his tea. "Thank you for the tea," he said, trying to catch the policeman's eyes. Victor looked down at the table. Melchior stood up and nodded to the man next to him, before walking along the wooden balcony and into the eating house. Michel had the radio turned down and he raised his eyebrows when the priest walked over to him. "I see Rweru has come to honour us," he said mockingly. A young man called Nbizi, standing at the counter and drinking a Primus beer, laughed out loud, perhaps in disparagement of the visitors, but Melchior was pensive and did not answer. He ate his meal on his own and when he had finished, he ventured back out onto the balcony. The group was no longer there and the Pajero was gone.

The priest made his way up the unlit road, walking carefully to avoid falling or twisting his ankle in the ruts and holes. The air was heavy and wet, filled with the threat of more rains to come, and the heat closed in around him. The cicadas fell silent as he passed near them, only to resume their grating calls as soon as he was a safe distance away. The night sky was dark and filled with the wisps of gathering clouds, giving the half-moon a halo of fine light. Despite the tepid air, he suddenly felt chilled and wrapped his arms about his torso. He had felt distanced from Victor, even more than usual when he sat listening to his former friend's self-absorbed reveries of life in the big town. He had always, in his adult life, felt some barrier between himself and Victor, as if the more worldly man secretly both patronised and envied him.

Melchior soon realised that Victor was in fact insecure in his successes and that he returned to Bukumara periodically to hold up his life to the priest, who had had none of the benefits, none of the luxuries, which formed part of the policeman's life. Melchior had chosen his simple life and, although he was interested in the events of the communal centre, he would never wish to take Victor's place. Perhaps that was what drove Victor, beyond apparent friendship, to return to the stone compound and berate the priest with stories of happiness and wealth, each time leaving with the nagging knowledge that the man was unpersuaded, even sitting in judgment of him after he had left. Plagued by these thoughts, Victor would keep returning to regale the priest with stories of his suburban enjoyments.

The priest was nevertheless always pleased to see him and to talk to someone from his childhood. It was important to him that he have someone whom he could regard as a friend, whatever the motivation behind the apparent friendship might be. But he often felt saddened on shaking Victor's hand and watching him make his way down to the village and back to his home in Rweru – a sadness at the needs and desires that wracked his friend's thoughts, the obvious absence of contentment that could salve the harshness that seemed to exist in his heart. Victor did not have a family life which could provide him with enjoyment in the evenings. He enjoyed recounting, in particular, his sexual adventures and the opportunities for uncommitted love in the big town - stories which he seemed to find all the more titillating because they were told to a man bound to abstinence by his own volition.

Melchior was not so disturbed by the lusty accounts of stolen maidenhood and forced liaisons as he was by the man's evident need to account to him. It was an unburdening of guilt and desire outside of the confessional: the unhappiness and dissatisfaction evident in the tales of purposeless but repeated coitus was obvious to the priest. These accounts clashed violently with his own tenderly-held visions of his love with Selena and their fleeting contacts over the past years, his yearning for her presence, his love and abandonment that seemed to be a martyrdom. He was unable to think of Selena opportunistically, crushed up against an alley wall with her skirt hoisted vulgarly about her hips. He saw her only in the duration of a lifetime, in which time was slowed down, in long moments without action, without words. He could not join Victor in his stolen scenes of punctuated sex, and his lurid descriptions seemed nothing more than the glimpse of a void.

Melchior moved slowly into the compound and across the open space towards his room, his mind filled with unnamed anxieties and a restlessness. Victor's visit had been different this time, not just because he was accompanied by others, or because he was apparently on some official business with the *nyumbakumi*, but because of the uncertain, pleading look in his eyes when he had first asked him to join their table. His expression had displayed a trapped, even frightened feeling, perhaps best described as desperation. His tone of voice had belied this and he had spoken firmly and with authority, but beneath the outward bravado, the priest was sure he saw an uncertainty, and a fear.

He lit the candle in the dark room and sat down on the cushions with the light next to his shoulder. He reached under the sofa and pulled out a letter he had received some days before, addressed from Butare. He opened the bent, thin pages and read the letter again, calming himself with the soft unspoken words.

'My dear Melchior, I am sitting at my small painted desk, with the sunlight falling across the unwritten pages of this letter, surrounded by exercise books which I shall have to mark this evening. They are piled in a daunting heap at my elbow, waiting like an impatient pet dog: if I listen carefully I can hear them whining. And so, if this letter is too long, it is because I am escaping my duties, and if it is too short, it is because my duties cannot be escaped.'

Selena understood him in a way that no-one else could, not any member of his family nor any past friend from the years of his childhood. She understood that he wanted to hear the simple details of chores, the mundane events of a clear day. He wanted to hear her tell of solutions to small difficulties - not the tensions of living but the daily pleasures of repeated gestures, routines and patterns which gave security and meaning, which provided sustenance and which drew him silently into her world. The living of an ordinary life.

'Today a student gave me a short poem that she had written. It was written on a piece of paper torn out from the back of a Bible. She is a diligent student and so I believe her when she tells me that she wrote it herself. It seems to be very grown up for such a young person, but I think that she has some talent. I will ask her to write some more and perhaps I can send you some examples for you to cast your exacting eye over. The exercise books which I must mark unfortunately do not contain anything quite so interesting. It is a comprehension test which I gave them on a French piece - they battle with the nuances of French expression so I can only imagine what some of them may have written.'

She did not express emotion in her letters. Instead she provided him with a factual account of her teaching, her pupils and girlfriends, her life. She still did not speak of any romantic interests, although Melchior supposed that she did have such interests. He in turn wrote to her of his life in Bukumara, filling his letters with funny stories of the village and its people. He liked to imagine her, sitting cross-legged on her bed, her hair falling about her face and shoulders, soft layers of black, woven hair, resting his letters on her lap, laughing out loud. He feared at times that perhaps she viewed his life and his letters as dull and parochial, and that she returned his writings only to avoid hurting him, a simple task to keep him satisfied whilst she enjoyed the lifestyle of a free and eventful town. They did not refer to their relationship in Butare. Melchior knew, in his heart, that Selena had moved on from her feelings for him and that, whilst she was happy to maintain a friendship, she would not and could not revive her former affection for him

'I am still hoping to visit you in Bukumara at the end of the year, before I go to my parents for Christmas. I do not think that I can get to your part of the world before then. You seem both so far away and yet so close. I do hope that this letter finds you well and contented. Kind regards, Selena.'

Melchior finished reading her letter, carefully folded it up and stored it safely under the sofa. The letter had calmed him and he felt more at ease as he prepared for bed.

The following morning brought its own events and he did not give any more thought to Victor's visit. He had just finished getting dressed and was waiting for the water in the pot to boil when Nbizi, the young man who had been at the bar the evening before, burst into the room without knocking.

"Father, please, you must come right away. My brother, Vincent, has been struck down, he's lying on the ground, he's not moving. He needs you, Father. Please, my mother said you must come!"

Melchior turned the heat off and hurriedly followed the young man out of the room. "Where is he?" he asked as they ran down the hill into the village.

"He is in the field behind my mother's house. He's not moving. I'm scared, Father. What if he's dead, what will we do then?" Nbizi was panting from the exertion and his emotion.

"What happened to him? What hurt him?" Melchior responded, avoiding answering the young man's own question.

"I don't know, Father. It looks as if he fell from the roof of the shed, or maybe he was kicked by the bull. There is blood on his head."

They reached Nbizi's mother's house, a series of three grass and mud huts linked together, facing away from the village onto a cleared field. On the one side stakes and reeds formed a rough enclosure for the livestock. Melchior followed Nbizi into the middle hut. Nbizi's mother, a stout woman with closely cropped hair and a wide smile grabbed him by the arm as he entered the poorly lit hut.

"Thank you, Father, for coming. But as you see, Vincent is all right, he just started talking now." A young boy was sitting on a bed, holding a damp cloth to his head. "The boy walked right behind the bull and one of the cows is in season. He knows that he must be careful when love is in the air," she cackled throatily and threw an old corn cob at the seated boy, "but he never listens and now he knows what love can do to you if you are not careful." The boy looked up miserably at his mother's joke.

"I'm pleased he is all right," Melchior smiled. "He gave Nbizi quite a fright I think. He is probably just concussed but you must watch him carefully. He should lie down on the bed and will probably feel like vomiting in a while." As Melchior spoke the boy started to retch.

"You see, Father, you know these things even before they are about to happen." She laughed again, now in high spirits, and turned to the boy. "Go outside if you want to be sick," she said unsympathetically. Melchior thought better of intervening. "Well, since we have brought you down here, Father, can I make you some breakfast? I have corn bread, some honeycomb and the water is ready for tea."

"Thank you," he said with genuine appreciation. He sat with the family for breakfast, crushing dripping honeycomb onto yellow chunks of bread and finishing three cups of rich spiced tea. The injured boy lay on the bed and slept, his forehead bruised and swollen where the animal's hoof had slammed against his head.

"Nbizi tells me that the communal police were here last night, talking to *Umuhutu*. No good will come of that, I tell you. I feel bad spirits in my bones." She was not laughing now and Melchior did not answer her, but their eyes locked for some time, until he looked away and busied himself with his bread and honey. Nbizi's mother had articulated his earlier unease and the bad spirits of which she spoke over breakfast were not long in coming.

A few evenings later he was sitting in the eating house finishing a meal of small potatoes and mashed corn when the music programme on the radio was abruptly interrupted by the agitated voice of a newsreader:

We have learned that the rebel force - Rwandan Patriotic Front - has downed the aircraft carrying President Juvenal

133

Habyarimana earlier this evening. The aircraft was hit by a missile fired by RPF insurgents outside Kigali causing it to fall just outside the city.

Michel rushed across to the small, portable radio with a speed that belied his large frame and turned up the volume. He waved his hand at his patrons to be quiet, but they had all noted the tremor in the reader's voice and heard the reference to the President and the RPF. Everyone was already listening with concern.

All of those on board the aircraft are believed to have been killed, including President Habyarimana and Burundian President Cyprien Ntaryamira. Members of the Presidential Guard were also on board the aircraft. Observers on the ground have reported seeing a missile launched from the outskirts of the city shooting across the sky and exploding into the side of the President's aircraft. The Presidential Guard, national police and senior officers of Rwandan National Army are on the scene of the downed aircraft. The reports are that no survivors have been located in the wreckage, which exploded in the air and continued burning on the ground.

President Habyarimana was returning from power-sharing talks, in Dar es Salaam, with the Tutsi RPF and was accompanied by the Burundian President and various other high-ranking state officials from Burundi and Rwanda. An interim government is presently being convened by the MRND executive in order to deal with the crisis.

The shocking news comes at a time when the President was attempting to reach a peaceful settlement with the RPF. It is a sad day for Rwanda when the betrayal of the Inkotanyi kills our beloved president. This planned assassination of our leader, at a time when he was sitting down with the RPF to discuss matters of importance, is unacceptable and cannot go unpunished. The RPF clearly had no intention of negotiating with the President, but merely used the opportunity to await a weakness in his defences, shooting him down and killing him like an animal. Tonight every loyal Rwandian will mourn the loss of our President. These killers are not umwaanzi, these are umubisha. The great majority, the nation itself, calls upon your action and your vengeance.

The news reader went on to explain the basis upon which the interim governmental committee had been established. The broadcast assured the nation that the governance of the country would continue without disruption, but few people in the eating house were listening anymore as an uproar of incredulous conversations took over. Michel looked at Melchior and smiled. "Our friends' sudden visit from Rweru looks a little more interesting now," he said tersely.

"What are you saying, Michel?" Melchior asked, genuinely perplexed at the connection made by the big man. "The communal police couldn't have known of the RPF's intentions, otherwise they would have done something to stop it. Surely?" Michel smiled ruefully at the priest and sat down next to him on the bench. "On my last visit to Rweru to get beer supplies, I heard things a little differently," he said. "The MRND is controlled by Hutu Power now, and ... well, they don't seem to enjoy Habyarimana's talks with the enemy. Perhaps a dead president is more useful..." Michel raised his hands to indicate that he would say nothing more and started to get up.

Michel displayed an insatiable love of scandal and intrigue. He would listen to the spy stories broadcast in French on the

135

national radio and he regularly proclaimed his understanding of the twists and outcome of the programme before it had finished. His endings were inevitably far more complex and disjointed than were those of the programme's, but he invariably provided his patrons with much amusement as they derided his attempts at plot-writing. Undeterred, Michel would embark on new plots the next week, the moment the first break in the story had been reached, pointing to the men seated around him and daring them to disagree with his conclusions.

But Michel's theory on this occasion had an ominous ring of truth - one that could not be easily discounted. It seemed unlikely that the RPF would have planned a missile attack on the President's plane from the outskirts of Kigali, particularly whilst they were in negotiations for a peaceful settlement. The priest soon left the noise and nervous agitation of the eating house and returned to the compound. The security of his life in Bukumara seemed, for the first time, to be tenuous and exposed.

Before

INTERNATIONAL CRIMINAL TRIBUNAL FOR
RWANDA

CASE NO. ICTR-98-3-1

In the matter of:

PROSECUTOR OF TRIBUNAL

versus

VICTOR BUSISWA MUYIGENZI

EXPLANATION OF PLEA TENDERED
IN RESPECT OF DETAILED CHARGE 2.4

The accused tenders the following written
explanation of his Plea of Not Guilty in
respect of indictment 2.4 (Crimes Against
Humanity (Murder) — Joseph Gatagero)
which explanation is tendered voluntarily
and in the knowledge that the accused may
incriminate himself therewith.

1. The accused was, at the time of the death of Joseph Gatagero, the head of the communal police for the prefecture of Rweru. The accused was responsible, inter alia, for the identification, location, containment and arrest of RPF rebels within the prefecture of Rweru.

2. On 23 April 1994, the accused personally received information from a confidential source to the effect that a RPF rebel soldier had returned from outside the borders of the country to his home village, Bukumara, within the Ngoro commune in the Rweru prefecture, with the objective of hiding arms in the area and recruiting young men and women known to him in the area.

3. The source of this information is not disclosed in this written plea explanation; if necessary to do so, the informant will be made available to the Court, on condition of appropriate protection of his/her identity.

4. The RPF rebel was identified as a young male Tutsi, one Joseph Gatagero.

5. On the same day the accused discussed this information with the prefect and his direct superior, Colonel Batho, in Rweru. It was decided that the accused would proceed to Bukumara the next day, with a contingent of communal police, in order to ascertain the accuracy of the information received.

6. On 24 April 1994 the accused led a contingent of four uniformed communal policemen to Bukumara. The accused was armed with his side-arm, a regulation issue 9mm pistol; two other policemen were armed with similar firearms, whilst the remaining two policemen brought wooden sticks.

7. The intention of the visit was: (a) to establish the accuracy of the information received concerning Joseph Gatagero; (b) to arrest Joseph Gatagero in the event of the information being found to be correct; (c) to establish the extent to which the RPF had recruited further members in the Bukumara area; and (d) to recover any arms that may have been brought into the area by the infiltrator.

8. The accused established the whereabouts of the Gatagero family house in the village of Bukumara and, upon their arrival in the village, proceeded by vehicle and on foot to the house.

9. The accused led the group to the house. He announced his presence and identified himself as a communal police-officer. There was no response to his announcement and he proceeded into the dwelling. Upon entering the dwelling he was confronted by a well-built male who attempted to strike him with a club. The accompanying members of the communal police came to the aid of the accused and a scuffle ensued.

10. The man with the club was subdued without suffering any serious bodily injuries and he was thereafter identified as Joseph Gatagero.

11. The said Gatagero admitted to the accused personally that he was a member of the RPF and that he had been sent to Bukumara to recruit members for the RPF. He further admitted that he had brought a quantity of arms which he had buried in the fields outside the village.

12. Gatagero agreed to take the police to the site where he had hidden the arms.

13. The accused and the four communal policemen were led by Gatagero to a field on the western side of the village. Gatagero took them to a point near the river, on the western flank of the field, and indicated that he had buried the arms in the soft soil on the side of the cultivated portion of the field. The point identified by Gatagero has been marked with an "X" on the sketch plan of the village, a copy of which is annexed hereto and which will be admitted into evidence as an exhibit.

14. The uniformed policemen started to push their sticks into the soil to locate the arms. Gatagero used the opportunity - whilst the policemen were so engaged - to draw a knife which he had hidden from the policemen in his boot and he attacked the accused. The accused anticipated the attack on his person and struck Gatagero with the back of his side-arm. One of the communal policemen struck Gatagero from behind with a stick and took the knife away from him.

15. At that point, Gatagero sat on the ground and cried. Gatagero told them that he had lied and that there were no arms hidden in the fields. He informed the accused that he was not an RPF soldier and that he had lied to them because he was afraid.

16. The accused and the accompanying policemen searched the edge of the field and did not uncover any arms.

17. The accused then decided to return to Rweru in order to discuss the matter further with the source of the information and with Colonel Batho.

18. The accused informed Gatagero that he was to remain in the village and that he was under no circumstances to consider leaving Bukumara without first informing the police.

19. The accused left Gatagero sitting on the ground in the field, approximately at the point marked "X" on the sketch plan hereto. Gatagero was conscious, lucid and was suffering from a small gash on the side of his head, which had stopped bleeding by the time the accused left him.

20. The accused had no reason to believe that Gatagero was suffering from any injury that was life-threatening and denies that he sustained any such injury as a result of the actions of the accused or the actions of the communal police under his command at the time.

21. The accused was informed of the death of Gatagero only three days later. The accused does not admit the cause of death alleged by the prosecution.

22. The .accused accordingly admits that:

(a) he detained Gatagero for a period of approximately 30 minutes;

(b) he was involved in a scuffle with Gatagero at the house;

(c) he struck Gatagero in self-defence after Gatagero had attempted to strike him with a knife in the fields;

(d) Gatagero was struck by a member of the communal police under the control and command of the accused, and in his presence, in defence of the accused and after Gatagero had attempted to strike him with a knife in the fields.

23. The accused further pleads that:

(a) Gatagero received no serious injuries during the scuffle in the house;

(b) Gatagero received no life-threatening injuries as a result of the incident in the field;

(c) any injuries that Gatagero may have received from the accused or the policemen under his command, were inflicted in self-defence and were lawfully inflicted in the circumstances.

24. The accused denies that:

24.1 he assaulted Gatagero;

24.2 he assaulted Gatagero unlaw-fully;

24.3 he inflicted any injury upon the person of Gatagero that did or could reasonably have resulted in his death;

24.4 he had the intention to assault or murder Gatagero;

24.5 he murdered Gatagero or is causally responsible for the death of Gatagero.

25. The accused accordingly pleads not guilty to indictment 2.4.

26. The accused pleads in the alternative that, should it be found by this Honourable Tribunal that the accused and/or the policemen under his direct command were responsible for the death of Joseph Gatagero in circumstances which constitute unlawful conduct (which is denied), then such conduct constitutes an isolated incident relating to the ongoing civil war in Rwanda at the time between the forces of the national government of Rwanda and the Rwandan Patriotic Front and that such incident accordingly falls outside the jurisdiction of this Honourable Tribunal.

T F H Grenoble QC
Counsel for defence
3 March 1998

Chapter Five

He was careful not to touch the torn head - for fear of being contaminated by the destruction that had been inflicted on the body and perhaps still lurked in the cold flesh. But he could not stop staring at the deep welts, the cruel indentations across the forehead, the sagging skin strung across the broken skull. He was transfixed by the violence which still seemed to shroud the dead man - in death he was not at peace but rather a battered testimony to viciousness. He had been beaten with brutality and without mercy, the blows breaking his body apart and leaving his face disfigured and almost unrecognisable.

The priest shuddered at the apparent ease with which a young man had been reduced to a crushed outline of thickening blood and flesh, the heartbeat stilled and his thoughts stamped under foot. He wondered too at the ability - the willingness - of others to produce such a result, to strike a being with such force, for such a period of time. Humanity was held together by the thinnest of gossamer, it seemed, silk spun in the air by principles and theories no more substantial than a morning mist, no weightier than the orb spider's last strand. People trod lightly and with gentleness not out of respect for others, but from an ever-present mixture of fear and self-interest.

Social values fell across the shoulders of humanity in a thin veil, resting across the heads of those who allowed it a place; a veil that was easily cast aside. It could be torn by the slightest shake of an individual in the crowd and ripped into great lengths by the movement of a group, shredded into light strips that fell unnoticed, unwanted, to be trampled into the dirt and mud.

The church, he knew, when he confronted his greatest doubts and most intimate thoughts, presented its social discipline on the same basis of deterrence and self-interest: an unsubtle combination of fear at the consequences of contrary actions and a desire to benefit, now and in the hereafter - a reward for acceptance, a payment for moderating one's own desire to succeed. But success could only be measured against the failures of others and the unity of one group necessitates the exclusion of another, the benefit of the one requires the deprivation of another.

Melchior wondered what goals the young man had been seeking before he was taken from his home and savaged by his fellow humans. His eyelids had been brushed closed, but the one had lifted at the corner, showing the dark cavity beneath a thin layer of skin, an empty void without thoughts and feelings: darkness and perhaps the reward thereafter, the priest thought sadly.

The church had no ropes with which to bind the congregation, it had no sanction for breaches of its feeble attempts at order. He could not keep one man from throwing the veil to the ground and seeking his own interests. He could not prevent the death of a young man like Joseph. There must be a balance between the fear and the self-interest, and the fear must be of real and immediate sanction, for when the lives of ordinary people become swept up in change, threats of punishment in a future life are no threat at all. The sanctioning body is itself a human function, motivated by the same selfish desires and as capable of digressing. Who watches the watchers, the priest wondered.

Joseph's death was confusing, as much because the young man was reported to have been a member of the RPF and had been hiding in the village, as the violence of his execution in the fields. At some point, supposedly, Joseph had decided to take up arms against the ruling government and to join the band of rebels that plagued the northern region of the country. Melchior knew nothing, or very little, about the RPF or what might have motivated Joseph's decision to join, but a time must have come when he took that life-changing, or -ending, decision. The decision to beat him to death with clubs and leave his smashed body in the stream could have been taken before the party left Rweru. Or they may have decided to complete their efforts only while they watched him squirm in the dust at their feet. Someone may have said something, voiced their decision, or it may simply have materialised as a logical end to their actions. However the conclusion had been reached, at some point the group of men from Rweru had decided that Joseph's life was unimportant and that they were entitled to take it away.

No doubt it had made it easier, in principle, first to label their victim *icyitso* - not to call out his name but call "*Inkotanyi*", to beat him with accusations, "*inyangarwanda*", and to denigrate him until he was no longer a person worthy of life but merely a nuisance, a parasite, *inyenzi*. Once he had been stripped of his human form, then perhaps the act became possible. The *inkotanyi* were reputed to have the tails of animals – but when they struck his body and kicked him to the ground, the priest thought, there would have been no animal features, but just the young man, the same man now lying in the open wooden box. The *inyenzi* were said to steal Hutu children to keep as slaves, or to sacrifice in bloody rituals, but when they took Joseph from his home, they would have witnessed the simple properties common to all of our lives: they would have been confronted not by demonic cunning, but by his mother, scared and alone, his little sister, crying under the bed. It is devastating that, in the face of such individual vulnerability, one person before another, people should still be capable of such brutality, he mused.

The priest drew his hand across his face before crossing himself. He lowered the lid across the box, throwing the young man's battered face into shadow, then covered by the light-coloured rough wood.

Joseph was buried in the small graveyard next to the church compound that afternoon, with a small smooth rock for a headstone and a small bouquet of forest plants and flowers. Melchior looked into the bewildered eyes of Joseph's mother and read from the Bible. He made milk tea for the family and they sat outside in the shade of the eucalyptus tree, talking quietly of the tragedies that had befallen them. He learned from the family that the policemen had arrested another young man who had been away for several years and had recently returned. They had taken him back to Rweru for questioning. His fate was not known. They had apparently questioned Joseph immediately and, by the time they were finished, he was dead. A friend of the family, an elderly woman named Rosalie, told him that she saw them beating the boy in the field. She said that she had seen Victor in the same grey Pajero, but she was frail and her eye-sight was poor, the priest doubted whether she could have seen what had happened. But there was no doubt as to what she had found after the group of policeman had gone: she described the mangled body lying in the stream, limbs askew, water washing the blood away.

The family left and Melchior recorded the burial in the church record books: cause of death, beating by communal police, he wrote.

There was a tension in the village in the days following Joseph's death. The policemen did not return, but one villager reported seeing thick black smoke rising from two different places somewhere in the direction of Rweru. The village seemed very quiet. The fields were left unattended, watched only by the storks and plovers, walking like school teachers, hands behind their backs, bent forward and concentrating. The dull hum of insects and the heat was disturbed only by the occasional click of brids' beaks and the rustle of goats, untethered in the bush, standing on their back legs to reach the young leaves. The eerie stillness was unbroken even by the troops of vervet monkeys scampering in the tree canopy above - an uneasy and predatory quiet.

Melchior walked to the stream where Joseph's body had been found. There was no sign of the events that had surrounded the killing of the young man. The small stream flowed unconcerned, clean and cold, over and around the same rocks that had felt his weight, leaving no trace of blood or mark. He sat on a rock and looked out across the unworked field. An ibis stalked across the uneven ground, its thick curved bill prodding the ground, flipping small stones over, working a restricted square area in front of its feet. The sheen across the bird's smoothed feathers and its singular concentration made Melchior think of Selena's words, when they had sat watching the sunbird in the poinsettia tree. He longed to talk to Selena now and he felt a warmth well up in his eyes - to cry, alone and without an obvious reason, seemed indulgent and weak, but he was unable to resist the slow rise of sadness, tears cupping on his lids and then trickling, almost unfelt, down his cheeks. He cried for himself and he cried for Joseph, wordlessly.

He recovered his composure after a while and blew his nose on a piece of cloth from his pocket, startling the ibis into taking flight for a short distance. It landed again and continued its relentless hunt. Melchior smiled, sad but lighter after the release of emotions. He rose and plucked a small yellow field flower that was growing next to the rock. He placed it in a slow-flowing pool on the side of the stream and watched it eddy and swirl before disappearing in amongst the grass and reeds along the bank. Tonight, he thought, I will say prayers for Joseph and for Selena.

The day slowly drew to a close, the sky thinning out to the palest of blues, darkening suddenly without the slightest glow of red. He walked down to Michel in the early evening, accompanied only by a small group of chickens, scratching in the silted mud on the side of the road and throwing up small sprays of dirt. A dead adder, beaten and crushed, lay in the road with its mouth split open, large black ants feeding off its intestines. The eating house was almost empty. Two young men from the village were seated near the counter, drinking together and talking in low tones. While Melchior was eating, a few villagers arrived, greeted him with a nod of the head, finished their meals quickly and left again for their homes.

Michel came to sit with him after a while, heaving his weight between the bench and the edge of the table top. He too was upset by Joseph's death and shook his head like some beast of the savannah, trying to shake the emotion from his mind, holding his beer in both hands on the table. Michel told him that the radio had been carrying heated broadcasts following the death of the president, blaming the RPF and its supporters and calling on the populace to rise up in anger against the threat. Michel told him of vitriolic speeches he had heard during the broadcast, berating the Tutsis for undermining the stability of the country, referring to them as foreigners.

"They keep using the word - *gukora* - as if there is some national outcome we must all work towards, but it doesn't make any sense the way they are using it. I think there is something else happening, my friend," Michel looked serious and slowly raised the bottle to his mouth, drawing a large mouthful of beer, swilling the liquid in his mouth and squeezing his eyes, drinking from necessity, drinking his medicine in huge gulps.

"The one woman, a woman mind you, not a man, a woman on the radio, she said the time had come for *itsembatsemba*, a time to wipe them out. She was talking about killing people just because they are *umututsi*, she said nothing about the *Inkotanyi*. They use words differently, they are speaking in a new way, Melchior. I can't understand what they mean anymore: they talk about 'work' but they mean something else. I think there is something happening in Kigali, something not good. I just hope that we are too far away for it to reach here."

Melchior had nothing to say to his friend - his fear, his anxiety at the death of Joseph, his insecurity, all fluttered about his tongue, pricking his tongue tastes and tickling the inside of his lips. But he could not open his mouth. He could not start to tell Michel of his sense of chaos, the knowledge that the killing of Joseph made further killings possible, that a tear had been rent in the fabric and which allowed ever more people to enter a world where life could be dismissed. That with every deed the hole grew bigger, until there was no fabric, only the absence of fabric through which they all would pass. He wanted to tell him of his fear that humankind was in reality an abomination, gifted with thought and cursed with raw desire, untamable, unpredictable. But his cross bore heavily upon him. His spiritual functions required him, he felt, to maintain serenity even in the face of weakness, to display an unwavering loyalty to destiny and thereby to instill calm and faith in those in his church community. Honesty, when it involved the recognition of doubt, was not a virtue to be espoused on the brink of a storm. So he nodded in unspoken agreement with Michel, as if he was already privy to the information and was not disturbed by it.

Michel did seem calmed by the priest's quiet demeanour and ended the conversation by repeating his words: "We are probably too far away for anything to reach us here." He laughed and added: "We are lucky even to get some news here now and again, never mind the attentions of government." Melchior also laughed, a snorting sound, which was cut short almost as soon as it had left his mouth.

Bukumara was not too far to be reached by the catastrophic events which engulfed the country. Within a few days of their discussion, the first sign of the events in the heartland of Rwanda arrived at the village. Late in the afternoon, a middle-aged woman was brought into the village with a baby tied on her back with a dirty-blue knotted blanket. A young girl, perhaps twelve years old, wearing a pink cardigan with cloth flowers stitched onto the shoulders followed her, carrying a large packet with a few belongings, clothes and another blanket crushed into it. A villager returning on his cart with firewood had found the family alongside the road, exhausted, and given them a lift for the last kilometre to the village. He brought them to Michel at the eating house. The young girl had large wet blisters on her feet which had been rubbed raw during the long walk. The woman's own feet were swollen and inflamed. She was incoherent with fatigue and emotion. Michel brought them to the church compound, without food and with nowhere to stay. The small group sat together in the yard, gulping down tea and broken lumps of corn bread.

After a while the woman started to tell the two men of their flight from a village on the road to Rweru. The woman's speech was often unclear and her story was disjointed, jumping from scenes in her village to her tortuous journey along the paths and roads to Bukumara. Two days before, some young men in her village had been identified as *ibyitso* and had been taken away by the police. There was a rumour that they had been killed. Some houses had been set alight; a group of policemen, drunk and smoking marijuana, had attacked the village leader's house and taken away his belongings. She had been part of a group who had fled, fearing further attacks, but they had become separated when they reached a roadblock along the road.

"But why were they attacking the village? Surely they were only searching for rebel soldiers? Are they saying that the whole village helped the RPF?"

The woman became increasingly tearful and agitated as she tried to explain her story to the men. "I don't know, I don't know", she kept repeating, shaking her head. The young girl started to shake uncontrollably, her eyes dry and unseeing, slapping her hand against her mother's bare leg over and over again.

Michel intervened and abruptly told the woman to stop her story: "You must rest, mama, and in the morning you can tell us more about what happened to you." The two men looked at each other.

The priest nodded. "You are safe here," he said calmly. "You can stay here tonight. I will make you and your children a bed in the office. You don't have to worry, you are safe here."

The woman said nothing and they drank their second cup of tea in silence, the unfinished story hanging in the air between them. The woman made no attempt to comfort the girl and seemed unaware of the small child on her back. Melchior took the girl's hand and held it between his two palms until she had stopped shaking. He looked into her eyes - she seemed dried up inside, as if a great dusty plain had filled her and reduced her to a crusted shell that rustled and shook in the breezes of her mother's garbled memories. Melchior smiled at her but received only an empty stare in response. He left them sitting together and made a bed of blankets and cushions for the family in the office. The girl fell asleep before she could take off her cardigan, her small hands clasped about her head as if she was in pain. Michel looked at the sleeping figure and shook his head again.

"Dear God in Heaven," he said, squeezing the priest's arm with his strong hands, "that a child must be punished by the madness of adults." Then he turned to the priest: "Father, they will be all right on their own for a while. I think that you should come and listen to something."

The two men left the sleeping family and walked down to the eating house. Michel took the radio into the house and they sat around his kitchen table. Michel's wife, Felice, put two large mugs of beer in front of them and this time the priest did not refuse. Michel said nothing and adjusted the radio.

"There is a radio station called RTLM – Radio Television Libre des Mille Collines. I don't usually listen to it because it is run by the national government, or it is certainly linked to the MRND, but the *nyumbakumi* said I should start listening to it. I was interested to know why, so last night I tuned in. It is that same woman I told you about; listen to this..." Michel carefully turned the tuning button until a woman's strident voice crackled through the speaker.

The graves are not yet full, brothers and sisters.

Our beloved President has been dead for over a week, but still the graves are not full. You will remember when the great Leon Mugesera told us two years ago that the foreigners must be sent back to Ethiopia by throwing their corpses into the River Nyabarongo: take heed of those words, my friends. The river is flowing and waiting for its cargo.

The enemy must perish, all must be eradicated. Not with expensive bullets, don't use money to kill these inyenzi. Would you kill a cockroach with a gun? No, cut them to pieces with a machete.

Turatsembatsemba abatutsi !

This is radio RTLM, the official voice of Hutu Power, broadcasting out of Kigali. And now I will play for you again: "No Present to the Enemy". To work, my brothers, to work.

Michel turned the radio off. No one spoke for a while.

"You are a Hutu, Michel," the priest said, breaking the silence. "Do you have any idea what this madwoman is speaking about?"

"I don't know anything more than you do. This woman says she represents Hutu Power and she is trying to stir up the people to attack anyone who is a Tutsi, whether or not they have a connection to the rebels. It looks as if Hutu Power is trying to run the Tutsis out of the country: Kigali is mainly Hutu, so if·I was a Tutsi there I suppose I would leave until this was all over. I don't understand why somebody doesn't stop her from saying these things. Where is UNAMIR, where is the interim government? Surely she can't be allowed to say these things on national radio."

"Unless the national government approves of her conduct," Melchior said gravely.

Michel took Felice's hand, holding her fingers between his two meaty palms. "I still don't understand how she can be allowed to say these things. If I tell my neighbour to kill you, and I keep on telling him to do it, surely that can't be allowed. I don't know, I'm not a lawyer, or a politician, but I don't see how that can be allowed."

Melchior slept fitfully that night, dreaming of his brother. He awoke and walked barefoot across the compound to the office to check on the sleeping family. They were sleeping heavily: a whistling sound emanated from the woman and the children were not moving. They were so unnaturally still that he placed his hand on the baby's chest to feel his breathing. He returned to his bed but the traumatised girl played on his mind. In the early hours of the morning he fell asleep. He dreamed that he was walking across the stream, placing one foot in front of the other across the stones, the water lapping at his toes. He saw something floating towards him, turning slowly in the water, catching on the rocks, circling in the eddies, moving ever closer towards him. He knew what it would be, even before it was near him he knew. He stood on the rocks, unbalanced and swaying, waiting in resigned anticipation until the girl's small body floated to his feet and dragged against the stone he was standing on. Her face was smooth and pale and her eye sockets empty, the water pulling at her hair and dress. The stone tipped under the weight of her body. He lost his balance, toppling and falling towards her dead face, towards the deep black holes staring up at him. He awoke with a ringing sound in his ears, unsure as to how loudly he had shouted, breathing quickly and straining for the sound of anyone about in the compound.

He got out of bed and rubbed his face with cold water from the enamel basin. His mouth tasted sour and his shoulders felt bruised. When he opened the door he saw the little girl, still wearing her pink cardigan, sitting in the first rays of the sun and scratching in the dirt with a stick.

"Hello," he said, smiling. She looked up at him but did not say anything. "Would you like some tea?" he asked. The girl nodded her head. "Can you help me make the tea?" She nodded again and got quickly to her feet. He had not expected her to be forthcoming - the tea was already made and only needed to be warmed, but her eagerness at his suggestion seemed somehow significant, the holding out of a hand to him, an acknowledgment. "I will bring you the kettle for the water," he said, striding back into the room. He poured the cold tea into his enamel basin, the honey-brown liquid blooming in the cold soapy water, and took the emptied tin kettle outside. The girl was waiting, standing in the sun.

"There is a water tank near the latrines," he said, handing the kettle to the girl. Her thin hands held the worn handle tightly in front of her, her knees knocking against the tin sides as she walked quickly around the corner of the sacristy. When she returned, the gas hot-plate was burning brightly. He beckoned her to come into his room. She placed the kettle on the hot-plate and sat on the soft chair, staring at the flames hissing under the tin.

Melchior was about to ask the girl to wake her mother, when a loud knock on the door startled him. The doorway was filled by the large figure of Michel. "Hotel Bukumara open for tea?", he asked, feigning good spirits. "I see your pretty guest is already working hard in the kitchen," he said grinning at the girl, who looked away. He continued undaunted. "You just tell the hotel manager what you want and he will take care of it, don't you worry, little one." Michel walked into the room and lifted the lid of the kettle. He caught sight of the murky water in the enamel basin and raised his eyebrows at the priest, but said nothing.

"I didn't want to wake you last night, but another group arrived in the middle of the night. Two women and some children. They are still sleeping in the house, but I'll bring them up here." Michel's jovial tone was for the benefit of the girl and underneath his banter Melchior noted a more serious mood.

Michel took his arm and led him to one side. "I think this may just be the beginning of a lot more people looking for somewhere to go, somewhere away from whatever is happening in the towns. This group also told me about an attack on their village, and about barricades on the roads. They say that others are also on their way into the forest villages, looking for shelter."

"There is not much comfort to be found in the compound," Melchior answered. "I can take a few more people here, I suppose, but we will have to find other houses where we can put them up for a while. How long do they want to stay here? Are they just moving through?"

"The new group is just as frightened as the first. I don't think they have any plan really, only to get away from their village and find some safety here. They say that the communal police were helping in the attack - I can't understand this." Melchior heard a scuffle of feet and turned to see the girl disappearing out of the door. The water boiled over on the hot-plate, spilling and hissing. The two men looked at each other forlornly.

Melchior accompanied Michel to the eating-house. The morning was clear and bright, the sun warming the damp earth. The smell of wood fires and baking corn bread filled the air. The reported fear and chaos of the city seemed very far away. But as they approached the eating-house, Felice came out to meet them, distraught.

"They have left, Father. The women said they were too scared and they wanted to move deeper into the forest." Michel took her by her shoulders. "The children seemed so tired. They could hardly walk and their feet were torn and scratched. I pleaded with the women to wait until you came, but they wouldn't listen to me. They were so frightened, they just kept saying that they must go further into the forest." Tears started to run down her cheeks. "I went to the kitchen to make the little ones some food, but when I came back they had gone already. They didn't have anything, Michel. What are they going to do running into the forest? The smallest one was only two years old and his mother is too weak to carry him. Must he walk all the way to Uganda?"

Michel drew her closer to him. "Perhaps they will come back to us," was all he could say.

Melchior returned to the compound, but within the hour he received word from Michel. His young son ran into the compound panting and asked the priest to come: "My father says the people are here," the boy panted.

"The same people from this morning?" the priest asked, but the boy shrugged and ran off.

Melchior hurried down to the village again: he was disappointed to find that it was not the same small group from the morning that had returned. Instead, a larger group of eleven adults sat on the benches, with children and babies. Bags and rolls of blankets lay scattered on the floor at their feet. The children were not playing, but sat exhausted resting their heads on the table tops. He counted nine adult women and two elderly men.

The group nodded a greeting to the priest as he stepped up onto the balcony. One man had a deep gash across his shoulder and back, old blood crusted on his clothes, a wet patch still seeping through the faded cloth. His faced wrinkled in pain as Felice tugged at the soiled fabric, wiping the wound with a wet cloth soaked in vinegar. One woman wept quietly and the rest looked on wordlessly.

"We have been walking through the night." A large middle-aged woman got to her feet and approached him, her skirt swaying from her wide hips. Her hair was bunched into small squares, beaded and pulled tight, leaving a symmetrical criss-cross of bare scalp across her head. Her face was lined with dust and her eyes were grave. "My name is Rutayisire. I have escaped the killing in Pukuma, near Kigali, and I have met these people along the way. We need a place to stay, Father. We are all too tired to go any further. The people on the road say that the only safe place is a church."

"If we are not safe in the sight of God, then we cannot be safe at all," he replied. "There are already some people in the church compound and there is not much space, but you are welcome to join them there."

Michel helped bring the group to the compound, and brought some mangoes, bananas and bread in a bag. The new arrivals were greeted without enthusiasm or resentment by the woman in the compound - the arrival of more refugees was met with a resigned expression of understanding and pragmatism. They arranged some blanket beds in the corner of the office. Melchior made rough divisions between families using chairs and boxes.

Rutayisire immediately assumed a dominant role. She moved her substantial weight about with surprising agility, chiding the younger women and attending to the wounded man, scolding the children for spreading the dust of the compound, organising water and directing the families to their different

162

areas. Melchior helped her clean out the store and set up a rough bed for herself. She worked with quiet determination and they did not speak further about her escape or the events she had witnessed.

The rainy season was drawing to a close, but the purple-black clouds still gathered in the afternoon heat, blocking out the sun and thundering in the sky above them. They quickly finished their work as the first languid drops plummeted to the ground, plopping in the dust around the compound. Rutayisire looked up at the dark clouds. A few hailstones clattered on the tin roof of the office block. She moved off to her room, without a word to the priest, and lay down on her bed. She left the storeroom door open to the compound and quickly fell into a deep and noisy sleep. Melchior could hear her sucking breaths, wheezing and whistling, from his own room. She lay on her back and drew the air about her into her body in great heaves, expelling it in equally passionate clouds.

The compound was empty and utterly quiet now, save for the slow pattering of afternoon rain. The open doors of the rooms and the whistling sigh of the sleeping woman were the only signs of its guests. Melchior lay on his bed without sleeping, lying in the darkened room and listening to the irregular beat above him. He thought of Selena, caught in the upheavals in the cities. He wondered whether she had gone to Kigali to her parents, or whether she had stayed in Butare, holed up with other teachers at the college. He knew that she still saw Gratian from time to time and he wondered if she had not perhaps found refuge with him at the seminary. Faced with an onslaught based upon fear and self-interest, she was more likely to confront her attackers than seek safety. He wished he knew where she was and that she had taken the danger seriously. He tried to force his mind to move away, but the vision of her standing up, defiant and challenging, her long braided hair proclaiming her ethnicity, daring her attackers to do their worst, kept returning. In his vision, the men grabbed at her, pushing her to the ground, their ugly scarred bodies straddling her and pinning her down. One took a machete and sliced through her hair, as if he were cutting through a tied bundle of wheat, holding it over her face and letting the strands drop thickly onto her face. He felt tormented and unable to escape his waking dream, which played over and over again in his mind as he lay trapped by his own fearful imaginings.

The children rested and slept for hours, but by the later afternoon he started to hear their stifled giggles, the shout of playful instructions, and an occasional peal of laughter. He got to his feet thankfully and went outside. The compound seemed cleaned and freshened by the short downpour. One of the small boys was peeking through the doorway at Rutayisire sleeping in the storeroom and he ran away squealing. He returned with a friend and they stood at the door, playfully pushing each other forward. The whistling sound paused for a second and the two boys were suddenly quite still, the one clutching the other, tensed like prey, waiting to bolt at any movement. Then a deep nasal snore bellowed out from the sleeping figure and the two boys scampered across the compound, exuberant and screaming with fearful delight.

Bent figures appeared from the open doors, stretching, rubbing their heads. Someone helped the injured man outside into the sunlight and sat him down on a pile of folded blankets. Slowly the compound came to life again. Finally Rutayisire lumbered into the light, unaware of the commotion she had caused. She paused and nodded towards Melchior.

Then she gestured towards the low-walled entrance to the compound. Melchior turned to look. Michel stood at the entrance, nervously surveying the scene, flanked by two uniformed policemen – Inspecteur de police judiciaire. Melchior walked across the compound to meet them. One inspector was noticeably older than the other, a thin quiet man who looked down at the ground. The other was younger than Michel, little more than a teenager, yet his manner was openly aggressive. His holder-clip over the butt of his pistol was unclipped and one of his hands rubbed the end of the magazine continuously. This seemed to provide him with a sense of authority and security while at the same time affecting an unspoken intimidation of everyone else.

Nonetheless, the two inspectors seemed to pose little threat to the families in the compound and Melchior smiled, about to invite the men in for tea. Michel stepped forward and raised his eyebrows. Melchior thought he detected a barely perceptible shake of the head and he stumbled over his words as he retracted the invitation that was about to roll off the edge of his lips.

"Would you ... are you here ... can I help you in any way?" he said mildly, turning from the one uniformed man to the other.

But it was Michel, not the two policemen, who responded. "The inspectors want to see how many families have congregated at the compound," he said. Michel hesitated and seemed to consider his next statement carefully, before proceeding: "The inspector tells me that the displaced and rotted reeds in the river tend to clump together in predictable inlets along the river bank." His eyes were wide and focussed on Melchior. "They tell me this is a good thing when it comes to cleaning up the river."

The younger policeman stepped forward and pushed Michel back with his arm roughly. The white-heads of adolescence were still evident against his dark skin and spittle collected at the corners of his mouth: his words were a sour breath on the older man's face, his unmeasured voice shrill and grating.

"It is necessary for our work that all displaced persons collect in designated places of safety," he had paused before using the word 'safety', but his eyes cut deeply into the priest, "and in this village this compound will be the collecting point for all persons arriving in the village. We will be back to assess the position here. You will be expected to keep proper records of all such persons as part of your work. This is what is expected of you." Again the use of the word *gukora* for 'work', Melchior noted.

The young inspector tried to push past Melchior but he held him back with a forced smile. "First of all, I need your name. And secondly, I need to know who your superior officer is."

The man seemed taken aback at first and stepped away from the priest. His head moved about on his shoulders as if disconnected, bobbing from side to side as rage and insecurity grappled uncertainly for control.

"I take my orders from Captain Venant," he hissed like an animal. "And my name is *Amasusu*. For you, my name is *Amasusu*. You remember my name, Father. You remember that name."

He pushed past Melchior aggressively and entered the compound. The children scattered into the rooms or cowered behind the adults. The inspector moved swiftly around the compound, his hand gripping the pistol menacingly, glaring

166

closely and without shame at the women sitting on the ground, like a dog unabashedly inspecting about the quarters of an intruder. Melchior almost expected to hear him sniff the wind about the injured man - instead he peered intently at the wound, examining it closely, before moving on with a grunt. His energetic pace was comical in the small confines of the compound: he moved as if he had a great distance to travel, as someone would who is in a large market but is only looking for rice or a particular fruit, and within a short time he was back at the entrance to the compound.

"Open the church," he barked. Melchior protested that the church was empty but the inspector insisted and so the church was opened and similarly inspected. His colleague hovered at the door, uncertain and torn between joining in the irreverent search and the respect to be accorded to the humblest of religious places. The youngster stalked into the sacristy but found nothing of interest and stepped out of the church into the strong afternoon sunlight.

"Soon you will need this hall, that I promise you now," he said loudly and insidiously, seemingly addressing the small group of people in the compound rather than the priest himself. Then they left, moving quickly down the road with Michel wedged reluctantly between them.

No-one in the compound spoke to him about the policemen's visit. They busied themselves with making small cooking fires in the centre of the compound, ringing the fires with rocks and stones lifted from the dried mud and fine dust at the side of the road. Smoke drifted up through the eucalyptus leaves, filling the compound with a calm sense of living, a domestic contentment that comes from families conducting the simple acts of preparing food, caring for their children, talking to friends whilst tending the flames of the open fire.

Melchior looked about the compound and suddenly felt a sense of purpose, albeit displaced. The compound had never seemed so homely, so lived in, as it did at that moment - the policemen gone, the two children playing with small round stones, the wounded man lying quietly in the softening sunshine, the women nursing the small fires, sun beams streaming and catching in the blue smoke. He stood as the master of his small world, caring for his newly adopted flock, providing shelter and security from whatever harm it was that lurked and stalked through the bush outside the confines of the compound. He had joined the church essentially as a protective act designed to shelter his own vulnerable self: now it appeared to him that there was perhaps a far greater, worthier cause. He wondered if this was not, by chance, what he had been striving towards all along, whether his desire to protect himself was not merely an individualist indication of his broader desire to protect all those weakened about him. He had not stood up to the policemen, he told himself: the inspector had represented no threat to the people under his care, but had on the contrary, implicitly recognised his role as a protector for 'displaced persons' in the area. People would seek out his church and accept that he had the power to provide them with security and comfort.

He walked over to Rutayisire, who seemed neither young nor old, but captured in a moment of motherly ageing, overweight and with large soft breasts that moved like water-filled bags when she worked. "How are you here now? Will you be all right to stay here for a while still?" he asked, benign and smiling.

She looked up at him with intense eyes. "We have no food, we have left our homes as they stand, we have only the clothes on our back. You say that if we are not safe before the eyes of God, then we cannot be safe." She did not smile and her full face looked tired and drawn as she spoke. "I am, no I was, a nursing sister in a clinic. My life has been broken, smashed like an old clay jug for which you have no use, and now this" – she waved her arm towards the church building – "is all I have. You are right to say what you do. This place does not say that I am safe; all it says is that if I am not safe here, then I am not safe anywhere. I accept that, that is the truth. And what it means is that I am not safe. I am protected only by the hope of safety. Our country has gone crazy: perhaps crazy people will respect this sanctuary, but probably they will not. If your church cannot protect us Father, then you cannot protect us."

She prodded the fire distractedly with a stick, the small embers sending up a thin line of bluish smoke. "Your church was founded in another country, where people strive for a life of spiritual purity and happiness. Here in Africa, Father, we strive only for a life at all."

Melchior did not respond. But her words struck deeply. The woman was right, of course; he could offer this new community of fugitives little by way of food or real safety. He could give them shelter, water and the guise of protection, a transient shield. He represented a power, or perhaps only a symbol of power, that could protect the people now in his care. Protection only existed provided that the symbol was recognised and accepted by all the players in this traumatic drama. Yet it seemed that the authorities recognised his as being a necessary and useful function - the young policeman may have been right, maybe the compound would fill with many more, as a collecting point for the displaced and wounded. The national authorities were promoting this function. Inherent in that must be a recognition that the church is sacred, the property of the church is a sanctuary.

But these rational thoughts belied the underlying dread that was growing inside him. He was filled with a terrible anxiety that he would be overwhelmed and unable to overcome the fate that awaited him. It was the same desperate feeling of helplessness that he had felt at the death of his brother who had been taken from him - despite his prayers and his commitment that it should not happen. No matter how determined he might be in his own actions, he could not conquer the will of God, the ordained steps set out in time. He had lacked not the will, not the desire, not the energy, but simply the power to prevent his brother's death. His power did not seem, in reality, any greater now. He felt alone, as alone as he had felt as a child.

He left Rutayisire tending her fire and entered the quiet and privacy of the sacristy. It was here, on occasion, that he was able again to capture that feeling of ease and warmth that he had felt in his days with Selena at the seminary, sitting beside her in the shade of the mpingo tree, listening to her melodic talk. He knelt before the small statue of the Virgin, his eyes closed, waiting for a state of reverie to overcome him, an absence of memory. But his thoughts wandered. He felt the burdening presence of his brother and he clenched his hands tightly together, trying to squeeze his thoughts dry. He saw clumps of braided hair that fell like strands of blood, splashing and twisting on the ground, turning into small black snakes scattered about his feet. He got to his feet suddenly, exasperated, the blood rushing from his head and leaving him dizzy.

Melchior pulled the sacristy door firmly closed behind him. As he turned away from the door into the hall, he was jarred by a series of sudden cries that sounded from the compound. Amid the shouts and calls he could hear the shrill wailing of a woman, uncontrolled and desperate. He half-ran across the hall and opened the wooden door of the church onto the compound. He was met by swirling clouds of red dust that filtered thickly down through the air, catching in his nose and falling evenly across his hair and shoulders. The dust was drawn into his throat and lungs with his first breath: dust caused by a crowd of nearly a hundred people treading up the road and flooding into the church compound, pushing and limping and bending down, shouting and saying nothing, looking backwards and moving forwards. An inexorable force of people that parted those already in the compound and slowly filled its borders.

The priest stood still, without any movement, his hand on his mouth, disbelieving. He breathed deeply with consternation despite the dust. He registered only an undefined mass of people, like a stream where no one portion of the flowing water can be distinguished from any other. His unfocused eyes swept blankly across the crying baby on his mother's back, the lost child walking in a daze, her knees bleeding, alongside a man pushing a wheelbarrow holding a goat, tied at the feet, its small voice drowned in the collective murmur of people on the move, the woman pulling at her torn hair, wailing and shaking her head, the old man with cracked skin and flies about his eyes, the little girl in the pink cardigan replicated tenfold - none of these things were noticed by the priest, only the dreadful, sickening flow entering his home.

Melchior did not know how long he stood at the church door, scanning the arriving mass of dispossessed people, but eventually the flow halted, unable to force any more people into the open compound. Rutayisire shook him by the arm: "I think we must open the church for these new people," she said simply. The priest nodded in agreement, without parting his dried lips, and stood back into the shadow of the hall.

The flow of people started again, this time into the church hall, unfolding blankets, staking small plots of floorboards between benches, until that too was filled with clusters of people, preparing their makeshift beds, holding their crying children, sitting staring not at the wooden cross on the front wall but at the floor, exhausted. No one spoke to the priest: his presence was taken for granted, he supposed, as the benefactor, the ever-present figure common to every village throughout Rwanda, every hilltop church building, every seminary and church school. The task of caring for a small group of refugees had previously provided him with some form of meaning and solace: now it took on the dimension of the impossible, the extent was overwhelming and without any meaning, a solace that could not be performed.

Rutayisire was still by his side, silently watching the broken families make their homes amongst the bench legs and brick walls. "Where have all these people come from?" Melchior finally asked despondently.

"We are all *umututsi*," she said simply. With that answer she turned and walked across the compound, now a sea of lying, sitting, squatting, sprawled beings, her small cooking fire crushed beneath the dust and feet of the newcomers.

A few families sat outside the compound, crowded close to the entrance and looking furtively into the compound, fearful at being disconnected from the crowd. Melchior walked carefully around the people in the church and opened the sacristy door: "Some people can sleep in here," he said, his voice cracked and trembling. The nearest group of people picked up their belongings without a word and moved into the sacristy, their place soon to be taken by others camped near the door of the church.

Melchior collected his keys from his room, stepping over limbs and bodies in the compound, gently pushing past women, standing, nudging children out of his way, returning to the classroom and opening the door. No words were needed and the small room was immediately filled with people keen to escape the crush of the open compound. The office and the store-room were already filled with refugees, most of whom were lying on the floor, apparently sleeping. There was a sour edge to the air and shiny-green flies buzzed around his face and settled on his shoulders. He stood at the door of the classroom and looked out across the compound. There was nothing more he could do.

He turned to his own room. He was grateful to find that no-one had taken over his own space. He nodded to some of the people sitting against the wall of the room and closed the door behind him. The solitude of his room filled him with relief after the chaos of the compound and church. He felt uncomfortable at the simple luxury of his small room, the excess of having his own sprung bed and a bowl of clean water, but the day had left him exhausted. He felt numb and emotionless. His anxiety at having to feed and care for the people now in the compound had left him, from fatigue rather than a sense of peace or resolve.

He cupped cold water in his hands and splashed it over his face. The water coloured from the dust on his hands and the sides of the bowl were streaked with dirty brown lines. He lay down on his bed without getting undressed. The murmurs of the people outside combined into a low drone and he fell asleep immediately.

Melchior slept soundly and deeply this time, physically exhausted and drained of all thought. He slept without dreaming and without disturbance. Then, in the early hours of the morning, he was awakened by a hand gently shaking his shoulder. He opened his eyes tiredly - his body craved both sleep and the escape it offered, and he reluctantly looked up at the person standing at his bedside. She looked down at him frowning with concern. A young boy stood next to her, holding her hand tightly.

"You look so very tired, Melchior," Selena said softly.

"EXHIBIT M24"

Gure, kuwa 3/05/1994

REPUBLIKA Y'U RWANDA
PREFEGITURA YA RWERU
KOMINI Y'UMUJYI YA GURE

Bwana Zukisisi wa
Senje
GURE
Prefegitura ya
Rweru
Komini Y'Umujyi
ya Gure

Impamvu : Umuganda we
Kuwa 6/05/1994

Bwana Zukisisi

Inama ya Perefegiture ushinzwe
umutekane yafashe ibyemeze bye
utmeshe ibihuru byese mu mujyi wa
Rweru ne mu nkengere zawe. Ni muri
urwe rwege twifuza ke kuwa gatanu
tariki ya 6/05/1994 guhera saa meya

hazakerwa umuganda aha hakurikira :
Umuhanda wa Rwabayanga uva muri GBD
ugana mu Rwabayanga, hazakerwa
n'abaturage bahegereye cyane eyane
abe mi cyaraby nab'i Gure.

Abaturage ba Tumbe naba
Cyarwa-Sume bazarkora umuganda we
gutema ibihuru ku muhanda we kuri
nkambi iimpungi.

Nsabye abajyanama kubimenyesha
abaturage bakazaza ari benshi;
ibikareshe bazitwaza ni imihore,
imipanga na ze coupe-coupe.

Prefet wa
Rweru
Batho,
Col

Bimenyeshejwe: Bwana Muyigenzi,V Wa Rweru

_Order from Prefect (Rweru) to councillors
and communal police to have population
turn out in large numbers with their
machetes to "cut the brush" on 6 May 1994
at 7 o'clock in the morning._

Chapter Six

The early morning light fell across the face of the small boy as he slept with his head on the priest's pillow. He breathed evenly with an open mouth, a small bubble of saliva rising and disappearing in the corner of his mouth. He slept deeply, drawing in the sleep like an elixir: his body was still, his darkly black hair curled closely against his scalp and the skin on his face pulled smoothly over his round cheeks and upturned lips. A peaceful figure caught momentarily in a circling pool, surrounded by thrashing water, waiting to be sucked back into the currents and to be swept away downstream again. Small pieces of grass stuck to the back of his head and his neck was pale with yellow-red dust.

Melchior was unprepared for Selena's sudden arrival. He was filled with conflicting emotions at seeing her at his bedside: he saw in her a purity that was uncorrupted by sordidness and suffering and he viewed her, unrealistically, as being exempt from the miseries of human conduct. In his fraught dreams Selena was threatened and defiled by imaginary attackers, but in his conscious thoughts, she remained as clean and untouchable as the first day he had seen her walking across the grounds of the seminary. Her unexpected presence in the compound, now the very definition of chaos and baseness, left him feeling unbalanced and uncertain.

His confusion and fatigue caused him to react distractedly towards her at first. Selena was wary at first as well, unsure herself as to how to deal with the unfamiliar conditions thrust upon them. They sat on the bed next to the sleeping boy and talked until the early dawn. She told him of her journey and her experiences in Butare and, as he listened and watched her movements, he felt his defences slowly receding. But his numbness was not replaced by a closeness or affection, but rather by an anxiety drawn from vulnerability. Selena was exhausted and scared: he could no longer see her as removed from the suffering of those around him. Like the refugees outside in the packed compound, she had sought him out in the hope of finding some protection. The refugees were unknown to him and he had no connection to them other than his representative status, but with Selena, his standing in the church meant nothing, and his emotional attachment was compelling.

Selena had cut her beautiful braided hair, leaving a thin stubble of dark hair clinging to her rounded head. His eyes kept wandering from her face, stricken by the violence of the change. It was necessary, she explained, to avoid being immediately identified as a Tutsi: her tall thin features were dangerous enough in themselves. Her hands explored her scalp while she talked, running over the coarse surface and brushing against the small cuts and uneven patches. She spoke in quiet whispers, touching her head or holding the small boy's hand in hers, running her fingers along his smooth palm and wrist, anxiously retaining her physical contact with him.

She had left Butare in the early hours of the morning, she told him. She had heard the news of President Habyarimana's assassination and within hours roadblocks had appeared on all the main streets leaving Butare. The smell of burning rubber and creosote poles, torn from the fencing along the government properties, had filtered through the air, catching at the back of her throat. The *Interhamwe* youth had placed burning drums and concrete blocks, pulled from the broken walls of houses, blocking the road except for a narrow pass for carts and wheelbarrows to pass. The roadblocks seemed to be a spontaneous and disorganised reaction to the news of the country's loss. The barriers were often placed almost on top of each other, different groups merging into one in places, then leaving tracts of open road and paths entirely unguarded - disorganised save for the arrival of sharpened machetes, bandanas and Habyarimana portrait pins. Some civilian *Interhamwe* even sported grey grenades clipped onto their belts. FAR soldiers, Kalashnikov rifles strung across their backs, stood watching the operation of the barricades from a distance.

Selena had been unsure as to the purpose of the burning roadblocks. From her window she had watched youths piling wood and grass onto a large barricade in Avenue des Libertes, intent only on building the fire higher and higher and without particular regard to the movement of people around them. She could see bands of militiamen moving through the suburbs and the commercial district and, in the early dawn light, the smoke rising from a number of houses in Buye. The morning had brought wild stories which circulated throughout the day: that the RPF had attacked the city, that the Burundian army was planning to enter from the south and was massing at the border, that Tutsis were being hunted down and killed in their homes, that Hutus were being slaughtered on the streets. Selena stayed inside and waited.

Then a colleague from the secondary school had arrived, knocking quickly on her door and slipping into the room.

"Turn on your radio, quickly, you must hear what they are saying on the radio."

The woman tuned Selena's radio to the station RTLM. Selena listened, stunned, as the announcer howled and cried, her every word filled with harshly pitched hatred, calling for the extermination of all Tutsis. Selena described the same rabid entreaties of "*gukora*", to work, to take up arms and perform the work of the Hutu nation, to work for your community by killing, 'until the graves are full', that Melchior had heard sitting in Michel's kitchen. Selena felt an involuntary shiver across her shoulders – 'until the graves are full'. Then she had known that she had to leave Butare.

She had drawn the curtains and cut her hair, sitting in front of her small mirror and twisting her head to get to the base of the braids. Her body had trembled from fear and she jumped whenever she heard a shot or explosion close by, half-expecting the sound to be followed by a cry at her door. The wind blew the black smoke from the large barricade in the avenue, pushing the ash and soot against the window panes, forcing the bitter smell under the seals and poisoning the air in the room. Still she waited, imprisoned in her room while the *Interhamwe* went about their business outside. A thunderstorm brought some relief, heavy drops of water pounding on the ground and clearing the air. But the rain was short-lived and the barricades were rebuilt and kindled with renewed vigour: by evening the air was thick with smoke again, and filled with the noise of chanting, singing and breaking glass.

Selena had not slept that night. She lay on her bed with her arms hugging her body, waiting for the night to pass. The next morning, before dawn, she slipped out into the back streets of

Butare, carrying a small bag of food and wearing plain dark trousers and a man's jacket. She managed to avoid any streets with barricades, withdrawing into the dark corners and backyards when she heard someone coming. She dropped into one of the valleys slicing through the town, stumbling along a half-overgrown path and pushing through bushes and grass in the thin moonlight. At one point she heard a shot ring out behind her and crouched down in the brush. Then she heard someone running towards her, panting wildly, a noise filled with fear. She shrunk further into the bushes and lay still. The fleeing person changed course and descended away from her, crashing noisily further down into the valley. When it was still again, she proceeded, half-seeing, half-feeling her way along the side of the valley, constantly pulling at the vegetation to keep her balance. On the ridge above her she heard people moving about, patrols of men and boys talking excitedly together, scanning the valley and the ridge on the opposite side.

The side of the valley evened out towards the edge of the residential area. Selena chose a small dirt track which ran past the veterinary school towards the Rwakabuye River. Flanked by banana trees and tall uncut grass, she was able to move quietly until she reached the boundary road which led to the communal offices. But she still had to cross the road to reach the relative safety of the river and its thicker bush. Fires flickered along the road, clearly visible through the tree trunks. She could hear voices and, some way off, a group of men were singing drunkenly. The smell of marijuana and beer mixed with the acrid smoke that drifted down the road in ghostly forms towards her.

She crawled alongside the road, using the grass and trees to shield her, until she found an unmanned barricade in a curve in the road, a thin line of smoke still drawing from some abandoned embers. She crawled on her hands and knees, ever closer to the barricade, trying to look only in front her.

"The barricade was made of bits of wood and stones, blackened from the fire. I was half-way across the road, crawling low down, when something caught my eye. I couldn't help myself, I didn't want to, but I just looked to my side. They had packed the wood around bodies, about seven bodies," she told him. Her eyes filled with dry tears. "Do you know what had made me look? A face, a child's face with wide open eyes looking right at me. Lying in the barricade. I screamed and got to my feet. I didn't care if I was seen, I just had to get away. I got up and I ran, I was in such a panic I dropped my packet of food. I ran and ran, through the bush. I don't know if I was still screaming out loud, but inside I was crying as loud as I could. You cannot imagine it, you can never imagine such a thing, Melchior. Children hacked with machetes, hacked by boys not much older than them, children who once played with their older brothers and teased little girls, now lying in the mud and dirty water, flies feeding off their cut faces, children spilled open on the ground."

She groaned as the visions, unbeckoned and unwelcomed, flooded her mind, filling her with nausea and desperation. "Oh, Melchior, what can become of us when our children kill and are killed like that, without any compassion, without any feeling. I saw young boys standing side by side with *Interhamwe* militiamen, chanting, spewing hatred, sharpening their knives and waiting for their next victim. They sang '*tura tsemba tsembe*', 'come let's kill them all, let's kill them all'. What do they know of killing? What do they know of such hatred?"

"Where are the Belgians, where are the blue helmets?" he asked gravely.

Selena looked at him, struggling to answer him calmly. "Melchior, I love you and I will always respect you, you know that," - he felt uncomfortable under the intensity of her unwavering gaze - "but you cannot always rely upon the intervention and control of forces beyond ourselves. I saw no god at the barricades, I saw no restrictions on their behaviour, there was no distinction between the acceptable and the unacceptable and no-one to enforce such a distinction should it even exist. The life or death of anyone who passes through the hands of *amarondo* is governed purely by chance and the whim of the hunters. You must understand this. One of them may take a liking to you, take you into the bushes and rape you before letting you go; another may think your hair just a little too straight, your nose a little too refined, or that you may have had an easier life than him. Perhaps you own some cattle. Your life is decided in the blink of a stranger's eye, in a momentary impulse, the glimpse of a thought - you are either walking alone down the path, free for now, or you are lying in the dirt, grass in your hair and your blood leaking into the earth.

"The blue helmets cannot help you now - they have been confined to compounds in Kigali and Butare, in the town itself. I heard someone say that the blue helmets had been chased into the compounds like goats, and that some had been killed. I cannot say if that is right, because I did not see a single UNAMIR soldier all the way from Butare to here. I saw some FAR soldiers driving a truck with UNAMIR emblems on it, that was all. The people on the road, they refer to the blue helmets as *minwa*, spoken about but never seen."

Selena looked at him in silence - he suddenly felt defensive of his naïvete and beliefs. He remembered her challenging way at the seminary, when she asked him about his studies, sniffing out the inconsistencies in factual statements, looking for the lie in belief. An answer based on faith would not suffice: "You can't plaster over a crack in a foundation with paper. Faith is just a shield behind which you can hide. All you are saying is: 'I choose to ignore this absurdity because I want to ignore it'. You can make that choice if you want to, of course, but don't then tell me that your choice is right and everyone else has made a mistake."

Melchior had always been wary of her debates and, as a student, he had resigned himself to retreating and conceding many of her challenges. However, after some years with his own ministry and as the church leader of his community, he could no longer pretend to laugh at his foolishness and wonder at her sharp intellect. His choices had turned into a responsibility. He looked at her now, trying to gauge the harshness of the criticism she had placed before him.

"Do you think God is *minwa*? That we have been forsaken?" he asked.

She paused before she answered, taking up his hand in hers. He noticed the lines of dust and the long scratches from the bush marking her forearms. "We have different outlooks when it comes to faith. Since our earliest days together we have each loved the differences in the other."

There was still an adult distance between them, but Melchior felt warmed by her words. "But what I saw outside Butare has nothing to do with those differences, Melchior," she continued. "I saw ordinary people who had forsaken themselves. They had let themselves off their own tethers and were running unrestrained and without morality, like a pack of street dogs. They were wild and buoyed by nothing more than being part of a group. Perhaps they will turn the corner and come out from the shadows into sunlight and realise that they cannot carry on like animals. But I have never seen a pack of dogs stop their rampage until they are faced with an adversary that is not a victim, an adversary that will crack a whip at them and send them fleeing, their tails between the legs, meek once more. Perhaps God will send such an adversary. Perhaps their appetite for killing will run out on the outskirts of Butare and Kigali. Perhaps we will be able to return to our former way of life, looking back on the events of the past few days as some inexplicable and momentary aberration.".

"But what do you think? You have seen the *Interhamwe* at work, you have travelled from Butare into the countryside. Is this madness going to carry on? Surely, ordinary people behave like this only out of some demented anger, which must pass. Once they see what they have done with their own hands, they will disown this movement and it will peter out."

"*Turatsembatsemba abatutsi*," she said.

She paused while the impact of these words was felt by them both. "That is the standard greeting now between *Interhamwe*. They sing songs about exterminating each and every Tutsi in the country, they say that the Tutsi are foreigners from the north and that their ... our ... bodies must be thrown into the Nyabarongo River so that our bloated corpses will float down the Nile. They say they are *rubanda nyamwinshi*, the great Hutu nation who are entitled to the fruits of Rwanda without the interference of pests, *inyenzi*. It seems almost overnight a new culture has burst out, like pus from a sore that has festered beneath the skin and has suddenly been released. And now it dominates, even amongst the 'ordinary people'. It was the 'ordinary people' who were running about Butare, possessed by this evil. From what I have seen, this is something more insidious than a momentary outburst of hatred or discrimination. I hope so terribly that I am wrong - for all of us - but the songs, the killings, the propaganda, it all points in the wrong direction." Selena took a long drink of water, and then continued her story.

"When the sun came up I had cleared the outskirts of Butare. The heat and humidity was stifling. I could hardly walk any further. There were other straggling groups on the road, but I tried to keep apart, hoping that I wouldn't be noticed. A few government trucks came past and sometimes the soldiers would shout abuse at us, but no-one stopped. A civilian truck passed and the driver gave me a lift, I think because I was on my own and I didn't have any children to worry about. He took me until we were close to Gikongoro. We both saw the barricade burning in the distance. The driver didn't say anything, he just slowed down on the side of the road and I jumped out while he was still moving.

"The barricade was manned by a big group of *Interhamwe* militia. It lay between me and the road north towards Rweru. There was no way to pass during the day, and so I hid in a sorghum field close to the road. I crawled along the field until I was closer to the barricade, so that I could crawl past when night came. I could see part of the barricade from where I was lying. I put my hands over my ears and I closed my eyes, but still I heard and saw things ..." Selena breathed deeply and ran her hands over her eyes, but gently pushed away the priest's comforting arm when it was proffered.

"There was a hail storm while I was lying in the field. The hailstones pounded my body and smashed against my head. The ground turned muddy underneath me and beetles and ants came out of the wet earth and walked over me. I couldn't move. I just lay there, being hit from above and bitten from below." She gave a weak smile. "I was miserable, but I couldn't cry or make a noise.

"Then the storm passed and the sun came out. The barricade came to life again. There was a dwarf, a lunatic, from the hospital cells. The *Interhamwe* had released him and brought him to the roadblock. They gave him a machete and *ntampongano* and cheered him on, like children at a soccer match, urging him to strike out at people who were brought by the patrols to the barricade. He was deformed, with a small twisted body and a grotesque head. I could hear his cries, like a tortured animal, as he danced around striking the ground, spitting. He urinated on a woman who he had beaten on the ground and they all roared with laughter. Then he struck her on the head with the club. I pressed my hands against my ears, but I kept hearing his grating bark, I couldn't keep it out. I cried and cried, silently to myself, until I felt numb and empty. Still his demented cries reached me where I was lying in the field. I had to keep myself from jumping to my feet and running at the dwarf with a stone to crush his skull, just to stop his noise.

"Finally, in the late afternoon, they took him off to carry on his work somewhere else, leading him away the way you would lead a dog. They killed over twenty people that day, while I was hiding in the field. The men brought a woman into the field, close to where I was, and they all took turns to rape her. I heard their laughs and their grunting as they rutted like pigs. Then they killed her with a sharp knife. She hadn't

187

made any sound at all the whole time." Selena looked up at him and held his eyes with hers. "I said 'that day', but the strangeness is that it was only yesterday. How quickly things can change in your life. How horribly suddenly."

She fell silent and they sat, exhausted but unable to relax, the sleeping child lying like a barrier between them. She stroked the boy's head and pulled some of the grass sticks from his hair. Melchior watched her fingers at work, unthreading the fibres and teasing the dried mud from the knots. He was forced to ask the question he had been avoiding. "And the boy?" he said softly, touching the sleeping child's bare arm.

"Jaki is a cousin. He was living with my parents for a while and then outside Gikongoro, I must take him to his aunt in Rukubara." She sighed and added, in a whisper: "His mother is Tutsi but his father's sister is Hutu and they will care for him there. His mother is missing."

She gently shook the boy by the shoulders, but he resisted waking up, turning his face into the fabric of the pillow and boxing her hand away grumpily. "Jaki, time to go, little one," she said in Kinyarwandan. She lifted him to a sitting position, but his body flopped against her chest, his eyes pushed closed.

"I will make you both some tea to wake up," Melchior said, getting to his feet. His legs were stiff and he rubbed his thighs to draw the blood into his tired muscles. He felt more comfortable talking to her with his back to her, busy with the hot water and tea. "You must have seen all the people in the compound when you came in. The hall and sacristy are full as well. Michel thinks we will probably get even more people here tomorrow. They are all frightened and they need someone to tell them that they will be protected. When I walk amongst them, I see them looking at me for reassurance, watching my movements from the corners of their eyes. They are assessing my confidence. There is one woman, a nurse, who has been helping me: she sees things the way they are, I think. She scolded me last night for looking so dejected. I felt like a schoolboy again. She said that I cannot be expected to protect these people physically: such help is beyond the control of any single person, no matter who they may be. My role is to try and give them spiritual hope by projecting my faith onto them. But how can I march around the compound, brimming with faith and loyalty and confidence in the ways of the Divine, when all these people have come to my church and I cannot feed them? The water is running low, the surrounding fields have been plundered for fruit and grain, the pit toilets are filling and the whole hilltop is covered in a stench."

"Melchior," she interjected, "the nurse is right in a way. You have to define your role in the compound narrowly and with care for yourself and for those you wish to protect. If you exhaust yourself and overextend yourself, trying to do more than you possibly can, you will harm both yourself and everyone who is looking to you. There are terrible and powerful forces at work, Melchior."

He turned to face her, a cup of tea in his hands. "I want to tell you not to leave here, but I can't tell you that it is any safer here than anywhere else." He handed her the tin mug and put his hand on her shoulder. "It does feel a better place for having you here, though."

"Melchior," she smiled back wanly, "after I have delivered my little parcel to his family, I shall return to the compound. My parents have already fled Kigali and I cannot return to

Butare." She left her thought hanging in the air between them, unfinished. He waited but she seemed distracted.

"Let me make some tea for you to take with you when you go," he said, breaking the moment. She had never seemed so vulnerable to him. He could not bear to see her without her normal self-assurance, her strength and her passion.

The boy drank only half of his tea before falling back asleep. Selena glanced anxiously at the sky, brightening as dawn approached and roused him once again. Melchior made them buttered sandwiches and a cold-drink bottle of tea, the mouth stopped with a cloth. He wrapped some leftover boiled potatoes in paper and packed the provisions into a string bag. Selena used the hot water from the kettle to warm a cloth, wiping some of the dirt from the boy's face. He stood, uncomplaining, his arms hanging limply at his side.

When they were ready, they picked their way around the contorted forms lying in the compound. Streaks of light were already appearing in the sky and some of the sleepers stirred as they passed. One woman sat erect near the entrance, her blanket bundled about her, staring at the lightening horizon and rocking to and fro. They greeted her in a whisper but she did not look back at them. The open spaces of the village were a relief after the compound and they walked slowly, side by side, without talking. A dog barked in one of the yards, shielded from them by a fence of reeds bound together with sisal. The banana tree alongside Michel's house still bore ripening fruit and he added a hand-sized bunch of yellow-green bananas to the bag.

The air was still and the sky was tinged with orange. Brown parrots started to call to one another from the treetops and a small flock of ibises flew overhead, their wings beating loudly. The village was peaceful and quiet: it was hard to imagine the acts of human evil that Selena had described. The roofs of the huts shimmered and the dark shadows of trees peered and danced over their peaks. A strange and luminous time when the night hands over its charges to the day.

They stopped under a drooping pepper tree. A troop of grey vervet monkeys was moving about in the top branches, dislodging small leaves which tumbled to the ground. The young boy hugged the trunk and peered up, trying to pick the animals out against the sky. He bent down and picked up a smooth stone from the road. He steadied himself to throw it into the branches. Selena put her hand on his arm and shook her head slightly and he threw it spinning into the fields instead. Two white storks took to the wing, lifting off the ground with heavy strokes, only to land again not far away, rustling their wing feathers.

She turned to Melchior, tired but still poised. He saw now, in the moment of parting, that it was he who felt weak and fearful at the prospect of being alone again. "We must be going now, my friend," she said simply. Her sudden appearance and unsatisfying intrusion into his life in Bukumara, and her equally abrupt departure, left him feeling overwhelmed. He fought to hold his balance in a rush of emotions, a flood of feelings and memories, an urge for physical intimacy: he wanted to rush to her like a child and hold onto her. But the reluctant distance of adults lay between them now, a barrier of time and faded familiarity that held him back.

He longed for her to take the initiative, but instead she fussed with the boy and the string bag, glancing nervously down the road that awaited her. Eventually he reached out and took her hand. Without looking into her eyes he squeezed gently and turned on his heels. He heard the little boy say something softly - perhaps to her, or a whispered goodbye to him – he could not tell, but he walked back towards the village, forcing himself not to look around, his chest heavy and tight.

The village was still asleep, but soon the light would return and the day would start. He heard someone pouring out a bucket of water behind one of the fences. Whatever the day would bring, he knew that he would never see the village, or the country, in the same way again. The wakening noise and the smell of the overflowing compound greeted him unpleasantly as he trudged up the uneven road.

Before

CHAMBER THREE

INTERNATIONAL CRIMINAL TRIBUNAL FOR
RWANDA

CASE NO. ICTR-98-3-1

In the matter of:

PROSECUTOR OF TRIBUNAL

versus .

VICTOR BUSISWA MUYIGENZI

**INTERLOCUTORY JUDGMENT
STATUS OF WITNESSES DDD AND DDE**

Judgement delivered: 29 July 1998

The Trial Prosecutor has applied for the
inclusion of two further witnesses on the
prosecution's list of competent and
protected witnesses: the witnesses shall
be referred to herein as DDD and DDE
respectively. The defence has objected

to the inclusion of the two witnesses and has furthermore objected to their proposed protected status. The tribunal has heard the arguments presented on behalf of the prosecution and by Mr Grenoble for the defence.

The background to the prosecution's application for the late inclusion of these witnesses is comprehensively set out in the written application: in summary, the two witnesses were located by IBUKA, the Rwandan genocide survivors group.

Witness DDD was located in one of the refugee camps of eastern Zaire during 1996, where she had been sheltering for some time. An initial statement was taken from her and, although that statement has not as yet been placed before the tribunal, it will no doubt make an appearance should the prosecution's application succeed. Having given the statement, witness DDD then apparently took fright: there is no suggestion that she was threatened directly, but the continued use of the refugee camps by Hutu extremists was a source of great anxiety to her and she fled the camp. The prosecution, and IBUKA, continued their efforts to locate witness DDD and succeeded only recently in locating her. The witness remained reluctant to testify at the trial and was uncooperative. In the weeks preceding this application, witness DDD was brought to Arusha and has been receiving counselling, with a view to calling her as a witness. The application was brought once she had indicated that she was prepared to give evidence: it is to be noted that her agreement to testify is conditional upon her status as a protected witness being confirmed.

Witness DDE was unknown to the prosecution. She was found by soldiers when Operation Turquoise moved into Rwanda. She was seriously injured and was taken to the military hospital in Kigali. She was subsequently moved to a government clinic in Kuruja, where she spent a considerable period of time undergoing rehabilitative treatment. The nature of her injuries and subsequent treatment are not disclosed herein in the interests of her personal security. She thereafter moved to Tanzania, where her family had fled during April 1994, and she remained with her family until their return to Rwanda in 1997. She was located by IBUKA in the early months of 1998. The initial statement taken from her is short and lacking in detail. The statement has been placed before the chamber and has been subjected to intense criticism by the defence. The

prosecution has submitted that, for
various reasons including the inexpe-
rience of the investigator taking the
statement, the gender of the investigator
and the reluctance of the witness, the
statement does not reflect the true
extent of her evidence. Members of the
prosecution re-interviewed the witness
during the past month and apparently
realised at this stage that the evidence
of the witness was critical to the
prosecution.

The defence objects to the inclusion of
the witnesses on the grounds of prejudice
to the accused. A similar objection is
made in regard to the protected status of
the witnesses. Furthermore, the defence
argues that in both instances, and
particularly in the case of witness DDE,
there is evidence that the witness was
initially reluctant and that the extent
of the witnesses' knowledge of events was
limited. The defence argues that the
tribunal should find that a real danger
exists that the witnesses have been
coached by the investigator and IBUKA
into giving evidence against the accused
and that their evidence cannot be relied
upon.

The tribunal must assess the prosecution's application and the objections
thereto in the light of Article 14 of the

Statute of the Tribunal and the Rules of Evidence and Procedure adopted at the Fifth Plenary Session in June of this year. The duties of the prosecution must be weighed carefully in the balance against the rights of the accused. In doing so, one must guard against straying unreasonably in favour of the prosecution, on the grounds that the accused is charged with the most heinous of all acts, the 'crime of crimes', or in favour of the accused, on the grounds that he may face life-long incarceration as a result.

The tribunal has considered all the arguments raised by the prosecution and the defence in this application. The overriding consideration of the Chamber's is the simple fact that the Chamber is free to assess the probative value of all relevant evidence and that the Chamber will apply the rules of evidence and procedure in order to achieve a fair determination of the issues between the parties. The evidence of a witness is approached in a holistic fashion and the restrictive rules which might ordinarily apply, such as the rule against hearsay, are relaxed in order for the tribunal to reach a true assessment of the probative value of the evidence which it has heard.

The Chamber is accordingly free, and indeed is duty bound, to assess the credibility, reliability and truthfulness of the witness and the evidence adduced during the course of the trial. The evidence of the witness will be viewed in conjunction with the facts disclosed to this tribunal in this application. The initial reluctance of witness DDD and her flight from the investigators will be considered and no doubt she will be subjected to rigorous cross-examination on these issues when the time comes. Similarly, witness DDE will be required to explain her initial statement: if it appears from her explanation that a real possibility exists that her evidence has been manufactured, then it will be dismissed and the defence will suffer no prejudice.

The prejudice which the defence faces accordingly, in the Chamber's view, rests not in the content of the witnesses' evidence but in the lateness of their inclusion on the list of witnesses. The view of the Chamber in this regard is that the explanation for the delay, as furnished by the prosecution, is satisfactory in both instances. Therefore, if the prosecution cannot be held responsible for the delay, then the Chamber must simply determine whether the potential prejudice to the defence cannot be mitigated by time. Mr Grenoble for the defence has conceded, correctly I think, that in the light of the prosecution's undertaking not to call the two witnesses until the present evidential theme has been completed, he cannot contend that he will be unable to prepare to meet the new evidential matter.

In the circumstances, the Chamber is of the view that the two witnesses, witness DDD and witness DDE, should be added to the prosecution's list of competent witnesses. The probative value of their evidence will be determined by the Chambers in the fullness of time.

The status of witnesses at the tribunal has traditionally been a vexed one. The prosecution has sought full protection, including the non-disclosure of the true names of the witnesses to the defence team. The prosecution's application in this regard has been fiercely challenged by the defence and, in certain instances, I believe that the challenge is justified. However, the Chamber is of the view that the status of the two additional witnesses should, in principle, be that of protected witnesses. A summary of the evidence of the two witnesses has been provided by the prosecution: Mr Grenoble's protestations aside, I must accept for present purposes that the summary provided reflects an accurate version of the evidence which will be presented by these two witnesses to the tribunal. It must be noted that the evidence of both witnesses, and witness DDE most directly, pertinently implicates the accused in acts which, if found to have been committed by the accused with the necessary intention, would support a conviction on certain of the charges brought against the accused. That being so, and having regard to the personal history and circumstances of the witnesses, the Chamber accepts in principle that the witnesses should be afforded a protective status.

The prosecution is aware that I do not favour the non-disclosure of names and relevant information to the defence. I have already given a lengthy judgment in this regard in the matter of <u>Zumalo and others</u> (ICTR -98 -2-3). I reiterate the conclusions set out in that judgment. The failure to release the names of witnesses to the defence unreasonably curtails the accused's ability to instruct his defence on issues of bias, reliability and malice. The non-disclosure cannot in my view be condoned or supported in terms of the rules of evidence and procedure and constitutes an unfair and unjustifiable infringement of the basic rights of the accused. The prosecution's application in this regard must in my view fail.

The Chamber accordingly makes the following order:

1. The prosecution is granted leave to add witnesses DDD and DDE to its list of competent witnesses.

2. The prosecution's undertaking not to call either witness until such time as the present evidential theme has been completed is noted.

3. The two additional witnesses are granted the status of protected witnesses and the contents of the Registry's directive of 11 March 1998 in regard to such witnesses are formally brought to the attention of the defence team, the accused, the media and the public present in the Chamber.

4. In addition to the contents of the Registry's directive, it is ordered that:

    4.1 The true names and personal details of witnesses DDD and DDE

shall not be disclosed by any
party hereto in open Court;

4.2 The prosecution shall release
the true names and personal
details of witnesses DDD and DDE
to the defence team forthwith.

5. The statement of DDE is provisionally
entered into evidence before the
tribunal, pending the evidence of the
witness herself.

Saresh Villay
Presiding Judge
Trial Chamber Three

Chapter Seven

Melchior found the thick smells of human bodies and uncovered waste which filled the compound increasingly unbearable. The flies pestered the wounded mercilessly and children scratched in earth already wet from the overflow of the latrines and pit-toilets. He stood at his door and surveyed the disorder that had descended upon his formerly insulated life at the St. Jean Church. The noises of the compound combined, the talking and shouting, the moans from those in pain, the murmurs and mumbles of those who rocked back and forth in fear, and the quiet noise of those who sat staring with their empty eyes, pounding on the priest's ears. He could no longer differentiate any one group of refugees from another or distinguish any family unit from any other clump of bodies strewn about the ground. The small girl in the pink cardigan was lost amongst fifty, a hundred other small children clinging to the wreckage of the their parent's lives. The noise and the heat and the people all merged into an amorphous sea, rising and falling in swells, moving towards him and back again, out towards the compound walls where it rose and crashed against the hard stone, driven back towards him in waves. An unimaginable sprawl of rags and begging limbs.

His eyes travelled across the surface, unfocused, sweeping from one side to the other in desperation. Then, in the southern corner next to the scarred eucalyptus tree, he picked out the familiar bulk of Rutayisire, shouting at a young man for urinating against the stone wall. She shouted at the perpetrator and made her way menacingly towards him. The man dismissed her with a wave of his hand and escaped through the stone entrance out of the compound.

Rutayisire looked about her to see if there was anyone else she could vent her anger upon - finding no one suitable, she heaved up her bosom in defiance and strode towards the office buildings. Melchior called to her and invited her into his room. It was the one place where there was some freedom from the outside noise and smells.

The nurse anticipated what he was about to say. "We have to do something about this compound, Father. We are going to have cholera, typhoid fever and who knows what else springing up unless we clean this place up. The children are playing in the fouled water and the drinking water was finished this morning."

"We need a work-force of healthy men and women who can help us. How many younger people do we have who are not wounded?" He gave her a piece of paper and a pencil which she took with an authoritative air. While she sat working out a work-force, he sat next to her and drew a sketch of the compound and its few buildings.

"I can organise a group of about twenty-five people who would be able to help us," she said, putting her pencil down thoughtfully. She looked across at the sketch.

"We must divide the people into groups," he said, pointing to the various rooms and buildings. "Perhaps the sick and wounded in the classroom, the store and the office, away from the heat of the sun and the flies. Then we could put the elderly and those with children in the church hall and the sacristy. Then the men with minor complaints and the unaccompanied adults in the open compound itself." Rutayisire nodded in agreement.

"And those children with no one, Father? We have at least twelve children with no family whatsoever. They were abandoned in the villages and followed the refugee groups until they came here." Rutayisire cast her eyes around his room.

"Here," he said quickly, rather than waiting to be asked.

"I am afraid, Father, that it has come to that. I will care for the children in your room, we will make mats on the floor. We would not take your bed from under you, Father," she said, chuckling to herself and pushing his shoulder gently. "And I'll stay on the floor, Father, don't you worry." At this she let out a guffaw, opening her mouth wide and displaying a bright pink tongue and gleaming white teeth.

It took the rest of the day to move the people into the various designated areas. There were many more women with children than they had thought and some had to be placed in the open compound. Some of the men prepared a drainage ditch from the latrines and others dug some deeper holes outside the compound. Another group took turns in hauling water from the river in two buckets to fill the tank on the top of the latrines. The tank was small and had been designed only to meet the needs of the few who were likely ever to stay in the compound. It was quickly emptied by the refugees as they sat without cover in the sun. It would need to be filled at least twice daily. Shallow circular pits were dug in the compound for communal fires and ringed with stones. Piles of dry firewood were collected and stored against the walls.

Huge purple clouds plumed in the sky in the late afternoon, blocking out the sun and bringing temporary relief from the heat. Melchior and Rutayisire walked together around the compound, surveying the day's work. They both sensed a subtle change in the mood of the refugees: the beginning perhaps of a sense of community, an identification with one another that had resulted from their attempt to improve their conditions. During the first day, the refugees had sat, dazed and immobile, resignedly awaiting their fate without resistance like animals penned in an abattoir. The spirit of the people seemed to have returned. He noticed a young woman sitting next to an injured mother, breast-feeding the injured woman's baby whilst her own child slept in her lap. Two women carried a bucket of fresh water and were offering a drink to the wounded in the office and store-room. The disorganised scattering of individual fires had been replaced with three larger communal fires, tended by young boys who broke up the firewood and fed the fires with sticks and twisted bark.

When they had finished inspecting the compound, they walked outside to the cemetery at the back, where the men had dug new holes for latrines. The banana trees had been stripped bare, even the green fruit had been pulled down, leaving the leaves torn and the stems bent and snapped. The greatest difficulty facing the church and its inhabitants remained the provision of food.

Four fresh mounds of earth ran in a straight line along the side of the cemetery wall. They stood in front of the first mound without speaking. Then, as Melchior was about to say something to break the silence, Rutayisire held his arm.

"People are coming," she said anxiously. "Listen." A sound like someone chipping stone, a harsh sound of metal on rock, reached them in the cemetery. And then the murmur of tired voices.

They hurried back to the entrance of the compound, giving them a view down the hill towards the village. A group of some thirty people, women, children and old men, walked wearily up the slope towards them. They were being herded like tired cattle by a band of seven men, wearing yellow scarves and strips of material as head-bands. Some wore banana leaves strung around their waists. They held machetes, each striking the ground in turn, slicing the earth and clanging against the rocks. Behind the men, Melchior saw a solitary figure, walking with his hands behind his back, like a school teacher walking down the aisle of his classroom, letting his students get on with their work, watchful but not interfering.

"Victor," Melchior shouted, recognising the solitary figure. "Don't bring any more people up here, we are full. There is no space for anyone else here, I am sorry."

Rutayisire touched his arm: "Save your breath, Father. They are not asking you, I think."

Victor held up one hand towards the priest and continued following the group up the hill. Rutayisire stood her ground as they approached, but Melchior stepped to one side and pulled on the side of her dress. It was clear that the herders were not intending to stop and the group swept past into the compound. The men stopped at the entrance, still striking the ground with their machetes. The refugees accepted the new group nervously, directing them to an open space near the latrines. Melchior noticed stones and sticks in the hands of some of the men in the compound. The *Interhamwe* outside pointed their machetes and jeered at them with open mouths, showing their teeth like wild animals and daring them to come out and fight. The men inside changed their grips on the sticks, readying themselves. The heat pressed down on them and the insults between the antagonists increased.

Melchior took a step forward to intervene and calm the situation, but, as he moved, Victor barked a single command and the *Interhamwe* fell silent.

"Victor, what is going on here ? We can't possibly take on any more people. We should be finding other places for these people, not bringing more here."

Victor looked tense. "My friend, there are bad things happening in our country. These people were camping in the village – they are not safe there. The only place where runaways will be safe is at the church. I know it is difficult for you, it is difficult for us all. We all have our jobs to do. Think of it as *umuganda*." Victor was not smiling.

The two men stood silently, each waiting for the other to say something to ease the sudden tension and distance between them. Victor seemed uncomfortable under the gaze of both the priest and the woman, and the small band of men that he had brought with him, who stood jostling together, watching him. He pursed his lips as if in thought and then ordered his men to stay outside the compound.

"I have to talk to you, Melchior." He looked at the woman directly. "On your own," he added.

Rutayisire clicked her tongue in disapproval and walked back into the crowd of refugees standing anxiously watching the proceedings. Victor took Melchior by the arm and guided him into the road. "Walk with me, Father," he said firmly. The two men walked alongside each other, not touching but close enough to communicate in low voices. Victor started to speak when they were a safe distance from the compound. But as he began, one of his men called back him with a shout.

"Excuse me, Father, I will be right back." Melchior watched him walk swiftly back towards the compound. A short conversation took place between Victor and the man who had called him, and he came jogging back. Melchior noticed the well-defined muscles on his stocky body as he ran. The exercise had not even raised his breathing.

"Have you been getting fit, Victor?" he asked.

Victor paused before he answered, frowning, then forcing a smile. "Well, the ladies like me strong," he responded lightly. "Lushodayana," he added after a slight pause, separating the word from the rest of his sentence. It stood on its own, imbued with its own independent meaning. Melchior had not been called by his childhood name for many years. It made him think of the moments in their childhood together. Despite his bullying and aggression on the playing field, Victor had always had a certain charm about him. He had been able to ingratiate himself with the parents of friends, doing small chores, affecting childishly polite mannerisms which reaped the rewards of shared meals and indulgences. The adults tended to believe Victor's stories rather than the sniffled complaints of their own children who would accuse him of kicking them in a game of soccer or punching them on the nose during a play fight. Victor had the ability to seem sincere, widening his eyes and raising the pitch of his voice as he persuaded others of his genuine intentions. Melchior wondered if he too was now the recipient of Victor's deliberated sincerity.

"My unit now falls directly under the command of Colonel Batho," he continued. "You may have heard of the things that are happening in Kigali and Butare, the killings and the persecution of people that is taking place there." Melchior nodded silently. "The killings have spread into the countryside and you cannot consider that a village like this one, or even a town like Rweru, will be safe from these events. There are already barricades between Rweru and here."

The priest interrupted him. "What is behind these killings? You are in the communal police, you must know what is going on."

Victor responded quickly and aggressively. "The RPF and *inkotanyi* have infiltrated the population. We believe that the assassination of General Habyarimana was the beginning of an attempted take-over. Trained killers emerged from hiding amongst the population and set about killing government officials and attempting to disrupt the functioning of the nation. The interim government has responded by mobilising the army and police force to root out the problem. We are to be assisted in this task by civilian militia groups." Victor softened his tone. "It is difficult for us to identify *inkotanyi* amongst ordinary people, and some innocent people may have been hurt in the process."

The priest interrupted again. "But Victor, I haven't heard any accounts of an RPF uprising or of attacks on government personnel. The only stories I have heard about are of attacks on ordinary citizens of the country, attacks that are motivated purely by the fact that the victims are Tutsis !"

"What is the source of these stories? That is what you must ask yourself. Of course RPF propaganda is not going tell you the truth. They are not going to tell you about the massacres of children, the abduction of women, the killings of whole families. You are a Hutu. You cannot believe what you hear from the Tutsis. We are faced with an attempt to take over the country by force, and we must respond with force. Certainly, some people may be hurt in the fight, innocent people who are not directly involved in the uprising, but if a family hides an RPF soldier, they are *inkotanyi* themselves and they bring their own misfortune upon themselves. Those who do not associate themselves with the uprising and who are loyal to the nation of Rwanda must distance themselves from the *inkotanyi* and take refuge until the RPF has been crushed."

Melchior walked on in silence. Victor's explanation was plausible, he supposed - the displacement of Tutsi families would be a natural result of the counter measures of the government forces. But there was a current of menace that underlay his words, a zealousness that indicated that the speaker would justify attacks even on women and children in the name of saving the Rwandan nation. The tone of Victor's speech persuaded the priest that it would be futile to take the matter any further.

"It is at times like these that people need to make their allegiances clear, particularly those of us who are Hutu,"

Victor added. Melchior felt the menace clearly now, like a heat radiating off the man next to him.

"Victor, you haven't come all the way from Rweru to discuss politics with me. So what is it precisely that you expect me to do?" Melchior stopped walking and turned to face him. The compound and church buildings were out of sight, shielded behind trees and bushes. The conversation made him feel alone and ill at ease.

"Firstly, it is in the interests of both the government forces and the people themselves that any displaced persons congregate at identifiable and safe points, in this case within the confines of your church compound. This will allow the government forces to clear the villages and the countryside of the *inkotanyi*, without causing unnecessary harm to loyal families. When the RPF have been crushed, all the civilians can return to their homes, safely. But even more importantly, Lushodayana, we cannot allow the collection points to become bases for RPF activity and safe havens for the *inkotanyi*. While we need you to take in displaced Tutsis, we also need you to keep careful records of everyone under your care: where they come from, their family name, their identity card numbers. If you see any weapons being hidden in the compound, or if secret meetings are being held, you must inform us and we will take steps to rectify the situation. The activities of a single RPF terrorist can undermine the safety of an entire community. You must be aware of this and ensure that the circumstances of the compound remain safe."

Victor's deliberate use of his childhood name was conspiratorial: standing alone with him on the shaded road, listening to his speeches, Melchior felt Victor pulling him towards him, urging him to take a side.

212

"Victor, this is madness and you know it to be so," he retaliated. "I am a priest who is charged with the care of whoever may need it: I cannot take sides in a conflict like this. And what am I supposed to do with all of these people? What must I do for food and water? The compound is in a mess, there is filth everywhere, the hall is filled with children, in the office the sick are lying head-to-toe and you cannot walk without stepping on one of them. We have already buried four people who have died here."

"Do you think that this is a situation that I have chosen?" Victor pointed his finger aggressively and jabbed the priest on his chest. "These people are Tutsis. It is their brothers and children who are now trying to kill this country. They are responsible: I cannot help it if that makes life difficult for them - they should have thought of that before they tried to take this country away from us. These people associate themselves with killers. They provide homes and food for murderers. They send their sons off to be trained in Burundi and Zaire to return and steal our children and rape our wives. They teach their daughters how to seduce the souls of Hutu men, baring their stinking loins to the world. And now you complain that they have too little food and that their water is not clean !"

Victor clenched his teeth in an effort to contain his sudden rage. Melchior moved back, away from his growing anger and stabbing finger. The menace that he had felt tugging beneath the man's words was tangible, hissing like a venomous snake between them.

"I am going back to the church now," Melchior said and turned on his heel. He had not walked more than a few steps before he felt Victor at his side once more.

"I understand that the conditions in the compound are bad. I am not in a position to bring you food or water at this stage. Colonel Batho believes that the whole matter will be over in a few days, and then the people can return home. If not, I will talk to him about getting some provisions to the compound. But we need your co-operation as well."

"I am a man of the church and my allegiance is to God, not to Colonel Batho. You know that I will not turn people away if they need my help. As to the rest, I will have to see."

As the roof of the church hall came into view, Melchior heard shouts and screams from the compound. He looked at Victor but the man's face was blank. He heard a heated argument taking place between Rutayisire and one of Victor's men as they neared the compound. At the entrance he found her shouting at a thick-set man - the argument had brought out beads of sweat on his neck and he was waving his machete at Rutayisire. His arms were strong and muscled, and the machete blade sliced the air with sweeping cuts. A little way away, on the edge of the banana grove, the remaining *Interhamwe* stood watching. Melchior saw three bodies lying still at their feet.

"What is going on?" he asked loudly. The heavy man with the machete turned towards him, glaring. Melchior noticed that part of his hair was missing on the right-hand side of his scalp, an incongruous smooth circular patch that glistened with sweat.

"These men came into the church and took away three young men. They have beaten them with their machetes and they won't let them come back. They are bleeding and they won't let me look at them. I think they have killed them,"

Rutayisire shouted hysterically, pointing to the three bodies lying at the feet of the *Interhamwe*.

Melchior turned to Victor. "Is this how you want me to protect these people? What are you doing here?"

Victor did not answer but the man with the missing patch of hair came closer to him. Melchior smelled alcohol on his stale breath. "We searched your church for *inkotanyi* and we found these three men were being hidden here. They had weapons and we are taking them away."

"What weapons did they have on them?" Melchior asked, refusing to be intimidated.

The man dug into his pocket and dropped a small fold-up penknife and a bullet into his opened palm. Melchior did not bother to comment and dismissed the man with a wave of his hand. He walked past the man towards the *Interhamwe* standing at the banana grove. A powerful hand grabbed him roughly by the shoulder and spun him around. As the priest turned he felt the flat blade of the machete smack violently against his cheek and he fell backwards in the dust in shock. His back jarred against the ground as he fell heavily. He sat helplessly on the ground, dizzy and suddenly nauseous. His face felt numb. His eyes refused to open, screwed up tightly. Then the pain flooded into his body, making him shake uncontrollably. Tears welled up unwanted in his eyes. His cheek stung as if he had been burned with scalding water. Immediately his face felt massively swollen and he reached up and ran his hand delicately across it. The cheek was not swollen but the skin was hot and prickly. He could focus on nothing else except the burning pain and the stinging of his skin.

He felt the sun on his back as the clouds parted. A shiny black insect crawled up his leg. It seemed very still, but someone was screaming. He looked up and saw Rutayisire running towards him, her mouth open wide. The man who had struck him stood between the two of them and she had to pass him to get to the priest where he sat dazed on the ground. Melchior noticed the plastic beads bouncing in the light on her head as she took big running steps towards him. The man with the machete lifted the weapon, blade first, the muscles on his arm standing out in anticipation, ready to bring the edge down on her head. Melchior, unable to move or speak, watched the nurse move towards him, dust kicking up behind her, the machete held high in the air, the man's arm tensed for the blow. All he could think of was how his cheek glowed like hot coals. Everything seemed strangely quiet and slow. He felt like a child who had just fallen from a great height, watching his parents running to help him. He realised that he wanted to cry like that child.

Someone shouted behind him. Rutayisire kept running to him. The machete remained raised to strike, but the blow never fell. Sounds suddenly came rushing towards the priest as the woman raced up to him, holding his face in her hands, tears falling from her eyes and splashing in the dust.

Victor walked up to the man with the machete and ordered him to return to the group. Then he looked at Melchior. Everything seemed loud again: strong harsh sounds jarred on the priest's ears and hurt his throbbing head. Rutayisire tried to wipe his face with her dress. The cloth grated unpleasantly against his sensitive cheek.

"I am sorry that Zephir struck you, but you must understand that unless we have your complete co-operation, we cannot help you or these people. Now please, leave us alone to do our work and we will not disturb you further," Victor said coldly.

Victor ordered his men to take the three captives into the banana grove. One of the injured men lay limp and unconscious and they dragged him by his arms between the waxy stems of the trees. The other two were pulled to their feet and pushed, stumbling and disoriented, until they disappeared from sight. One of the militiamen remained at the edge of the banana grove to prevent anyone from following. Melchior waited at the entrance to the compound, resting his body on the stone wall and touching his burning cheek with his fingertips. He strained to hear some noise from the bushes, some indication of the militia's intention with its captives. But he heard nothing. One of the women brought him a cup of water. He gratefully drank some and poured the rest gingerly onto his cheek.

After a short while he saw the militia returning, without the captive men. Victor did not look at him again as they made their way down the hill. The men walked past one at a time, hitting the ground with their machetes. When they were out of sight, some of the refugees clamoured to search the side of the hill for the missing men. Rutayisire held them back.

"Father, we both know that we are not looking for living boys in those bushes. You go and look for them there. Come back and tell us what we already know. These people," she gestured to the refugees behind her, "don't need to see it with their own eyes. It will only make it worse for them."

The priest nodded resignedly. He walked, still dazed, along the path that the militia had taken between the banana trees.

They had killed the three men silently, cutting their throats cleanly with sharp hand-knives. The bodies lay slumped together amongst the bushes on the steep side of the hill overlooking the river. The eyes of two of them were wide open, as if caught by surprise. Very little blood had seeped from the wound on the third body. He was probably already dead when they dragged him into the bushes, Melchior realised. Their skin was still warm when he touched their faces and closed their eyes. He left them lying in the bushes. They could bury the bodies in the morning, he thought. Rutayisire was waiting for him when he emerged from the grove. He looked into her face and nodded. She let out a small sigh and followed him back to the compound.

"They are herding us like sheep, Father," she said from behind him.

"If you are found outside of the protection of this church, they will undoubtedly kill you. Muyigenzi has told me that we should encourage people to congregate at the church and that we will be safe here. I can offer the protection of God's will and nothing more. If it is His desire that we should be safe, then we will be safe. I have nothing more than that and my bare hands to offer you."

"Father, they struck you on your face as if you were an animal." The priest resisted the need he felt to touch his cheek to assess the swelling. He said nothing in response. The nurse was right, he thought to himself: he had not anticipated that they would strike a priest, with such force and aggression, and in front of witnesses.

"You must be careful, Rutayisire. That man was ready to strike you too, and not with the flat of the blade either."

"Pah !" she scoffed. "If he wants to kill an old woman like me because I am a threat to him, then let him do so. He harms no one but himself by doing so." They made their way past the people sitting in the compound, walking around the smoking evening fires. In his room, Melchior inspected his cheek for the first time: the blade had left a raised, darkened welt across the width of his cheek. The smaller corpuscles had burst around the edges and the bruising was starting to spread in a deep bluish hue across the side of his face. He dabbed the welt with a damp cloth.

Rutayisire was halfway out of the door when she turned to the priest. "No matter how well you think you know your dog, there will come a time when he will bite you. You can play games with him and listen to his stories, but watch out when the game starts to get too rough and the story runs on too long." Melchior was about to say something in answer to her, but at that moment she stepped out into the shadows to tend to the cooking on the communal fire.

The fires burned brightly as dark descended on the compound. The cicadas and night owls started calling and moths, attracted by the firelight, circled the seated figures. The bustle and fear of the day slowly eased, soft conversations started up. Children ventured out of the compound to collect sticks and the adults absorbed themselves in the simple tasks of preparing food from the few shared provisions.

Rutayisire brought him some ground corn bread and laid out blankets on the floor of his room for the orphaned children. After he had eaten, Melchior lay on his bed with the wet cloth pressed to his cheek. He dozed lightly for a while. The compound was still but he could hear the grunts and sniffs of the children asleep on the floor around his bed. After a while he sank into a deeper sleep but was wakened by a tentative knock on the door. The giant figure of Michel appeared in the doorway, carrying a large stick.

"Come in, Michel," he said thickly, wiping his mouth with the damp cloth. He found his box of matches and lit the candle. The flickering light from the candle threw the side of his face into dramatic relief and Michel immediately frowned in concern. "What happened to you, Father?" he said with genuine concern in his voice.

"Oh, don't worry, Michel," the priest responded, pleased to see his friend. "A small accident. Nothing more. What time is it?"

"It is late, Father. I wanted to see you once everything was quieter. I have something to ask you. The militia were in the village earlier this afternoon and they have recruited some of the men to set up a barricade at the beginning of the village, opposite Mama Butto's house. They say that the men at the barricade must check everyone's identity documents. If they find anyone who is a Tutsi they must keep them until the militia comes back. They didn't say so, but if anyone - any Tutsi - comes to harm, they would not worry about it."

"Who was in charge of recruiting people for the barricade? Did you see Muyigenzi with them?" Melchior asked.

"There was a group of three or four of them, led by a large man, with a scar on his head and a nasty face. They called him Zephir, a captain I think. I didn't see Muyigenzi anywhere." Michel sat on the bed and rubbed his thick thighs out of nervousness.

"He is playing things very carefully," Melchior responded. Michel looked at him quizzically. "Victor, Muyigenzi, he is being very careful not to get too close to things but still be in charge, jumping from one side of the river to the other. I spoke to him earlier today: he was like a crocodile lazing on a muddy bank, calm and ponderous, and vicious and brutal, all at the same time. The accident to my cheek happened both because of him and in spite of him. I fear for his soul."

Melchior stood up and took the candle to the mirror. The swelling had stopped but the bruising had turned a darker blackish-blue. The welt reached across his cheek to his ear. "What do you want to ask me, Michel?"

"The militia came to the eating house this evening. I made them food and gave them beer. I offered them banana beer but they demanded Primus. They drank nearly half of my supply. And they haven't paid me for any of it. But that is not the problem. They have told me that I am on duty at the barricade tomorrow morning. They have given me this."

Michel lifted up the stick he was carrying. The long shafts of a dozen steel nails and pins glinted in the candlelight.

"They told me this is my 'tool' for my work tomorrow. What do they expect me to do with this, Father?" Michel asked plaintively.

Melchior did not answer him. He brought the candle closer to the weapon. The nails had been knocked through the wood at one end and protruded almost three inches on the other side. The other end of the stick had been shaved and sanded to make a comfortable grip.

They stared at the weapon. "I cannot tell you what you must do, Michel. Whatever you decide to do will have some consequence for you. If you tell them that you will not stand at the barricade, they may mark you as being disloyal and make things difficult for you in the village. But if you agree to help them tomorrow, well, that club was made only for one thing. It is a weapon to inflict harm on other people. I don't think you can go to the barricade tomorrow morning, carrying that weapon, and avoid becoming involved in whatever is going to happen there. I cannot say to you that you should do one thing or another."

"What do you think will happen if I refuse to go to the barricade?"

"You are a Hutu, Michel. This madness is aimed at the Tutsis. They may regard you as being disloyal, but they cannot expect everyone to agree to fight for them. You can say that you support them, that you wish for the RPF to be crushed, but that you are not part of the army or the police-force and that therefore you cannot take up a weapon. You have provided them with food and beer, and you probably won't get paid for it. I don't see that they can, or will, do anything to you."

Michel sat despondently with the nailed-stick across his thighs. The priest tried to cheer him up, searching for conversation that avoided the present, conjuring up past stories that Michel had himself told in his eating house, "Do you remember when ..", or projecting a vision of a future returned to normality, "Imagine how it will be ...". But his heart was not in it and his attempts fell short, sounding hollow and forced. After a while he left the pretence alone and the two men sat without words, each immersed in their private and troubled thoughts.

The candle spluttered at the end of its wick, disturbing Michel from his reverie. He looked up at the priest. "I am sorry, Father. You must be tired and I am keeping you from your bed with my nonsense."

"It is not nonsense, Michel. I only wish that I could give you some guidance, but I am no better able to foretell these men's intentions than you are. We are like two small fish caught in an unknown current: I cannot tell you if the next bend will bring us into a still pond or whether we are headed towards some rocky falls. Only God knows that. He made the river and all I can offer is trust in Him. You are faced with a difficult choice, but it is a personal choice and no one can judge you, whatever you decide."

Michel rose to his feet, the stick in his hand. "I will give this back to them tomorrow morning," he said. He stopped on his way to the doorway. "I brought a bag of maize flour for the compound, it's just outside. I hope that it helps."

"You are a good man, Michel," the priest said. "May God and His protection be with you always."

"Thank you, Father," the big man replied, walking out of the room into the dark night air.

The militia did not return the next day and the atmosphere in the compound became more relaxed. The maize corn brought by Michel was immediately divided up and the warm smell of unrisen corn bread filled the compound by mid-morning. An early morning shower gave way to bright sunshine, which dried the earth and raised the spirits of those who had spent the night outside. Melchior organised a small party of older men to bring the bodies of the three captives out of the banana grove and to bury them in the cemetery. A fourth refugee, an old woman, had died quietly on the floor of the office during the night and they buried her as well. The priest said a prayer over each grave and some of the women placed small garlands of wild flowers and bright green leaves, picked from around the compound walls, at the head of each grave.

Melchior forbade anyone to wander far from the compound but allowed one group of men to search the surrounding slopes for fruit and tubers. They returned after some time with bags heavy with green bananas, small potatoes, earthy cassava and taro. The men reported that the fields seemed quiet and that they had not encountered any militia patrols. Two of the men left again for the fields and returned with a goat they had caught near the village, its throat slit to keep it quiet and its blood running over their fingers. The carcass was quickly dismembered and by lunchtime pots of meat and potato were stewing in the middle of the compound.

The priest sat on the step at the doorway of his room. Perhaps we can survive like this, he thought to himself. The bustle of activity in the compound, the sharing of food, the helping of others, reminded him of his village during his childhood – the energy of people, themselves faced with hardship, helping one another to survive. He felt warm towards these people. Perhaps he could be their protector after all, perhaps he could use his influence to help them weather the storm. In a few days, he could bid them farewell and watch them return, grateful and once more filled with faith, to their waiting homes. Perhaps God was testing him, providing him with an opportunity to return people to their faith with new commitment. These thoughts soothed him. Even his aching cheek felt less painful, and he felt a positive energy gather around him.

Rutayisire sat down heavily next to him and handed him a plate of goat's meat, potatoes and sweetened cassava. "You seem more rested today, Father," she said caringly. Melchior gratefully spooned the warm food into his mouth. The goat's meat had been cooking over a low heat for two hours and it was soft and full flavoured. The small round potatoes had absorbed the liquids from the pot and the soft brown flesh was delicately held together by the skins. She watched him eat with a smile on her face. He did not speak until the food was finished and he had cleaned the plate with a chunk of corn bread. He handed the plate back to her.

"Thank you," he said. "I don't know how we could manage here without your help."

The older woman nodded without replying. Then she pointed to the far side of the compound. "Father, you must know that this peace will not last. They will be back. In our hearts, you and I know that they will be back. We cannot sit on the ground and wait for them to take us away, one by one. We are not asking your permission, Father, and we do not ask for your help, but the men will collect stones and sticks this afternoon and store them at the entrance to the compound." He felt his mood darken once again. "They will be back and we must be ready to defend ourselves. I am sorry, Father, but that is the truth."

Melchior nodded resignedly. She was right, he could not expect them to await their fate meekly, letting the militia pick the men off in twos and threes.

"I cannot be a part of that, but I will not stand in your way," he replied.

During the course of the afternoon Melchior witnessed small groups of men leaving the compound and returning with fist-sized rocks and sturdy sticks stripped of leaves. By evening, the inside of the entrance to the compound was flanked by mounds of stones and sticks and branches, laid neatly in piles. Sentries were posted around the compound as the day drew to a close: young boys and old women, holding sharpened sticks and waiting for the onslaught to come. Children standing in small groups in the failing light waiting for God's will.

TRANSCRIPT OF COURT PROCEEDINGS

TO: **The Honourable Judge Saresh Villay**
ICTR Chamber Three

In the prosecution of:
Victor Busiswa Muyigenzi
Case No. ICTR-98-3-1

7 August 1998

Tape: 58:18:3 – 58:31:15

Witness: TP witness # 21
Protected witness DDD (adult female)

TP: What was happening in the compound
      at this time?

DDD: We were very afraid in the compound.
     The people were crying. We were
     waiting for the men to come back and
     take others of us. The priest from
     the compound seemed to think that he
     could protect us, but we knew in our
     hearts that they would not care
     about him. And we saw that he was
     scared. We had been through the
     barricades, we had seen what was

happening. He had not seen these things himself, not with his own eyes. We told him about what we ...(indistinct)... about them.

TP: Did the men return that day?

DDD: No.

TP: And during the night?

DDD: We had guards outside the compound during the night. I did not sleep well. I was worried that they would come back. And my sister was a guard during the night. I was scared that they would take her away. I just waited for her to come back to me.

TP: Did she come back that night?

DDD: Yes. None of the guards were harmed that night and they did not see anything during the night. When we woke up the next morning, two of the wounded people, a man and a woman, had died. But that was not from the *Interhamwe*. ... (indistinct) ... They had arrived at the church with the last group. They were brought by the *Interhamwe* and they were not strong. We could not help them and they died. We woke up early that morning because the wife of the man who had died was screaming. She cried for a long time.

TP: What happened that day?

DDD: We received news that the man who ran the eating-house in the village had been killed by the *Interhamwe*. I didn't know the man and I don't know his name. But he had helped us in the beginning and he was a friend of the priest. The priest was very upset. He put his hands together and walked up and down the compound very quickly. We watched him. I cannot say who killed the man, or who ordered him to be killed. I wasn't there. But they said that the man had refused to help the militia and so they took him outside his room and clubbed him with a *masu*. They dragged his body to the barricade and left him there, lying dead in the sun.

TP: Yes.

DDD: The priest was very upset and didn't say anything for the whole day. He stopped walking up and down and then he kneeled and prayed in the sacristy. There were people lying there but when they saw how upset he was, they moved away and let him pray in peace. In the afternoon he went into the village and persuaded the men at the barricade to let him bury the body in a shallow grave in the fields just outside the village. The priest came back after a while, when it was getting dark. He went to bed without eating any supper. We prayed for the dead man that night, even though the dead man was a Hutu. And for ourselves.

TP: Can you say whether the accused was involved in the death of this man?

DDD: No. ... (indistinct) ... I don't know who was involved in the killing of the man from the eating-house. The priest told me that they had smashed his head completely open, that you could not see him. He said he ... the priest said that he was responsible for his death.

TP: That he, the priest, was responsible? What did he mean by that?

DDD: I don't know what he meant by this. He didn't name anyone else. I don't ... (indistinct) ...

TP: What did he mean - that you could not 'see him', the dead man?

DDD: I think that you could not tell that it was him. He was so badly beaten.

TP: Where was the accused, Mr Muyigenzi, on this day?

DDD: I do not know.

TP: Was Mr Muyigenzi not present at the compound at any stage during the day?

G: I must object to this question, Your Honour. With respect to the learned prosecutor and to this Court, I accept and understand that it is custom in this Court to give some leeway both to the examiner and to the witness and that technical objections are not made and should not be sustained.

However, the witness has been asked a question and has answered the question asked: she does not know where Mr Muyigenzi was on the day in question. The question cannot be put again and again to the witness, in a subtly different form, in the hope that a more beneficial answer will be forthcoming.

The manner of the prosecution's questioning in this matter is indicative of the difficulty which I first raised in regard to the prosecution's application to have this witness joined to the list of witnesses at a late stage. The witness has, in my submission, been coached by the investigator or members of the office of the trial prosecutor: when she fails to give precisely the answer which they have provided for her, the question is repeated in the hope that her short-term memory (rather than her long-term memory) will be revived.

May I add further at this point, Your Honour, that the learned prosecution seems to be bent upon establishing my client's guilt based on isolated incidents against persons who were identified as being members of the RPF or as being sympathisers of the RPF movement.

The prosecution can assert, and it can be put no higher than this, that it has laid circumstantial evidence before this Court as to Mr Muyigenzi's involvement in the deaths of or assault upon perhaps four or five persons (the eating-house owner included). The evidence is scant as it is, but even were the prosecution to prove these acts of violence, it is to be accepted that the Tribunal was not established in order to meet complaints of individual acts of violence. One RPF does not a genocide make, to coin a phrase. These are matters for the Rwandan courts ... (interrupted) ...

Court: Mr Grenoble, you have made an objection to a particular question and I will deal with that objection. This Court is always eager to hear your erudite views, with or without the coining of phrases, on matters relating to the trial and the course of justice in general. However, this is not an appropriate moment for these considerations. The objection is upheld and the prosecution is requested to proceed with further questioning.

Chapter Eight

Umwanzi wacu n'umwe
Turamuzi
N'umututsi

"Our enemy is one
We know him
It is the Tutsi"

T he *Interhamwe* arrived the day after Michel's death.
The first sortie comprised twenty armed men, carrying
machetes and clubs. They came up the hill singing
loudly, whooping and shouting, running on the spot for five
beats, then moving forward for five beats, their feet kicking
up a trail of dust behind them.

"Turatsembatsemba, abatutsi abatutsi!"

The man in front carried an old Kalashnikov rifle and chanted
aloud, waving the rifle in front of him. He pointed the barrel
of the gun up the hill towards the church buildings and
stamped on the ground with his bare feet. A small figure
bounced energetically in the middle of the group, not keeping
within the rhythm of the group, jumping and screaming,

barking excitedly. The figure pushed towards the front of the men, then fell back. Springing dementedly, he barked like an attacking dog - *"abatutsi, abatutsi"*.

Melchior stood at the entrance to the compound and watched their progress up the hill towards him. His hands were trembling and he held them together to hide his fear. Behind him the compound had erupted. Men shouted orders, mothers screamed for their children, wails and curses rose and fell. Melchior took two steps towards the oncoming group of men. The uproar from the compound immediately dropped, reduced to a whisper of concerned questions and murmurs: someone called out to him in a thin frightened voice. The priest took another step forward, away from the compound.

"Abatutsi, abatutsi !"

The men kept advancing. Melchior's legs felt weak, barely able to carry him further, but he started walking down the hill towards the men. Each footstep he took jarred his body. He met the group halfway down the road. When they were a few paces apart he held out his hand to quieten them, but the chanting only became louder.

"Turatsembatsemba, abatutsi abatutsi!"

The man carrying the rifle was sweating and his body was slick and gleaming. The muscles on his dark arms stood out from the exertion. He stopped when Melchior's face was almost touching his. He drew deep heavy breaths and his reddened eyes bore down on Melchior with frightening intensity. The militiamen did not wait for their leader and kept moving up the hill towards the church. Their chanting was interrupted only by the grating shouts of the dwarf. The group split and moved around the two stationary men, closing again on the other side of them. The dwarf paused at the priest's side and cut the ground close to his feet with a blow from his machete.

"*Abatutsi, abatutsi, abatutsi!*" he yelled fiercely at the priest. Melchior looked straight ahead at the man facing him.

"What do you want?" Melchior asked, straining to project his voice above the noise of the dwarf and the shouting men.

The man said nothing. His only response was to lift up the rifle and point it at the side of the priest's head. Melchior felt the cool metal circle of the barrel press against his temple. His whole body went cold and he felt the blood draining from his face. The back of his eyes shook with dizziness, but he kept standing still, unable to move. He felt as if he was about to faint. The man kept the gun up high, pressing it hard against his head. Melchior focused on the butt of the rifle: a small set of letters - KL905/6 – written in white paint on the side. He wondered vaguely what the letters stood for. The last number was barely discernible, the top and side of the circle of the number 6 had been scraped away. Melchior kept concentrating on the inscription, waiting for the man to pull the trigger. A movement on the man's face distracted him, however, and his eyes were pulled involuntarily away from the butt and onto the man once again. The man was smiling, not a sneer of contempt or disdain, but a genuine smile of amusement, the beginnings of a laugh. The man's white even teeth appeared as his lips pulled back and his pink tongue clicked against his palate.

"Bang !" the man said softly. His smile grew wider and Melchior heard him laugh, a throaty, guttural laugh that emanated from deep inside him and then ended almost as soon as it had begun. The smile withered on his face and he slowly lowered the gun. He put his free hand into his trouser pocket and pulled out a small metal object. Then he stepped to one side to continue up the hill, stuffing the object into Melchior's cassock as he passed. Melchior fumbled in the folds of the cloth until his fingers closed around a cylindrical shape - an empty bullet casing.

His legs buckled under him and he sank to his knees on the road, the stones digging into his kneecaps and scraping against the top of his feet. Tears ran down his face and dripped onto the red earth. A wave of nausea overcame him and he started to retch. He wanted to run away, away from the compound, away from the village, away from men and their machetes and guns and the crazed dwarf.

The first stone fell behind him and skipped across the surface of the road, plunging into the foliage on the side. Like the first drops of a rainstorm, there was a barely perceptible pause and a moment of absolute silence, before the air hissed with stones hurtling down the slope of hill, cracking and splintering all around the priest. Sharpened sticks flung like spears traveled in arcs, cutting the air before striking the ground. One stick thudded into a patch of softer soil to the side of the priest. Shouts and screams of anger filled the air, wails of pain and noise of people running beat on Melchior's ears. A chip from a stone stung his hand and he drew his arms closer into his chest. Three of the *Interhamwe* came running past him: one was bleeding from his forehead and his breaths came in quick, high-pitched gasps.

Melchior half rose to his feet and turned to look up the hill. More stones fell about him and a stick came slithering like a yellow snake along the surface of the road towards him, turning slightly and stinging him across his ankles. He saw more of the *Interhamwe* racing down the hill towards him. The dwarf was nowhere to be seen. He shuffled to the side of the road, rubbing his throbbing ankles. Then he felt a tremendous blow to his head, striking just above his forehead with crushing pressure. He fell onto his side, dazed and bewildered. It felt as if he had been struck by a club. A warmth spread across his face as he lay, stunned, on the ground. His blood dripped off the end of his nose onto the large flat stone that lay next to him. It was quiet again, except for the shrill buzzing in his ears. He heard some shouts in the distance. It felt to him that he had lain on the ground for a long time before he felt the helping hands of the compound refugees on him. They lifted him up in a blanket. Someone wiped his head as he was carried up the hill, his helpers struggling to keep him from tipping onto the ground. He kept his eyes shut: he had to concentrate on clenching his mouth closed to keep from vomiting. Only when he felt the giving springs of the bed under his body, did he let himself drift off into a state somewhere between sleep and unconsciousness.

When he came to it was late in the afternoon. The soft touch of caring hands wiping his face drew him from his semi-conscious state. His head pounded and he still felt nauseous.

"When I left you, you were fit and healthy. Now you look as if you've been attacked by a pack of wild dogs." Selena was seated on the bed next to him, gently wiping the dried blood from his face with a cloth. "I have safely delivered Jaki to his aunt, only to return to find you unconscious and bleeding." The light hurt his head and he closed his eyes again, enjoying the soothing feel of her attentions. He touched his head lightly and felt a cotton bandage covering his forehead.

"What was it?" he asked, his tongue thick in his mouth.

"A stone," she replied without embellishment. He did not ask to explain any further: his conduct on the road that morning made him feel foolish and afraid. He watched her strong features as she moved about over him. She finished cleaning his face and took the bowl of water away. He drifted off to sleep for a while until Selena returned with a cup of warm tea. He drank the tea gratefully, taking comfort from its familiar aroma and the bite of cloves in the back of his throat.

She looked at him with a look of affection and concern mixed with reprimand. "You cannot try and intervene any more, Melchior. I know that you believe your duty is to stand between those in conflict, but this is not some marital dispute. This is not a fight between two members of your church. This is not even a fight between two drunks in a bar. This is different, and the reason you are hurt is because you don't seem to appreciate what is really happening here. You could – you should – have been killed today. You cannot think that your cassock and your cross will protect you anymore. They have used you, Melchior, they have used you to keep the goats together for the slaughter. They don't need you anymore and if you try and stop them they will kill you. You must see that."

"You are right that they may kill me - I saw that on the face of that man with the gun. He could have killed me. I saw that in his eyes. But what am I to do ? I am a man of the church, Selena. I cannot take up weapons, even a simple weapon like a stick or a stone, and fight against these men, no matter how evil they might be. God did not put me here to fight with my hands like all the other refugees in the compound. I have something different, I have my representation of the church.

I am God's representative in this village and, whatever my human failings, I cannot turn away from that."

"It is not a blessing, Melchior. But it may be a curse," she said looking at him intently. "If you sit in the middle, you will be caught by both sides."

"Yes, it may be a curse. When life is good and righteousness abounds, it is a blessing to be associated with all the forces of good, but when evil is stalking about, then the righteous are duty bound to use their faith to fight it. It is an obligation that may be a curse."

"You sound like a preacher, now," Selena said sharply. "Full of words of faith and righteousness: 'the forces of good' – for God's sake, Melchior, what 'forces of good' do you see here? You are housing a group of women and children, unfed, ill and dying, a group of terrified people who have no defences against an army of madness. Yes, they drove off a small band of their attackers with sticks and stones. And tomorrow? Do you think the same small band of men will return tomorrow? No, Melchior, tomorrow we will see how they have multiplied like vermin overnight. We have no forces to fight this: UNAMIR has fled the country. The RPF are in exile. The world is asleep."

"What do you suggest that I should do? Run away and leave these people to face their fate without me? Where would I run to? If I run from this obligation, when will I stop running? I have chosen this path for my life, and I cannot forsake that choice because now it places me in some danger. I am not a brave man. I was shaking and vomiting on the road this morning. If my legs had felt stronger perhaps I would have run away, but I cannot leave these people on their own."

"You are as brave as any of the men who lost their lives this morning, braver and more foolhardy, that is what makes me so afraid for you."

Melchior's face fell. "I thought the militiamen had been chased away ... were some of our people injured?"

"I am told that you were further down the road with the one with the gun. The rest came up and attacked the compound. They dragged three of the young boys away and killed two of them before they were driven off. The third boy died this afternoon - there was nothing the refugees could do to save him. Some of the others received wounds from the machetes." ·Melchior raised his eyes expectantly. "All of the militiamen got away, although apparently some of them seemed to have been wounded."

"And the dwarf?"

Selena sighed and fingered her hair away from her face. "I arrived after it was all over and I didn't see him. I don't know if that is the same one that I saw at the barricades. It could be. The people described the same grotesque look to him, and the same harsh bark. I don't know, how many people like that could there be? They say that he came up the hill with the group and came right into the compound: he didn't seem to feel the blows of the sticks. He was so excited he jumped around, striking out at anyone near him with his machete, screaming. The women beat him with sticks on his face and head and he was bleeding, but he wouldn't back away.

"Someone, Rutayisire I think, said she struck him with a rock and he howled at her in rage. They said it was like trying to ward off some crazy animal that did not feel pain and would only stop if it had won or it had been killed and its body burnt. Then the *Interhamwe* ran back down the hill and the dwarf lost all his energy. He was like a young child left behind by his older brothers. He screamed after them and ran out of the compound clutching his head. He even dropped his machete. Some of the men chased him and he ran into the bush. They searched for him for a while but it is not safe to venture too far. They never found him."

They sat drinking their tea in silence. Then Selena leaned forward and kissed him gently on his forehead. Her neck grazed against his nose as she pulled away and he felt the warmth of her smooth skin. He longed for a moment of quiet, free from the unrelenting horrors of the deaths around him, a moment in which to reach out and take back what he and Selena had enjoyed before.

"You need to rest now. I am sorry that I got cross with you. But you are not always realistic: sometimes that is endearing, but sometimes, Melchior, it can be so very dangerous." He did not reply. He watched her wipe the cups clean and collect the bloodied cloths on the floor.

The *Interhamwe* did not return that night as Selena had anticipated. The following morning started with a dense cloudburst: deep black and purple clouds thundered in the sky and drenched the village in mist and spray. They slept head to foot in the bed, the warmth of their bodies soaking through their clothes. Melchior was exhausted and he slept fitfully. He awoke with a start, disturbed by a vision of the black barrel of a rifle, moving slowly and deliberately to face him and envelop him in its musty interior. It was a recurring vision, but in the last dream before morning, the metal rim of the rifle had changed into the soft petals of a flower, hovering before his face seductively, before being whisked away from him by a naked figure. Her warm brown breasts caught the sunlight and her smooth body swayed before him, her legs opening, revealing herself, red, the colour of blood. Then the body jerked away, struck by empty bullet casings, tarnished brassy yellow beetles that burrowed into her body, Selena naked and writhing on the ground in pain as animals buried themselves in her soft flesh.

He woke clawing at the blanket, gathering it up under his body with desperation. He lay panting, listening to the rain drum down on the metal roof above him. Selena slept peacefully, her breathing clear and even, her body still and warm beside his. His hand felt around her foot and he squeezed it gently. She did not stir. It had seemed natural, inevitable, that they should have collapsed into bed and slept, facing opposite directions, beside one another. But in the morning light it struck Melchior that he had not ever shared such prolonged contact with Selena before. Their one moment of physical intimacy was a powerful memory for him, but it had been short and surreptitious, a stolen moment before they parted. It was incongruous that then, in a time of calm, he had not used the opportunity to enjoy the quiet comfort of her body, but had instead been ravaged by the passion and newness of the contact. Now, in the midst of the tumult, the opportunity had been thrust upon him in a situation he could not have anticipated and could not control. He lay for a long while, enjoying the early morning quiet and the comfort of her body next to him.

A thin crust of dried blood lay on the pillow, but the wound had closed during the night. His forehead was bruised and tender. Selena winced as she changed the cotton bandage.

Old bandages were washed and re-used and even the fresh bandage on his head was grey and discoloured. Selena had gentle, healing hands and the ache in his head started to clear once he had drunk some tea, thickened with crumbs of maize bread, for breakfast.

When he ventured into the compound, the bodies of those killed the day before had already been removed and buried. The refugees had retrieved the stones and sticks used to ward off the first attack. In the mid-morning a small deputation of militiamen was spotted coming up the hill and, as the lookout cried out, the compound erupted into activity. Melchior heard the commotion and went to the entrance to the compound. He saw Victor in the front of the group, holding his arms up in the air as he walked to show that he was not armed. Only four men accompanied him, one armed with a rifle. This time Melchior waited at the compound, but told the refugees to put their weapons back on the piles. Some of the men kept the sticks in their hands, but it was clear from Victor's approach that the men had not come to attack the compound.

Victor had come to talk to the priest, but Melchior was the first to speak.

"Victor, you must tell me what the militia's intentions are in regard to these people. If they are to be attacked and picked off one by one, then I must tell them to disperse and leave the compound. You told me they would be safe here, but yesterday we were attacked by your militiamen and three of the refugees were killed. One of the men threatened to kill me. I cannot stand by and allow this to continue!"

Victor held up his hand. "May I come inside and talk to you, Father?" he asked.

Melchior hesitated. "Given what we have been through, I think it would be better if you told me what you have to say out here. Perhaps you could address all of the people here and tell them, not just me, what your intentions are."

Victor looked across the compound with obvious distaste. "Then I will talk to you out here, alone."

The two men walked along the length of the outer stone wall of the compound until they were out of earshot of the compound entrance. A blue-tailed skink scuttled across the warm rocks at their approach.

"Lushodayana, you must draw a distinction between the *Interhamwe* youth, and the militia and municipal police. We fall under the control of Colonel Batho and I take my instructions from him. What happened yesterday was a case of over-exuberance and it is not my, or Colonel Batho's, intention to use your church as an abattoir." Melchior shivered inwardly at the man's choice of words. "However, the fact of the matter is that *inkotanyi* from your church left the compound two nights ago and attacked militia members and their families in the village. They raped two young girls and cut their breasts off and they stole some cattle and grain." Melchior started to protest, but Victor would not let him interrupt. "The *Interhamwe* came to look for the perpetrators yesterday and, when the people in the compound attacked them with spears, they retaliated – that is unfortunate but, at the end of the day, they have no-one to blame but themselves." Melchior looked at the ground, his face grim and set against the lies he was hearing.

"You must understand, Father, that tempers are raised and things are very, very sensitive out there. The militia and police can only contain things if we have your complete co-operation. I have told you before, if the compound is used as a base for *inkotanyi* then I can offer no protection at all. These latest developments make me fear for the continued safety of those innocent people who may be living in the compound. You must urge these Tutsis to give up the *inkotanyi* amongst them. It is the only way that I can guarantee their safety. If there are any more attacks on the village, I do not think I can hold back the *Interhamwe* youth. The consequences will be terrible."

"You are lying to me, Victor." Melchior was surprised at the force in his own voice. He wavered for a moment as he saw the man's face darken with anger but then continued. "There was no attack on the village two nights ago. There are no spears or weapons here. The *Interhamwe* came to attack the compound and were surprised by the force of the defence they met.

"These people do not have weapons. They have some sticks and a few stones picked up from the ground, and with that they defended themselves against a vicious and unwarranted attack. There are no stolen cattle here in the compound. We have almost no provisions left and there are no stolen bags of grain lying here. The militia and Colonel Batho have done nothing to assist matters here. There has been no food brought here, no medical supplies, nothing except violence and abuse. You say that you can only protect us if we co-operate, well, we have co-operated and done nothing to harm you or your militiamen. There are no RPF hiding here, these are innocent men and women who want to be left alone..." Melchior felt his emotions rise and fought back tears of pain and desperation. The wound on his head started to throb and he pressed the palm of his hand against the bandage.

Victor cut him short. "I did not come here to argue with you," he said angrily. "I came here to tell you that unless these attacks on the village are stopped, this compound will be regarded as being a threat to the security of the area and we will act accordingly."

Victor turned on his heels and shouted to his men to follow him. He turned back to Melchior: "I will want to see all the records of the people staying here. Make sure they are up-to-date and I will send someone tomorrow morning to come and collect them."

Melchior watched the group make its way back towards the village. When they were out of sight he walked wordlessly to the office. Men with festering wounds, children with sores, lay in rows on the floor. He stepped over them carefully and picked up a bundle of papers that were stacked in the corner. Once outside, he walked across to Rutayisire's fire and placed the pile of paper on the glowing coals. Acrid smoke rose quickly around the paper. He stopped and blew on the embers and watched the flames spring up and take hold. Rutayisire sat cross-legged and nodded in approval through the curtain of smoke that rose from the fire. Together they watched as the edges of the pages blackened, creeping along the priest's scrawled handwriting – neat columns of names and identifying information cast onto the flames. Rutayisire picked up a long stick and stoked the coals beneath the papers, breaking the bundle open and exposing the inside of the documents to the fire. Flames burst out from the middle of the pages. They waited until all the paper had been burned. Then the old woman patted the ashes with her stick, breaking the flimsy paper fragments into a black dust, which swirled and rose in the heat of the fire. Only when there was no trace left did Melchior turn away.

Melchior told Selena that night that he had destroyed the records. She frowned with concern at his news but did not say anything.

"I have resolved to go and see Colonel Batho tomorrow in Rweru," he said, taking himself aback almost as much as he surprised her by his words. He had, in that instance, come to the firm conclusion that a visit to the colonel would be the only way to ascertain the *Interhamwe's* intentions and to secure some form of protection for the compound.

Selena disagreed with him. She argued that it was too dangerous, that the Batho would have him killed.

"I am a Hutu and I am a priest. If that counts for nothing on the roads to Rweru then we are all as good as dead anyway," he said sincerely. "I have failed these people. I fear that I have been used for the work of evil. I must do something now to try and stop what is happening."

The more they spoke about his plans, the more they exposed their own affection for one another. Melchior spoke with honesty and emotion, Selena responded with concern and sincerity. They spoke in hushed whispers, their eyes drifting from one another to the sleeping children on the floor of the room. Rutayisire was sleeping outside in the compound. She had left the two together, without a word, quietly rolling up her blanket and stepping outside into the night air, closing the door behind her. Their fingers touched lightly as they spoke of the dangers on the road to Rweru. They discussed Colonel Batho and his possible intentions. They talked about Victor and his strange desire to appease the priest, his ambiguous play act. They spoke of Selena's parents, of Michel, of Gratian, of their past together.

"I often wonder what has become of Gratian," he conceded. "Especially now."

"He was a clever man. He would not have been caught up in this. He would have moved on, well before anyone else saw this madness coming." Although it was said without conviction, Melchior felt the better for hearing the words: it was comforting to think of Gratian, the mentor from his past, safely in exile in Bujumbura. He would be regaling church brothers with stories of seminary life in Butare, belittling pompous leaders and ridiculing the political elite of the day. A memory from his past safely stored away.

"I remember when I first spoke to you, in the market," she laughed lightly, and then harder as he began to blush. She stroked his arm lightly. "You looked so terrified that day - you wanted the strips of cloth to leap up and hide you behind their curtain." They laughed out loud, giggling and snorting, trying not to wake the children, their eyes filling with tears from the effort. But with each breath that burst from their mouths, with each tear that formed in their eyes, a world of tensions was dispersed. Their laughter stopped, momentarily, as they reflected on the fortuitousness of their encounter in the market. Their shared joy had released their fears: they found themselves starting to laugh for no reason, the one feeding off the laughter of the other. They rocked on the bed, crying with their mouths open, tears running down their cheeks and their eyes locked onto each other. The torrent of emotions kept bubbling up in them and bursting out, slowly diminishing into hiccups of mirth that exploded on the surface, until eventually they both fell silent, their energies spent.

They stayed like that for some time, holding hands, wiping their faces from time to time, looking at each other with renewed intensity and wonderment at their being together. Intimate and unspoken feelings flowed between them, without being expressed, memories of past intimacy not fully appreciated. Selena smiled knowingly and broke the trance.

"Isn't it strange how you only come to appreciate a particular time when its death is upon you and how suddenly you are filled with shame and outrage at how you have squandered the ease of its opportunities until then. At its death you try and grab hold of it for the first time and make it your own. We are perverse, Melchior - not us, but people, all people, I think."

"Do you think we are at its death now ?" he asked sadly. He looked away, not wanting her to answer. She opened her mouth to say something then, thinking better of it, lifted his hand up to her lips.

Selena's thoughts struck Melchior with a clarity that had often escaped him in his conversations with her since she joined him at the church. Somewhere deep inside he felt immediately connected to her once again. "I lay next to you in bed this morning and I didn't squander the opportunity. I lay quietly and absorbed your closeness with every part of my body - I drank you in as you lay next to me. You were asleep and you didn't know. But I do not regret that moment at all, on the contrary I will hold that close to me always."

He felt light-headed and isolated from the outside world. His focus was limited to the person sitting in front of him and the room behind her seemed blurred and without consequence. He remembered the time he first saw her standing at the gate to the seminary, how her surroundings had melted away around her. The air seemed cleared of the breath of sleeping children. The noise from the compound outside ceased to intrude into the room, and a space of pure intimacy arose between them. Selena filled him with passion and wonder. He stroked her strong face, his fingers brushing against her lips. He allowed his hand to explore her cropped hair for the first time.

"Oh Melchior, I have missed you so much at times," she said, placing her palm against his cheek. "I don't know if we are at the death of our time. What is important is that we are together in this moment. Whatever happens to us after this, I will have a piece of you in my heart forever."

Melchior's chest ached with sadness and with love for her. They drew closer, Selena holding his head gently in her hands. His fingers stroked up and down the sides of her body, from the smooth skin of her waist to the hidden heat beneath her arms.

Selena shuddered and smiled at him. "This time is ours and we will not squander it."

Chapter Nine

The truck made its way slowly along the winding road. The wheels kicked up dry dust at times and sank into slick tracks of mud at others, as the road descended into the valleys. The engine jerked and spewed diesel smoke as the old vehicle strained up the hills on the other side. The truck was from the tea plantation, old and faded green with wide wheels and rusted doors. The mudguards had come loose and flapped against the metal side, clanging in protest at every stone in the road. Melchior sat on a wooden crate in the middle of the back-load of the truck, his hands gripping the wide sides like a crucifix. He had accepted Victor's offer of transport without thanks, climbing on the back amongst empty wooden crates and rags, resignedly accepting that the militia's use of the truck would ensure that he reached Rweru safely.

The militiamen had come for the church records that morning, but he had distracted them with his news that he was leaving the compound to visit Colonel Batho. For the first time it seemed that they listened to him respectfully. They escorted him to Victor so that the priest could personally inform him of his decision to visit the colonel. Victor made no mention of the records and he immediately supported the priest's decision.

"That is an excellent idea, Father. I have told you that I am only here on the orders of Colonel Batho. He is certainly the best person to give you whatever assurances you may seek. He is in control of this area and he will explain to you exactly the difficulties facing the interim government in this region. I think you will find that he will be quite open to meeting you. He will listen to your concerns."

Melchior considered Victor's enthusiasm sceptically as he bounced along the track through the forest. But although the man's eagerness that the priest should leave the area was perhaps cause for cynical concern, Melchior was far more unsettled by the fact that the militiamen had seen him say goodbye to Selena. They had hugged each other inside the compound grounds, unaware that they were being watched by a militia patrol headed by Zephir, standing at the very entrance to the compound. When he looked up he saw their cold eyes on him, registering his affection for the tall Tutsi woman. The moment had been forgotten when he blurted out his plans to travel to Rweru. As he left the village, however, he saw Zephir conferring with Victor: both men had looked in his direction as the truck accelerated out of the village.

The truck passed through the barricade outside the village without incident - the barrier was unmanned so early in the morning. The priest held the cloth of his cassock over his mouth as the sour, offensive smell of rotting flesh rose from the bodies lying amongst the concrete blocks, springs from burnt-out mattresses, rocks and car tyres. He closed his eyes and pressed the cloth against his face until the air felt clearer. But when he looked up he saw the burnt shell of a hut, close to the road, its roof gone and the walls blackened and crumbling: outside the front door the small frame of a child lay on the ground, awkwardly bent and still. The men inside the truck said something and laughed. Melchior thought of Selena and their night together. He felt all the more alone for the memory.

The truck was stopped briefly by an *Interhamwe* patrol, just as the road pulled away from the forest and the open plains of grass, rice fields and scattered camelthorn trees began. The hills were densely populated on the plains, cut thin by grazing goats and scarred by paths and eroded tracks. People lived on top of each other, their huts clutched to the sides of the ravaged hills, the red earth uncovered and streaming into the thin valleys and ditches. Broken sticks knocked into the ground marked the rough boundaries of small individual plots of corn and bean plants. The mud huts with their grass-thatched roofs were strewn haphazardly on both sides of the road. Some had been burnt and broken down, looted and abandoned. Lone acacia and nyala trees rose up from their littered yards like bleached skeletons.

The patrol shouted for them to stop and its leader spoke to the driver aggressively for a while before they were allowed to pass. None of the militiamen said anything to the priest and he avoided making eye contact with them. They looked wild and unkempt. The leader was perhaps twenty years old, but the rest were still adolescents, boys with strong arms and sharp knives.

A little further, past a small village that encroached onto the road, they came across a UNAMIR supply truck lying on its side across half of the road. It looked like a pathetic stranded animal, the pale blue paint and UNAMIR emblem staring up at the sky. A young boy sat on top of the toppled vehicle and shouted when he saw the militia truck approaching. *Interhamwe* men appeared from behind the shadow of the truck, where they had been drinking banana beer and playing cards in the shade. They waved at the driver to stop, before pulling open his door and trying to force him out of the truck.

"Where is your identity, you whore," one militiaman screamed at the driver. "We will slice you into pieces and feed you to our dogs." The man swayed on his feet and wiped his mouth unsteadily with the back of his dirty sleeve. The men around him laughed menacingly.

"*Inkotanyi ! inkotanyi !*" the young boy shouted from the upended supply truck, pointing at Melchior and jumping up and down with childish excitement. The *Interhamwe* men left the driver and came around to the back of the truck. Melchior stared in disbelief at the child, who was still pointing and shouting at him.

The drunk man smiled, showing his yellowed teeth. "I haven't killed a priest today", he said. He strode up to the truck, waving his machete, and heaved himself onto the back of the vehicle. His trousers caught on a rusted flange and he lost his balance, stumbling back to the ground. The laughter of the men around him turned to uproarious mirth and they slapped each other in delight and jeered at the drunk man. He swore loudly and clenched his machete still more tightly in his hand. Again he attempted to heave himself up to reach the priest, but he was unable to swing his leg over onto the back of the truck. He remained teetering uncertainly before careering backwards, striking the ground off-balance at a half-run. He lost his footing after two steps and sprawled backwards onto the road.

Melchior did not know where to look for fear that he would enrage the man even further. The man tried to get to his feet but a crimson stain spread across his leg - he had fallen across the blade of his machete, cutting deeply into his thigh. When he saw the blood he howled like a child and started to cry uncontrollably, pleading for help in a piercing, high-pitched voice. The men became all the more hysterical, pushing each other and hitting the ground with their machetes. One them started coughing uncontrollably and sank to the ground gasping for breath. The militia truck seemed to have been forgotten in the confusion and the driver slid back into his seat. Melchior lowered himself onto the floor of the truck to escape their notice, but the men did not turn around as their vehicle edged past the stranded UNAMIR truck, engrossed as they were in taunting the bleeding man. He watched with relief as the overturned truck and the dancing figures slowly receded into the distance.

The road to Rweru left him in no doubt as to the extent of the madness that had gripped his country: the stench of corpses, left to rot in the sun, filled the air along their journey. Bodies lined the barricades and lay piled in muddy ditches and fields. There had been no attempt made to hide the killings. Instead, the bodies were put on display, as a warning, or just left where they had fallen, in the road, pushed flat into the earth by passing trucks. A stout sausage tree had been adorned with the bodies of victims, strung up on thick ropes and left hanging like grotesque fruit in the fetid air. Houses and huts had been razed to the ground. Melchior saw men removing furniture and supplies through a window of a house even while another group built up a fire around the front door. Groups of youths wearing bandanas and strung banana leaves roamed along the road and the paths, waving sticks and knives. He saw a young boy beating the corpse of a woman with a stick, shouting obscenities at the dead body while a group of older boys looked on blankly.

The priest was witness to a depth of depravity that left him aching and devastated by the time they passed through the last barricade at the entrance to Rweru.

Rweru itself was a relief after the horror of the journey through the villages: the town seemed calmer and the groups of *Interhamwe* youth that marched along its streets were silent and more disciplined. The houses and buildings were intact and he did not see any bodies on the short drive from the barricade to the headquarters of the municipal police and the *bourgemestre*. Some of the small stores were open for business, although there were few people on the streets other than those forming part of the *Interhamwe* patrols. Children watched, without expression, as the truck drove past their open doorways.

The *bourgemestre's* offices were housed in an imposing red-brick building. The driver slowed down and beckoned wordlessly to the priest to disembark. As soon as he had clambered off the back, the engine revved and the truck pulled away in a sticky cloud of diesel smoke. Melchior stood on the side of the road for a moment. The neat garden and the row of blooming white rose bushes flanking the path to the offices belied the anarchy that he had witnessed since leaving the village. He noticed that the earth at the base of each rose bush had been recently turned and scattered with dried bark. The garden had been watered that morning and the clipped grass still glistened. The path was firm and his shoes crunched pleasantly as he made his way to the building.

The doors were made of a dark, polished wood. The brass handles shone in the sun. The doors were heavy and swung open slowly as he pushed them. He tried to close them behind him but the hinges resisted being pushed back.

"Don't worry, Father, they will close by themselves," a neatly-dressed woman said to him, crossing the tiled floor and extending her hand in greeting. Her hair was pulled back into an austere bun and her rouged cheeks seemed to glow eerily from within. "We were told to expect you and I am very pleased to see that you have made it safely to us." Melchior frowned uncertainly and the woman continued, in answer to his unspoken question. "We are in contact with the Head of the Communal Police who informed us of your desire to meet with the *bourgemestre*."

"I hadn't realised that there was that kind of communication," he said, feeling foolish and out of place.

"Never mind, Father," she answered, rather patronisingly he felt, as she escorted him into a small waiting-room. The table in the middle of the room was set out with fresh coffee and biscuits. Chairs lined the wall and a low side-table was stacked with popular magazines. A radio on the windowsill crackled unintrusively.

"The *bourgemestre* is eager to meet you. Unfortunately he is a little busy right now, but he will be with you as soon as he has an opportunity. Meanwhile, please make yourself comfortable here."

She did not wait for his reply and closed the door behind her, leaving Melchior alone and deflated in the small room. He had expected a confrontation and had steeled himself against weakening before Colonel Batho, who was reputed to be a fearsome and domineering man. The woman's mixture of cordial aloofness and disregard left him unsure of himself. He paced the width of the room for a while, trying to focus his thoughts once more.

By lunchtime the coffee was cold and the biscuits all but eaten: nevertheless, he was reluctant to leave the room and seek out the woman again, placing himself once again at her favour. He opened the door and looked outside. The entrance was still and the corridors were clean and empty. He was about to close the door again and return to his uneasy solitariness when the woman appeared from around the corner, startling him.

"Are you looking for anything, Father?" Melchior was flustered and shook his head. "The *bourgemestre* hopes to see you shortly, Father. If you don't mind waiting a little longer."

Chastened, he returned to his seat next to the magazines. He was beginning to feel isolated from the realities of the compound and the village that had steered him to Rweru in the first place. He tried to imagine the tense heat of the compound, the claustrophobic closeness of the hall. He searched to find the right words to articulate the fear that the refugees felt. He tried to describe to himself the assurances that he sought from the *bourgemestre*. The sedate coolness of the building, the measured manner of the woman, the neatly arranged coffee service, all colluded to undermine his efforts and intruded on the clarity and passion of his arguments.

How can you meet a man in these surroundings, he thought, so clean and calm, drink his coffee and eat his biscuits, and then seek his assurance that he does not intend to murder hundreds of women and children ? But does the order and the control mean that Batho would be above acts of barbarism ? Perhaps he is all the more able to carry out such acts, he thought. As the afternoon stretched on towards evening, Melchior tormented himself with doubts and self-deprecation. He felt tired and irritable. He was frustrated more with himself than with the *bourgemestre* - for travelling to Rweru with unreasonable accusations, for failing to appreciate the communication that existed between Victor and the *bourgemestre* and for not understanding the nature of the hierarchy of command to which Victor had referred so often. He could not comfort himself even with his thoughts of Selena. It only aggravated him further to think that he had left her alone at the compound and that he could not be with her.

He stepped outside the room in the late afternoon, in search of a toilet, and was again met by the officious secretary. She directed him to a clean-smelling bathroom: a fresh towel embroidered with flowers hung next to the washbasin and a new bar of soap, unmarked by water, nestled in the dipped porcelain next to the tap. Melchior washed his face. The discoloured water fell into the basin and swirled in front of him before gurgling down into the drains. It suddenly dawned on him that he had not washed properly in days and that, after the events of the last few days, ending with the journey on the back of the truck, the officious woman would have been presented with an ill-smelling, unwashed and unkempt man who was unable to articulate even the simplest of his desires. Melchior strangely felt his spirit lift rather than fall at this realisation, as if he had suddenly been able to place his hands on the reality that he had been struggling to find in the sterile room. The dirt and smell that he carried with him were the realities of the compound and whatever the purification he was expected to endure whilst awaiting the great man's arrival, the new soap bar and embroidered hand towel and cool running water would not be able to cleanse him.

The secretary was waiting for him when he came out of the bathroom. "Can I see Colonel Batho now, please," he asked in a bold manner. She looked at him with renewed interest.

"I do understand that you have been waiting all day, and I am sorry for that, really I am. Unfortunately, the *bourgemestre* has been called away on urgent business and will only be back in office tomorrow morning. He has asked me to tell you that he would appreciate it of you would come again tomorrow and he assures you that he will see you early in the morning." The woman paused while the priest considered this news. He started to object but she anticipated him, cutting him short. "I can assure you in any event that there is no possibility of returning to your church tonight: there is a strict curfew in Rweru and you would not be allowed to leave. You can only return tomorrow morning. I have made arrangements for you to stay in the police hostel behind this building. There is a single room available for you and I think you will find that it is comfortable. Please come back here at nine o'clock tomorrow morning."

The hostel room was comfortable, as the secretary had promised, and its clean sparseness reminded him of his room in the seminary. However, he slept fitfully and awoke during the night, lonely and increasingly anxious. Images of the journey from the village crowded into his dreams: the drunk man jostled for position with the body of the woman being struck by the young boy. Corpses rose from nowhere and leered at him, blood flowed and thickened, then turned into flames. The priest tried to summon up positive images to counter his nightmares, conjuring up the innocent faces of children, only to have their smiles distort murderously. A naked body appeared repeatedly in his dreams and he fought off looking at the face, fearful of its identity.

He awoke with a start, fatigued but relieved that the battle of the night was over. It was still dark outside when he switched on the small light next to the bed. He was disconcerted to find that someone had placed a tray of food on the floor next to the bed while he was sleeping. Fresh fruit juice and a flaky croissant with jams and cheese were arranged on a pretty cloth. The priest felt like a hunted animal, bewildered and mocked by his unseen antagonists. He ate the food hungrily, however, and washed his face and torso with soap and cold water in the basin.

His heart sank when he returned to the familiar room in the *bourgemestre's* offices to find fresh coffee and biscuits waiting for him. The woman smiled thinly and moved towards the door.

"Excuse me, but you must understand that I am not going to spend another day in this room. Please inform the *bourgemestre* that I will be returning to my village before lunch today. If he is unable to see me before then, I am afraid that we will both have missed our opportunity." He felt in control again and pushed his unexpected advantage on the woman. "Will you give him that message. Please, if you are not going to give him that message, I might as well leave right now and not waste my time any further."

The woman frowned at him with disdain, but acquiesced. "I will give him your message. Wait here." She left with a flick of her head, but the door was closed carefully and without any noise.

Melchior had to wait for over an hour before the woman returned. She beckoned him to follow her and they made their way through the cool interior of the building. Smooth floored corridors stretched in different directions like the inside of a large hospital. But no-one appeared in the labyrinth and all the doors were closed. He wondered vaguely whether it was a public holiday for the administrators of the town. The woman's hard-heeled shoes clattered noisily as she led him through the maze of passages. She knocked tentatively on the last door and waited for a response. The priest heard a gruff answer and she opened the door for him, standing back to allow him to pass. He heard the door click closed behind him. Her heels clipped away from the office down the corridor.

The *bourgemestre* was sitting behind his desk, leaning back on a reclining leather chair, his eyes now fixed firmly on the man who had just entered his chambers. His bulk filled the chair and the muscles on his one arm pressed out against the short sleeves of his shirt. The thought crossed Melchior's mind that that this was not the type of man to fulfill his duties from the comfort of his office. His massive head was smooth and bald, giving him an aggressive and dominating air.

"Sit," the large man said, gesturing towards the row of empty chairs in front of the desk. He had not risen from his seat. Melchior nodded and chose a chair directly in front of the colonel. "Can I offer you some tea?" he asked. Melchior was unsure as to whether or not he had caught the beginnings of a smile on the square-jawed face. He allowed himself a slight smile in response and declined the offer.

"I am Colonel Batho. And you are Lushodayana Thomas Ngonzima from Bukumara. Tell me, Mr Ngonzima, are you aware of the story of the queen mother Kanjogera?" Melchior did not know the story and the *bourgemestre* did not wait for his response. "History has it that, as the Tutsi queen mother grew old, she found it increasingly difficult to rise from her imperial throne with the same ease she had managed when she was younger. In order to assist her, she had two Hutu children placed just in front of her, one on either side of her throne and slightly in front of her. Each child was impaled with a long sword, the handles reaching back towards her. When she wished to rise, she needed only to grasp the handles of the swords and lift herself up, pressing the blades ever deeper into the children's backs." The big man flicked open a brass cigarette case and offered the priest a cigarette. The priest declined but the *bourgemestre*, unperturbed, proceeded to choose one for himself, gently knocking the end against the desktop. He placed the cigarette between his lips, thoughtfully, using the same hand to bring the lighter up to the cigarette. Only when it was lit and he had inhaled his first languid draw, did he speak again, smoke funneling out with his words.

"What do you think of that story, Father? What does that story tell you about us?" Again, he did not wait for a response. "It tells me two things: that the self-interest of the Tutsis is ultimately self-defeating – one day the swords will slide to their hilts, into the backs of the two innocent children, and her royal highness will fall in trying to reach the handles to lift herself up. And secondly, it reminds us that the distrust of Tutsis by Hutus is deeply ingrained and does not arise from any one person's political ambitions."

The *bourgemestre* took another long draw on the cigarette, savouring the dense smoke and heat. When he spoke again his voice seemed even deeper and more resonant.

"Look at this picture and tell me what you think of this, then." He sat up and pushed a thin newspaper across the polished desk to the priest. Melchior did not pick it up but bent forward to look at the front page lying on the desk in front of him. The crudely-drawn picture on the front page depicted Mary and Joseph standing together, with halos around their heads. The sun was shown shining brightly in the top corner. Joseph was holding the Christ child while Mary looked on, smiling benignly. A line from the child's mouth led to words scrawled in Kinyarwandan: "Hutus should learn to love one another". A line from Joseph's mouth lead to the phrase: "Yes, you must tell them to unite."

Melchior looked up at the *bourgemestre* quizzically. "This newspaper is *Kangura*, the voice of Hutu Power," the colonel said, taking back the newspaper. "So you see, we have Christ himself calling for the Hutu nation to unite. Are you aware, for instance, Father, that Hutu Power has issued its own Ten Commandments, aimed at maintaining Hutu purity and outlawing the contamination of any Hutu by marriage or relationship with a Tutsi? Are you aware Father that the Archbishop of Kigali wears a portrait pin of assassinated President Habyarimana on his cassock whilst saying mass? Are you aware even that the official position of the Catholic Church in Kigali is that the suppression of a Tutsi uprising after the assassination of President Habyarimana should be supported?"

The colonel's presence was overpowering and Melchior's struggled to stop his voice from trembling as he retorted: "Why are you telling me these things, Colonel? No, I did not know most of the things that you have told me now. And I cannot say whether what you tell me is true or not. If the Archbishop wishes to display his support for the murdered President then he must be entitled to do so. If some writer wants to publish a bad depiction of Jesus Christ on the front page of his newspaper and put words into his mouth, then I suppose he may do so. None of this has anything to do with why I have come to see you."

The colonel smiled and sat forward to face the priest directly. "Now that is where you are wrong, Father. These facts have everything to do with you and why you are here. To put it simply, Father, you are out of touch with the reality of Rwanda now. You are ignorant of the position of your own church and you are operating from a position of ignorance and not from one of knowledge.

"You have travelled all the way from Bukumara to see me because your church compound is filled with Tutsi refugees hiding from the storm of outrage that is passing over them. You have come from Bukumara because you seek assurances from me, but you come to me with empty hands. You have come from Bukumara because you are not prepared to accept the word of my head of police. You have come from Bukumara to make demands on me and yet you make no demands on the Tutsi rebels who hide under your cassock in your compound!"

The colonel rose from his chair aggressively. Even from the other side of the desk, he towered over Melchior who sat wide-eyed and reeling from the tirade. "You have come from Bukumara to make demands about that of which you have no knowledge. You know nothing of the uprising, you know nothing of the murder of President Habyarimana, you know nothing of the plans and intentions of the rebel forces and the *inkotanyi* in exile. You see, Father, while you are in a position of ignorance, I am not!"

The colonel sat down in his chair and, in an instant, was calm again. He smiled warmly towards the priest. "I apologise Father, perhaps I have been in politics too long. I am given to lengthy speeches when what can be said should be conveyed in a few short sentences. The people in the compound will be safe provided that they co-operate with the militia and police and provided they turn over any RPF soldiers or sympathisers to the *Interhamwe*.

"The entire operation throughout the country is being managed by the interim government. My head of police is, as you know, currently in Bukumara. I have given him clear orders in this regard. He is also a member of the ruling party and a member of Hutu Power. He is a responsible and ambitious political animal and he will not jeopardise his career by acting foolishly or disregarding my orders."

The colonel rose and Melchior understood by this that the meeting was over. He had hardly said a word himself. As he reached the door he turned to say something, but the *bourgemestre* interrupted him.

"Just remember, Father, not to lean on the handles of the sword when you try and rise from your altar." The big man smiled and closed the door prematurely, forcing the priest to shuffle backwards out of the way. Once outside, he remained standing in the corridor for some time, reflecting on the *bourgemestre's* words and the impending journey back to the village.

Arusha
18 October 1998
Draft article for Nairobi Daily News

****

"The *Interhamwe* arrived that morning, soon after the priest had left us.

"We heard them singing and chanting in the village. We ran to get more sticks and stones and we hid the children in the sacristy. Some of the women refused to get up off the ground in the compound. They just sat there and wept. Some other women went to sit in a row at the entrance to the compound, to try and block the killers when they came."

The Courtroom is very quiet, except for the clear voice of the witness, standing erect in the witness box. The witness, protected witness DDE, tells her story in educated French, simply and directly. The prosecutor is sitting down and letting her proceed without interruption. The Judges have stopped taking notes and all three are watching her, listening to her account. The defence counsel is also listening. Only the accused seems to be distracted.

"We saw them coming up the hill: there was a large group of them with a truck in front. Then we heard the noise of chanting and shouting from the other end of the road, where it dips away into the forest. There were more coming from that direction. Then we knew that our time had come to an end." The witness pauses, naturally and not for impact, but the effect presses on everyone. The omission is still obvious. She has made no mention of the accused.

"Some of the women ran out of the compound with their children and into the banana grove. I saw some women trying to climb over the wall around the compound. Some children climbed up into the big eucalyptus tree in one corner of the compound. But most of us got ready to meet our attackers. The truck stopped near to the entrance and the two groups of *Interhamwe* met along the road outside the compound. They were singing: *turatsembatsemba, abatutsi, abatutsi.* It had a rhythm that was almost seductive, but the words were spat out with such venom and glee that it filled us all with terror. They waved machetes in the air and one or two held rifles up over their heads. Their feet kicked up the dust and the wind was hot.

"Their cries rose and rose, louder and louder, until they had driven themselves into a frenzy of stamping and shouting. They danced and waved banana leaves, around and around, chanting and screaming. They almost seemed oblivious to the compound, they were so absorbed in their own singing and dancing. Then a man stepped forward, I think it was the one they called Zephir, and threw something into the compound. I didn't know what it was, I thought it was a stone, except that they all watched him step forward and throw it, like it was some kind of ritual. It looped through the air and landed against the wall of the church. It bounced back amongst the people who were packed in the compound. It exploded with a terrible crackling sound and my nose filled with a chemical, powdery smell that was biting and made my eyes water. There was a lot of smoke from that part of the compound. I could not see what had happened, but I heard people scream in agony and I knew then that it had been a grenade. That was the signal for them to attack."

The witness pauses again and she turns and looks towards the accused. He keeps his head straight, staring forward at the floor in front of the trial Judge's bench.

"The man who threw that grenade is known to me. His name is Victor Muyigenzi. He was the head of the communal police for the prefecture. He was in charge of the militia and the *Interhamwe*. He is the accused sitting before you now. He launched the attack on the compound. He initiated the massacre that day. He is a *genocidaire*."

Now the accused looks up at the witness. His expression is one of bafflement, as if he is hurt that this woman should point him out above others as being worthy of special sanction. He rubs his forehead with his hand and looks down at the ground again. His counsel is making notes now.

"The women sitting in a line in front of the compound entrance were all hacked to death in seconds. We had hardly thrown any stones before they were upon us, slicing and cutting as they rushed into the compound. Some fought back with sticks, but the machetes broke the arms that tried to hold the sticks. Sick old men and frightened women are no contest for grown men who are filled with madness and hatred. We tried to put up some resistance but, after perhaps ten minutes, a kind of tired resignation came over the compound. People ·simply knelt down and let the blows come down on their heads. They dropped their stones and threw down their sticks. Some lay down as if they were already dead. The smoke and the dust rose up so thickly in the compound that you could not see the people in front of you. Some of them were trampled to death, especially the smaller children. Especially the smaller children," she repeats, frowning to herself. The chamber is quite still, glimpsing the horror that the witness is describing.

"Then another grenade went off. I don't know who threw it or whether it was a mistake or not. There was a bang and my ears hurt and were humming afterwards. I think it was quite close to me, but there were so many people squashed together that only the people next to the grenade were killed. Whoever threw that grenade made a mistake though, because the smoke from the grenade, together with the dust, the ash from the fires, the smoke from the scattered embers, all became so thick that no-one could see anything any more. I could see shapes running and moving just in front of me, but they could have been refugees or *Interhamwe.* I couldn't make them out.

"The slaughter slowed down then. I think most of the *Interhamwe* left the compound and waited for the smoke to clear. It was too thick to carry on in the compound. Some of the refugees climbed over the wall at the back, near the latrines, but the militia were waiting for them. I heard them being beaten. The smoke started to clear after a while. You could almost see across the compound again. Bodies were strewn about the compound, groaning in the mist. I heard the chanting starting again. Then they came running back into the compound."

They respect this woman's testimony: the measured manner, the logical sequence, the unemotive narrative - all this captivates the audience listening to the story unfold. The room is very still and even the defence counsel sits motionless, save for the occasional scrawled note.

"Then I saw the dwarf come running into the compound. He was surrounded by *Interhamwe*, but he was looking for someone in particular. I saw her with a stick in her hand – she knew he would be coming. He screamed, perhaps with delight, or fury, I don't know, and ran at her. She struck out at him with the stick, but she did not have the strength to ward off his determination. The dwarf killed Rutayisire. He hacked at her, breaking her arm and throwing her to the ground. He stood over her and chopped at her body as you would chop at a log of wood. He was not aiming fatal blows, just chopping at the part of her body nearest to him, her legs, her arms, her chest. I suppose eventually he struck her by chance across the neck or on the head. She may have already been dead a long time but that did not stop the demented creature. Eventually one of the *Interhamwe* pulled him off her devastated body and pushed him away." She pauses again.

"But the madness was not limited to the dwarf," she says evenly, looking again at the accused.

"They raped a lot of the women in the beginning. They started by dragging them away from the massacre, outside of the compound. I could hear their cries of pain and distress. But after a while they did not bother even to take them away and just raped them in the compound, while others went about their work of killing. They mutilated the women and often they did not bother to kill them, they just left them to die on their own.

"Then a strange thing happened. I saw the accused standing among the bodies. He was holding a machete and he had a gun pushed into his belt. I had not seen him in the compound itself before this. He shouted at the men who were sprawled on top of the crying women. He said that they did not have time for this and that they must stop wasting their energy. It seemed strange, because really they had as much time as they wanted. The compound entrance was blocked and the walls were too high for the refugees to climb over. We were caged in our safe haven, easy victims waiting for our fate in turn. They really could take all the time they wanted. But he was worried about time."

He is looking at her with open, vulnerable eyes: she has said something that has awakened him. He is watching her now, waiting to see what she will say. And his counsel is watching him out of the corner of his eye. The Judges are watching his counsel, and her. They are waiting for her to answer the riddle. She is master of the story.

"Then I understood – the priest."

She does not say anything more. Instead she waits while the chamber considers her statement: the priest who would be returning. He is still watching her warily - he has hate and surprise in his eyes. She looks past him and then continues.

"I hid in the priest's room, where the children had been sleeping on the floor. Some of the children were still there, lying under the bed and behind the chairs. I watched through the door as they herded the refugees into the church. Those who resisted, who moved too slowly, who could not squeeze through the packed door, they slashed with their knives and left squirming on the ground. The compound was littered with bodies piled one on top of the other: children, women, old men, all still except for the slow dripping, the draining of blood from their bodies. The compound was wet and sticky with their blood. The earth had been churned into mud but no rain had fallen.

"When the last person still alive in the compound area had been forced into the church or cut to the ground, the doors were pushed closed. Nothing happened for a while. I heard orders being given and some of the men moved off. After a while, one returned with some long nails: he slammed the thick iron nails into the wood with the butt of a rifle. They threw stones through the few unbroken windows of the church hall. I didn't know what they were doing.

"Until I saw the men returning, dragging dry branches and grass behind them. They doused the grass with paraffin and pushed the branches, woven with the wet grass, through the windows. Then they lit the grass."

Witness DDE looks at the judges. She is going to give them something more. She is waiting for them to appreciate this. One judge nods almost imperceptibly towards her, 'go on, tell us' his expression says. DDE sighs and takes a small sip of water from the glass in front of her. Her fingers clench the glass tightly.

"The man who lit the grass, he took a cloth and soaked it in paraffin. He held it on a stick and lit it with a cigarette lighter. He had a smooth head and was strongly built, although one of his arms was withered away. I had not seen him before. He lit the cloth and threw the burning bundle into the church. He watched for a while and then he left." The judges are not satisfied. She continues.

"I believe that the man who lit the bundle was Colonel Batho. I am not able to identify Colonel Batho but Mr Muyigenzi will be able to help you." Again the witness pauses, waiting. "Mr Muyigenzi was standing next to him when he threw the bundle into the church. When the colonel left, Mr Muyigenzi saluted him and shook his hand. He seemed very eager to please him." The press staff are writing notes in their ring-bound notebooks.

"The colonel left in the truck and Mr Muyigenzi," she nods towards the accused to make sure that no-one is in any doubt as to whom she is referring, "stayed behind at the compound. The fire burnt for a while and everything was still in the church. Then I heard wailing and crying. The fire never really caught properly - it burnt the window frames and the roof started to smoulder. But it seemed to make more smoke than fire.

The smoke was black and very thick. It poured out of the windows and through the burning holes in the roof. I saw it seeping under the door, like water. The roof crackled and splintered. It became very quiet inside the church. I heard no noises. The men stood around and watched the slow progress of the fire. One of them brought some beer and they stood drinking, in silence. They seemed tired after the exertions of the day.

"I lay still in the room and I stopped watching them after a while. I looked up when I heard them cheer - the roof of the church hall collapsed, sending showers of sparks into the compound. One beam from the roof stayed, pointing up at the sky, burning along its length. They didn't bother to open the door of the hall. They knew that they had succeeded. They just kept drinking their beer and watching the smoke and flames."

Her hands are trembling. But she is as strong as iron. She stands upright and looks straight at the Judges. They look back at her. Nothing more is to be said today. She is the master of the story. The Courtroom is the audience and the accused the only participant.

Chapter Ten

A stillness spread tightly over the village, a stillness rather than a quiet, the absence of sound rather than the presence of comfort. It was the kind of stillness that forces you to look over your shoulder in a darkened lane, or glance up at the sky before bolting your door. It held down the birds from flying up, forced the monkeys deep into the corners of boughs. No sounds of ordinary activities broke through. An absence of sound, an absence of life.

Melchior had walked the last few kilometres into the village and felt it the moment he saw the abandoned barricade. The trucks which had been parked in the shade of the trees near the councillors' houses were gone: only a few darkened oily patches marked the place where they had once been. The bodies were gone from the rubble of the makeshift barricade, dragged away and buried, or dumped in the fields somewhere. Banana leaves littered the ground and shuddered in the warm breeze, their corners lifting and falling, like living creatures on the ground. The air was sour: it was filled with a strange and rich smell which caught in his stomach rather than his throat. A broken machete blade lay forgotten across one of the stones on the barricade, chipped along its edges and snapped clean at the handle: when Melchior saw the blunted instrument, he knew.

He started to run through the village, his hand covering his mouth to stop himself from screaming out loud. The houses and simple huts passed by him, a blur of browns and blacks as he stumbled and thrashed along the road towards the hill, and the compound. His mind felt empty, a hollow shell burnt and scoured like the looted huts he had seen on his journey. No thoughts came, just the roar of emptiness crashing in beating waves.

When he reached the start of the hill he stopped running. His chest heaved and he stood panting with his hands on his hips, looking up at the outline of the church building. He wanted to run away, to avoid confirming what he knew to be the truth, to deny a betrayal by refusing to witness it. But he had witnessed it already: he could see the collapsed roof of the church and the pervasive smell of blood and death filled his mouth and nose. A dark river had flowed from the compound entrance, like a snake disturbed and winding unevenly down the road towards the priest. His eyes took all of this in: the burnt church, the smells, the stillness in the air, the dark river flowing from his compound. But he felt nothing at all: no fear, no anger, no sadness, just a crushed acquiescence, an uncomprehending horror.

The compound could have been strewn with flowers instead of the hacked bodies of the refugees. The sticky drying blood under his feet could have been honey. The gaping body of the young girl thrown onto the compound wall could have been a woven blanket. It would not have mattered what scene greeted the priest in and around the compound – nothing made an impression anymore. The indescribable mayhem of the hell that was his church could not be grasped. It was not a reality that could be faced. The obliteration of Gomorrah would have looked like this - a few cryptic lines and the deed was complete: no fear, no anger, no sadness. God not only sanctioned this – this was God. The face of God stared back at him, upside down, spread-eagled in a cross hanging from the compound wall. Melchior stood in the middle of the compound, surrounded by bodies and limbs, the dusty ground hidden beneath cold skins and torn clothing. His eyes wandered like scavenging crows across the fields of war, picking out forms here and there, a hand, a distorted face, the fabric of a stained dress.

The door to his room swung open and, in the haze, Zephir stepped out into the sunlight. He surveyed the scene proudly, his arm outstretched and slowly sweeping in an arc, across the broken field of bodies. Zephir looked him in the eyes and smiled.

"Welcome home, Father," he said. "You must be tired after your long journey. Come …" he beckoned with a half-empty bottle of beer in his hand, "… come and join us in a drink to celebrate the end of the Tutsi nation. Come and relax with the victors!"

Melchior stood transfixed. He stared uncomprehendingly at the man who had to hold onto the doorway to steady himself, his skin glistening thickly with sweat.

"Come and join us in enjoying the spoils of war." There was a scuffle behind him and he stepped outside, to one side, letting the light stream onto the face of Selena. Her head had been shaved completely, pale and scarred by the careless hands of her captors. "You see, we have your friend, a Tutsi. But we have cut the last of her hair off, so she will not be able to seduce you any longer. Tutsi whore!" Zephir grinned and laughed. "The priest's Tutsi whore."

Melchior took a step towards Selena, but Zephir held up his hand. "You see, Father, we have always known that these Tutsi whores could seduce the simple Belgians, that is how they came to keep the Hutu nation enslaved. And we know how they can seduce the manly UNAMIR soldiers, opening and closing their legs like flowers, whispering in their ears and playing down in their pants. We have even seen how they can entwine some Hutu men in their spell, spinning a stinking web made from their own seed. Tutsi whores! But now we see that even a man of the church, a priest, a Hutu leader of his community, he too can be tricked by these clever whores, who wave their backsides in the faces of men like baboons in season. You too, Father, you have been playing with the enemy. That is treason, Father. Playing with a Tutsi whore, that is treason, Father!"

"What have you done to her," he managed to say hoarsely.

"Us, Father? Us? We have done nothing to her. We have shaved off her hair, certainly, so that she will no longer be able to spin her web about you. We want you to see her for what she is. We want you to be clear about this Tutsi whore."

Zephir turned and grabbed hold of Selena by her neck, pulling her out of the room into the shocking light. He thrust her forward over his outstretched foot, sending her tumbling into the dust between the two men. She lay still on the ground, one more silent body among the others, jumbled row upon row of corpses. Melchior looked at Selena on the ground before him: she had been beaten and dried blood had formed on her scalp and around her mouth. But they had not killed her along with the others. They had kept her for his return: this was his tool for her survival. He looked at Zephir and his heart felt hard and cold.

"Zephir, I am a man of the church, as you say. I am a priest. I may not be with a woman. It is forbidden. Now it is true that I used this woman to meet that need. I will not tell you that I do not, or that I did not like her. I did. She was attractive. She gave me pleasure. But she is, at the end of the day, only a whore. Whether she gives her favours to passing men in a drinking house, or to a priest who cannot keep his vows, she is still a whore, an inconsequential whore. She is what she is. She does what comes naturally to her, and she has not committed any evil by doing so."

"I don't know what you are saying, priest, but I will stand here and drink my beer and let you finish."

"I am telling you, Zephir, that this woman has not committed the evil of which you complain. What has she done? She has done only what all whores must do - found a willing man and performed her work. But now, you must ask yourself: what of the man?"

"Hah, what of the man?" the drunk man interrupted. "Indeed, what of the man ?" He lifted his beer in a toast to the priest and took a long swig, the yellow liquid dripping down the side of his mouth and chin. Melchior moved closer to him.

"The man has taken a vow, a vow not to you, not to his community, not to his country. He has taken a vow to God," he pointed above him to emphasise the point, "A vow to God Himself that he will not touch the carnal flesh of a woman. That is his vow and that is the vow he has broken. And therein lies the evil you should be complaining of. Therein lies the betrayal."

"Yes," Zephir shouted, pointing unsteadily at the priest.

"There lies the evil. *You* are the evil and we must kill you both!"

"No," Melchior said quickly, coming right up to him. The smell of unwashed sweat and drink swept powerfully over his face. "Here is my offer to you. You take me for her. You let the whore walk away, free, and you take me. She means nothing - she is nothing. There will always be whores, whether they are Tutsis or not. But the root of the evil here is the weakness of the man who has breached his vows. That is the evil which you will extinguish in exchange for letting this grain of sand, among so many others, fall from between your fingers."

"But I have you both," Zephir replied simply.

"Physically, yes, you have us both. But on what grounds will you kill a Hutu priest unless I give you this justification? I am a Hutu, Zephir, and I am the leader of this church. God will not easily forgive you for such an action. I am the one you want, you know that, but you cannot have me unless you are prepared to pay some small, trifling price. I give you the man who broke his vows to God. I give you the sinner. I give you evil itself. But you must turn away from this pathetic creature and let her scuttle off to hide under some rock. That is the deal."

Zephir drained the last of the beer from the bottle and threw it high in the air. It spiralled in an arc across the compound and landed with a dull thud amongst the bodies. He looked at the priest and scowled, a cloud of anger passing over his face.

"You are in no position to offer deals, priest. You cannot tell me what I can and cannot do. Look around you ... what do you see? Is this the work of a man who can be told by you what he must and must not do? I came into your church and I squashed the cockroaches that lived here, that had been feeding off your table, that you were living with, that you were filling with your rotten seed. I am the one who came into your church and cleaned it out. You had left your church to decay, overrun with rats and cockroaches. I cleaned it. Don't try and tell me what I can and cannot do. That is a mistake! You were breeding *inkotanyi* dogs in your compound - this was not a church, it was a whorehouse for *ibyitso*. And I crushed them one by one with my boot, my heel squashing down on their feeble bodies, their rotten juices squirting out underfoot."

Zephir bent down and grabbed the fallen woman by her arm. Melchior witnessed his strength as he pulled her up with one hand, holding her on her feet and pushing her close to the priest. When she was standing, facing him, Zephir moved his hand onto her shoulder and clenched the fabric of her dress in his hands. With a single pull he tore the fabric from her shoulder to her waist - it seemed to float off her, like silk, flowing over her skin, caressing the curves of her body as it tumbled to the ground.

Melchior did not look at her body, but instead for the first time looked up into her eyes. Her face was filthy; dried blood from the shaving scars had mixed with dirt and tears, the side of her lip was swollen from a blow. But her eyes stared back at him - the same eyes that he had first discovered and loved under the mpingo tree at the seminary, the same eyes that had looked up at him during their first furtive love-making, the same eyes that had awoken him from his troubled dreams in the compound. Her deep brown eyes stared back at him, unmoving and tearless.

Melchior opened his mouth to say something to her, to try and tell her of his regrets, his painful love for her and his fierce desire for her survival, but she widened her eyes and shook her head, slightly. Zephir saw that his moment of confrontation had been subverted and pulled her abruptly to one side, tripping her back onto the ground. She fell heavily on her shoulder, stifling a shout of pain. Melchior did not move.

"Now, Father, you were talking of a deal. Well, here is how things will be now." He shouted someone's name over his shoulder and a much younger man, almost a boy, came out of the room with a machete. Zephir took the weapon from him. He picked up the torn fabric of Selena's dress and folded it into a tight bundle. He looked up at the priest and then ran the blade slowly over the cloth. The blade was razor-sharp and pulled gently at the cotton, teasing it momentarily before slicing through one layer after another. By the time the end of the blade had reached the cloth, the bundle was cut halfway through. "He has been sharpening this blade for you, Father. So that you only have to strike once."

Zephir held the machete by the tip of its blade, angling it towards the priest. The handle bounced gently up and down.

"Only one strike to redeem yourself. Redemption could not be given to you more easily, Father. In your church one can secretly say your 'sorrys', hidden behind thick cloth and without any price at all. But here, Father, in my world, redemption comes at a small price. But then, Father, she is just a whore."

"Mary Magdalene was just a whore, Zephir."

"Play games with me, father, and I will kill you both, right here in the compound. And I will kill her first, so that you can watch. Take the machete and do what you know you must do. Rid yourself of this Tutsi. God and the entire Hutu nation is watching you."

Melchior reached out and touched the warm wooden handle. It was damp from the hand of the young man who had been sharpening the blade. Zephir pushed it further towards him, into his hand. His fingers closed slowly around the handle. He was surprised how comfortably it fitted into his grip. It was heavier than he had expected, weighted by the blade, heavy for chopping the brush.

"It suits you, Father," Zephir said, snorting with disdain. "When you are finished with her, we may have other work for you. Perhaps you will develop a liking for the job. There is little money, of course, but the beer is free." He laughed out loud, jeering at the priest with his wide-open mouth.

Melchior stood silently holding the weapon in his hands. Then he walked past the laughing man to the naked figure on the ground. He reached down and took her arm, helping her up as she winced and held her shoulder. But as he steered her past Zephir, the militiaman grabbed him.

"Where are you going with her?" he hissed aggressively.

"I am taking her into the banana grove," he said shortly, pulling away from the drunken man's grasp.

"You want to fuck your little whore one more time, hey Father?" The words grated harshly on his ears. He pointed the machete at Zephir.

"I am not like you and I will never be like you. You are a stupid and evil man. Your only future lies in the fires of Hell and Damnation. I will never kill people the way you do. This is not "work". You cannot hide from what you have done by calling it work. This is not *gukora*, this is murder. I am not a murderer, Zephir. If I must kill this woman then so be it: let God judge me for it. But I will not destroy her like some animal in a killing pen, surrounded by the dead, watched by their murdered eyes. I am taking her to the banana grove."

He did not wait for the response and turned, leading Selena by the arm, choosing a path between the crumpled bodies. He heard a noise behind him but he did not turn around, keeping his eyes focused on the compound entrance, waiting for the inevitable blow to the back of his head, imagining the sharp cut of a blade or the crushing blow of a *masu*. But it did not come and he reached the entrance safely. Once they were free of the bodies, he turned around and saw that they had been followed by the young man. He gestured to them to keep walking.

At the edge of the banana plantation they stopped. "I will wait for you here," the young man said. "Do not go far. I will come and get you if you are not back very soon. Just the time it takes to give a single chop." The young man was staring at Selena's naked body while he spoke.

It felt unreal to Melchior as they walked together between the banana trees. It was still on the hillside and between the trees they could see bodies scattered. The trees had been stripped of their fruit and the lower leaves had been hacked away. Many had been chopped clean through at the stems. They did not speak until they were out of sight, then without a word they turned to each other.

He held her quietly in his arms, rocking her gently backwards and forwards, the way one rocks a child to sleep. Selena pushed her face into his neck and they stood, holding onto each other, wordlessly.

"Where are you? Have you finished?" The voice of the young man sounded close.

"Just wait. I am coming now," Melchior replied, lifting his head. Then he pulled away from Selena and cupped his hands around her face. Through the dirt and the blood, through the fear and the terror, her strength and her beauty still shone. Her eyes were filled with tears now.

"You must go now," he said quickly.

She looked at him and her hand stroked his cheek. "They will kill you, Melchior. You know they will kill you."

"Perhaps they will not," he said, lying. "But you mustn't worry. I am ready. If you are free, then I am ready. Our time has come to and end. I cannot come with you. We wouldn't get further than this hill before they caught us again. You must go now. You can make it on your own."

Melchior let go of her and moved around a tree, where the body of a woman lay in the grass. He quickly pulled off the skirt and loose jersey, trying at the same time to brush off some of the dirt. Selena reached for the clothes without a word and held his hand for a moment.

"I will hold you for ever in my soul," she said, squeezing his hand between her palms.

"You have been my soul," he said. "You have been my deity."

Then he turned from her and looked back up towards the burnt church building, tears welling up in his own eyes. "I am coming. It is finished," he said through clenched teeth.

He heard Selena moving quickly down the hillside behind him. He waited, without turning, until it was quiet again around him. A grey rat scuttled past him, disappearing under a pile of debris. There were no other sounds. He knelt down next to the stripped body of the woman and, without hesitating, plunged the blade deep into her soft side. When he pulled it out, streaks of dark coagulated blood marked the blade. The blood did not look fresh and he looked around at the other bodies lying amongst the trees. The dead had all been in the grove since the previous day. There was nothing more to be done.

Melchior walked out of the banana grove and wiped the blade against the trunk of a banana tree. Then he handed the machete to the waiting man.

"It is finished," he said again. They walked back towards the compound, where Zephir was standing at the entrance.

"So you see, Father, it is not so difficult to kill a cockroach after all."

"Except, of course, that he did not kill her."

The voice, coming from the other side of the wall at the entrance, was familiar. Melchior stepped back from the entrance as Victor walked out from the compound. His hand held a cigarette to his mouth which he drew on strongly, his eyes on the priest. He blew the smoke out in a long stream before he spoke again.

"You didn't kill her, Lushodayana. Isn't that right? Lushodayana Thomas Nyonzima, the boy-priest of our village, the church's golden altar boy, the boy who would only do good. You would not kill her. Would you ?" He drew on the cigarette again. "But why am I so sure of that, you might ask? Is it because you are such a good person? No. No man is good or bad, he is always just a man. So, could it be because you are a man of the church, a priest? No. You have broken other vows of your church when your personal interest came first. So, is it perhaps because you are unable to resort to an act of violence against a woman? No again. All men, in the right situation, will happily strike a woman, rape a woman. Then why do I know that you did not kill this whore?" He paused and dropped his cigarette on the ground, grinding the life out of it with his foot.

"Lushodayana did not kill that woman because he loves her. Perhaps she is the only woman he has ever loved." Victor laughed nastily. "Is that so?" Melchior said nothing, silently imagining Selena scrabbling down the hillside towards the river: where would she run to from there? Which route would she follow? Would she be safer if she walked along the river bed? Or should she go up the other side of the valley and strike deeper into the forest, making for the border?

"Lushodayana does not want to speak to me now. He wanted to speak to me before, when it was in his interest to do so, to save himself, to save his scurrying Tutsi insects. But now he has nothing to say to me. You are a fool, Lushodayana. A fool! You think that you have allowed your woman to get away, but we have men waiting for her, in the valley, on the hilltop. They will bring her back soon enough. She is no match for them."

"Why did you let me take her into the banana grove then?" he asked, breaking his silence more to keep Victor talking than for any other reason.

"I knew that you would not kill her. I knew that you would let her go and bring me back a blade smeared with the old blood of some shrivelled corpse from the field. I knew that was what you would do. You do not control this situation. I control this place. I let you go into the bushes. I let you think she was escaping. I let you think that you had got the better of us. I let you do all those things, because I wanted them to happen. And you are too stupid and too arrogant to realise it. Where is your self-righteous god now, Lushodayana? Where is the mighty fist of your god to crush your tormentors, sweeping you to safety? You have built your life on sand and straw and the first wave of reality has washed the foundations out from underneath you. There is nothing now but a hole beneath you and you can do nothing but fall into it."

"Why are you playing at this pretence then? If you really did know all of these things as you say you did, then you are just like an animal playing with its prey, out of boredom or for some depraved pleasure."

"Your problem, Lushodayana, is that you underestimate the people around you. You are so fervent in your beliefs that you categorise everyone into either fellow-believers, those who are to be praised, or those who do not meet your standards, who are to be disregarded as the chaff. I am a believer.

I believe in God. I believe in destiny. I believe that the members of a community must care for one another. I believe that a community has a right to protect itself from an outside threat. I am not the chaff, nor am I the face of evil you think you have discovered. I am outside of your simplistic divisions, of black and white. I am the area somewhere between black and white, where most people live their ordinary and decent lives."

"Victor, look into that compound. Are you saying that that is the work of ordinary people living ordinary and decent lives? That is the work of madmen, that is the work of the Devil Himself." Melchior was surprised to see that Victor did not react to this response with anger: he shook his head in disagreement, in the measured way one might disagree with a point of view in an intellectual debate.

"None of us are monsters here, Lushodayana. Our community, the Hutu nation, is under threat from an external force and an internal rebellion. Our community has been subjected to the tyranny of the Egyptians, and we are rising up to fight for ourselves. This is a concept that is familiar to your God and mine." Victor paused and looked at Melchior. "And perhaps the Devil resides in all ordinary men and women." He paused, as if considering this last statement, before continuing.

"I cannot order the execution of a Hutu priest lightly, Lushodayana. You were right when you said that to Zephir. I was listening to you and I agree with you. But now, you have allowed an *inkotanyi* to escape from our custody - you took her from us on the pretence that you were assisting us, but instead you betrayed us and released her into the hills. She will be caught – she has probably already been killed – but that does not absolve you of your crime against your nation and your God. It is for that crime, and not for any other, that you will be punished. May God have mercy upon your soul!"

Melchior no longer felt the need to speak. Selena was either running free through the thickets of the forest, or she was lying slain upon the ground. He could not bear to think about her any longer: now he wanted his nightmare to come to an end. He turned to face the burnt-out roof of the church. The stone cross on the wall above the window was scorched and blackened. The last beam of the roof stuck out into the air. The priest thought he saw a wisp of smoke float up from the base of the wood. The interior walls of the church and the sacristy were exposed to the rain now. Soon the church would start to crumble. Birds would pick at the exposed bodies. The flesh would decay and be washed out into the ground. The priest knelt on the ground facing the church. He imagined the creepers sliding over the walls like green snakes, pushing through the broken walls, curling around the bleached bones. He could see bushes springing up in the compound, their strong roots cracking the caked dirt. Black crows nested amongst the burnt rafters, their droppings marking the cement floor below. He saw the compound wasting away. The bush slowly returned to cover humanity's menial accomplishment, reclaiming the shattered bricks as its own.

Melchior thought of a small porcelain statue, with a blue draped shawl and a creamy face, its eyes downcast in humility. He saw it lying in the folds of the roots of a big tree that stretched out of the middle of the church hall, rising upwards through the broken roof and casting its branches towards the heavens. He saw two pieces of a small wooden cross, carved so that they fitted together smoothly, without the need for glue or nails.

POSTSCRIPT

In the distance a woman bends over her fields, pulling tubers from the loosened reddish-brown earth. The soil crumbles as the strong roots give up their resting places, pulling up in a shower of loose dirt. The old woman shakes each plant from side to side. She places them carefully in a hessian bag, before shuffling forward without standing up, a footstep to the next plant. The fields are green and brown, filled with bees and buzzing insects attracted by the flowering crops. In the next field men and women work alongside each other, pulling up the beds of weeds and casting them to one side to dry in the sun. A young man on a bicycle rides past, sitting on a heavy bag of corn flour, his legs splayed out to the sides to reach the pedals around the sides of his load.

Selena enjoys the feeling of the soft dusty earth under her feet as she walks along the side of the road. Her four-year-old son bounces joyfully on his toes at her side, his hand firmly in hers. Her hair is cut short, held tightly against her head with butterfly clips. She walks slowly, enjoying the sun on her face and taking in the smells of the flowers, the sounds of ordinary people at work in their fields.

An older man stands on the side of the road, leaning on a hoe. She nods towards him and he greets her back. Where had he been? she wonders, looking at his worn face. Where had he been when the killings took place? Had he been one of them? Had he slaughtered and maimed, this man standing quietly on the side of the road ? She looks into the fields, at the men and women working there: Were they killers? What did they do when the genocide started? Does a killer look any different to anyone else?

She would not go back to Bukumara, not now. She has heard that the church compound has been left untouched, as a memorial to the victims of the carnage. She has heard that you can now walk into the compound and see the bleached bones of hundreds of people, cloaked in garments, lying in the church, in the sacristy, scattered about the compound. She has no desire to return to see the sight. She had looked at the burnt church building for the last time the day she had fled from the banana grove. Running through the bushes and stumbling down the hiilside towards the river, she had known in her heart that she would never return. She had paused on her way up the other side, having crossed the small stream and pulled herself up the steep banks of the valley grabbing hold of the creepers and the roots of the overhanging trees. She had turned and looked back. The church had been marked only by the top of a single burnt beam, visible above the trees. She had waited, standing still and looking across the valley, waiting in silent agony for the sound she so dreaded. A sharp crack, a single crack echoing across the valley, that was all. Then she had turned and run.

She had told the Court about that sound. She had tried to describe it to them. How short the sound had been. How final. She thought that she had failed to make them understand how terrible that sound had been. But in the judgment, it was stated in neat black print, recorded for all of time: "It is clear from this evidence that Lushodayana Thomas Nyonzima, the priest of Bukumara known as Melchior, was executed by or directly on the orders of the accused."

The boy at her side is pointing to something in the field. A white stork has caught a small lizard. She stops to watch as the bird snaps the small animal in its beak. Victor had tried not to look at her when she testified about the destruction of the church compound. He had looked down, or written notes for his counsel. But at the end, when her aunt had come into court with the boy, Victor had looked at her then. The boy had walked in front of her aunt and smiled at his mother. He had put his arms up towards her to be carried. The simplest of gestures that had captivated everyone in the courtroom.

"Is that your child in court," the judge had asked quietly, leaning forward. "Yes," she had replied. "You will see that he has his father's clear eyes." The courtroom had been quiet in the presence of the small child. Victor had looked straight at her, for the first time. She had seen the fear in his eyes.

During a period of 100 days, commencing on 6 April 1994, almost one million Tutsis and moderate Hutus were massacred in the cities, towns and countryside of Rwanda. Prior to the commencement of the planned genocide, the Canadian commander of the UNAMIR peacekeeping force in Rwanda, General Dallaire, sent a cable to the United Nations Secretariat, warning of the impending disaster. General Dallaire requested authority to intervene. He was of the view that he would be able to prevent, or greatly reduce, the extent of the killings. He remains of that view today. General Dallaire's cable was dismissed by the Secretariat in a reply prepared by Boutros Ghali's chief adviser, Iqbal Riza, and signed by United Nations Secretary-General Kofi Annan. Subsequent cables and reports suffered a similar fate.

During December 1999 an independent commission of inquiry headed by former Swedish prime minister, Ingvar Carlsson, and General Rufus Kupolato of Nigeria, released its report, stating that the killings in Rwanda "will forever be remembered as one of the most abhorrent events of the 20th century." The report slammed the United Nations Secretariat for its failure to take steps to reduce the scale of the disaster. "The international community did not prevent the genocide, nor did it stop the killing once it had begun." The report found that the United Nations and the Security Council and its members should formally apologise as one body to Rwanda.

On 16 December 1999, Kofi Annan accepted the report's conclusions and, in a prepared statement, issued a personal apology: "All of us must bitterly regret that we did not do more to prevent it. On behalf of the United Nations, I acknowledge this failure and express my deep remorse."

The criminal trials of perpetrators of the genocide continue at the International Criminal Tribunal for Rwanda in Arusha, Tanzania, and in the national criminal courts of Rwanda. Several of the sites of the massacres have been left intact: the bodies – now reduced to bones – of the hundreds of victims killed there, remain as a stark and graphic memorial to the genocide.